Elda,

Thank you so my books and sharing them with others. Your support keeps me going.

xoxoxo

C.J. Anaya

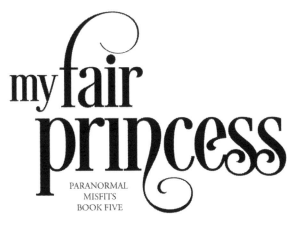

my fair princess

PARANORMAL
MISFITS
BOOK FIVE

C.J. ANAYA

Cover designed by Fiona Jayde
http://fionajaydemedia.com

This book is a work of fiction. Names, characters, places, and incidents either are products of the author's imagination or are used fictitiously. Any resemblance to actual persons, living or dead, events, or locales is entirely coincidental.

C. J. Anaya
Visit my website at http://authorcjanaya.com

Printed in the United States of America

First Printing: Aug 2019
C. J. Anaya Publishing LLC

ISBN-13 978-1-0897872-7-3

Contents

Crysta

"Crysta, wake up. Crysta, please!"

The urgent whisper was seriously unwelcome, cutting into my subconscious and rousing me from a place where pain, fear, and terror couldn't penetrate. I shied away from resurfacing as pressure in my ribs reminded me why the darkness felt so darn inviting. I was nearly pain free, sinking slowly into that coveted place of bliss when—

"We don't have much time. Princess, you must wake up!"

This was annoying.

The frantic cry ripped me from the darkness, forcing my eyes to blink once, twice, then snap open, awakening all my nerve endings. Trembling, I tried curling up into a tight ball to ward off the random stabs of pain, only to find my wrists chained above my head with my back flat against a hard slab. With bleary, unfocused eyes I gazed at the rawness of my wounds, torn and ripped just underneath the shackles. Blood encrusted the metal. I stared at it with a bit of detachment.

Is that my *wrist?*

It looked as if I'd tried and failed to rip my arms out of the restraints several times over. I couldn't remember the struggle, but delirium can cause you to do some pretty messed up things.

"Thank the goddess, you're alive. I couldn't tell with all that blood covering you."

Blood?

I slowly moved my head to the left—difficult since the muscles in them seized at the slightest movement—to see what looked to be a female Goblin in a similar predicament: chained to the same stone alter about a foot from me.

"You don't—" The muscles in my throat cramped up and I croaked, coughing up something that tasted coppery. I seriously doubted that to be a good thing. It took a moment for the Goblin to come into focus. "You don't have blood on you. Are you okay?"

She shook her head in frustration. I noticed she didn't have any problem with her neck muscles and felt an unwarranted stab of self-pity.

How come my neck feels like a vise is clamped around it?

Her large, pointed ears folded in on themselves. I found that fascinating for some reason and kept my eyes trained on them as their green folds rolled up and down in an agitated state.

Cool.

Goblins were cool.

I felt funny.

"No. Please don't lose consciousness again. We don't have time for that."

I blinked my heavy eyes open, unaware that I had closed them in the first place. I thought I'd been studiously analyzing the construct of her earlobes. Now I was blacking out again.

"What's happening?" I finally got out.

"You need to check on the Siren?"

"The Siren?"

Didn't ring any bells.

The Goblin tugged at her chains and tried to kick her legs out, which were also chained down. She writhed around as best she could considering her restraints. Were my legs chained down, too? I gave them both a good kick and immediately regretted it. They did not feel right. Fire enveloped my legs and side, jolts of agony following close on its heels. I wished I hadn't allowed this demanding Goblin to wake me up.

"The Siren," she said in exasperation. Then she nodded her chin in my direction.

I looked to my right to see a familiar figure chained next to me. It took a moment for that to register, and then the last forty-eight hours came rushing back to me in a tidal wave of horror.

King Moridan had prevented me from disapparating from his castle due to the vial of my blood he had collected. After torturing me for several hours in that dank, dark dungeon, he'd had me restrained and taken to this room of terror. It looked as if several ritualistic sacrifices had been made here.

Let's face it, they probably had.

The stone floors were stained in blood. Everything smelled musty, with a tang of ozone for good measure. It stung my nose and settled in. I'd be smelling blood for weeks, I just knew it. A myriad of torture devices lined the walls, each one of them encrusted with fluids I did not want to think about.

After bringing me to this room and chaining me down, Chantara and the Goblin female had been dragged in and chained with me.

Grizelda, the Goblin King's daughter. The joy I'd felt at seeing her alive had lasted two seconds. Then my back began to burn, bringing me to my knees...and...the memories were fuzzy after that.

Pain. Lots of pain. Lots of screaming. Holy crap, lots of screaming. A million questions about fated mate bonds and the diadem were thrown at me.

Right. Like I could answer them.

3

Stop stabbing me in the side, and I'll be happy to answer your questions, you psychopath.

He'd asked Grizelda and Chantara several questions about the diadem and its stone, but they were weird questions that had to do with the chemical compounds in the stone, the effects of Dark Magic being channeled through the diadem, and the diadem's ability to bring about eternal life. Since all I knew about the diadem was its ability to anchor the magic of fated mate bonds, I literally had no idea what to tell him.

Chemical make up? It's not like I aced Chemistry in high school.

Eternal life?

It wasn't like the diadem was the fountain of youth.

If he'd been so interested, and actually knew these items existed, why hadn't he acquired the stone and the diadem and found this out on his own? Did he really not know where they were located? Didn't he have Paio, Chantara's son, imprisoned because he thought Paio knew about the diadem?

My mind was fuzzy—on a lot of things—and my inability to answer his questions gave him more reason to inflict pain...for everyone. I might have been the one receiving the wounds, but Moridan had used magic to link Grizelda and Chantara to me in a way that tortured their bodies. They shared my pain when the burden became too much for me to handle. It prevented me from outright dying.

He was one sadistic faerie.

"Chantara," I said. I tried to move my arm just a bit, but the pain and the chains prevented it. "Chantara," I said a little louder.

She slowly began to stir. Grizelda let out a choked sob.

"I thought she was gone. I just wasn't sure if she had survived the last round of torture."

"It was that bad?"

Her eyes widened in shock. "He broke your legs and made Chantara feel the pain."

Huh. Definitely unconscious for that one. A wave of guilt bowled me over. I didn't want anyone suffering on my behalf.

"I think she is still feeling that pain because my legs only hurt if I try to move them."

"Either that or the damage is so extensive that your nerves are ruined beyond repair and you'll never walk again. Did he break your lower back? Paralyze you?"

Horrifying line of questioning.

"Your bedside manner needs work," I said.

"Huh?"

The thought of being paralyzed was scary beyond all reason. I decided to move nothing and simply brainstorm a plan to get us the hell out of this torture chamber.

"How long has Moridan been gone?" I asked.

"Thirty minutes."

"And what is the point of all this torture? I thought he wanted my blood to resurrect his dead wife. He has plenty of that, so what's the hold up here? Why am I still alive?"

"Honestly?" She shifted her broad shoulders and winced in pain. "Probably for the same reason he hasn't killed me yet. He is trying to learn everything he can about the diadem and what it can do. I have told him for months that I know nothing about the diadem, and I don't, but he doesn't believe me."

"He's had the scrolls this entire time. He could have sent anyone to claim the diadem and stone. Why is he pumping us for information when he could simply get it himself?"

Grizelda looked exhausted as she stared up at the stone ceiling.

"He seems to think this diadem is somehow tied to his dead wife, and for whatever reason, we haven't served our purpose yet. I don't pretend to understand it, or put any credit behind it, since there is no question the Seelie King is insane, but he thinks there is something to it, and that makes our situation very dangerous."

"Still, he has my blood. What is he waiting for?"

"I'm waiting for the rest of it," said a voice that would have made me fall off my altar if I hadn't been chained to it. My heart rate increased ten-fold as I stared at the apparated form of King Moridan slowly inching his way toward the end of my altar. "Your blood, and only your blood, can bring back my dead wife. It isn't a simple thing to raise the dead, young lady. One vial of blood will not do, and it must be tainted with pain, hopelessness, and despair for the spell to truly take effect."

I snorted, which hurt.

"I'm going to throw out some sound logic here in the hopes that it will combat this insanity, but do you really think any spell that requires a blood sacrifice tainted with pain, hopelessness, and despair is something you want to use to resurrect a loved one? No way your wife comes back a winner. She will be just as certifiable as you are if you attempt a spell like this."

A sharp slice of pain hit my leg, and I screamed in agony. Moridan's eyes gleamed with wicked delight as he watched my reaction. He held up another vial, one magically filling up with more blood.

"I think, Princess, that ought to be exactly what is needed."

I swallowed down another scream and tried to focus.

"You wanted me dead. You sent an assassin to kill me when I was a baby and again when I was a teenager. Why kill me if you needed my blood to bring back your wife?"

His eyes brightened momentarily. He actually appeared excited to talk about it.

6

"At the time, I had no idea your blood was needed. I simply wanted you dead. I still do. Your fated mated bond with Jareth is tearing this realm apart."

"I'm pretty sure the Dark Magic you're working is responsible for that."

He made a disapproving noise and gave me a condescending smile. "Poor Crysta, so misinformed on so many levels. Dark Magic is only dangerous if one isn't skilled in using it. My wife was a connoisseur of the Dark Arts. One of her many gifts she used to maintain balance within our kingdom before she was so brutally murdered by your father."

None of that seemed right to me. According to Jareth, Dark Magic was forbidden. If she had been working it for that long, someone would have noticed.

"You knew she'd been practicing Dark Magic when she was alive?"

"No. After she died, I found her spells. I studied her notes. I did all that I could to honor her and the valuable work she had contributed to our kingdom. Your union with my son would have disrupted the balance she'd fought to achieve, and my Seer saw that union as inevitable. I felt I had to get rid of you."

Crazy. The Lake of Beatha maintained the magical balance. Even I knew that, and I was a newbie here. So he had continued working Dark Magic and messed everything up. How convenient that he could blame the imbalance he'd created on my fated mate bond with Jareth.

"I thought you were dead, that I had solved the problem, but the imbalance continued. I worked for years to maintain order, but the imbalance became worse."

Because you were working Dark Magic, you moron.

It irked me that my birth had been blamed for mistakes he and his wife had both made.

"Several years ago, I discovered a spell so glorious, a spell so magnificent, it could accomplish what no other spell had ever been able to accomplish. Resurrection. I could bring my wife back. I knew if I did, order would be restored. With her ruling by my side, wielding her Dark Magic as she should, the realm would be healed."

"Why didn't you resurrect her right away if you've had this spell for so long?"

"That's where you come in. I had every ingredient but a specific type of blood that simply did not exist. I spent years sacrificing various faeries to come up with the right mixture of blood, but every attempt at the spell failed."

I bit my lip hard. He had callously sacrificed the lives of faeries to bring his dead wife back to life. He was beyond monstrous.

"Then I found out you were still alive, and I realized why I had failed at restoring order and balance, but here is the most interesting part of this entire tale, the thing that gives me great pleasure and a sweet sense of justice. You returned to our realm, your binding spell was released, your magic reawakened, and the Dark Magic within me sensed it. Suddenly, my search was over. I recognized your magical signature. I saw it for what it was. The blood from your parents, royal and rare. You may be the cause of this imbalance, but you are also the cure. Your blood will bring order to the chaos. Your death will give my wife new life."

I shifted a bit, tried to get comfortable, realized how stupid that idea had been, and opted for more conversation.

More talk, less torture.

"How does the diadem play into this?"

"You already know the answer to that. It's why you've been seeking it out."

Sure. I knew how it played into *our* end game, but I wasn't clear on how it played into *his*, other than preventing us from acquiring the means to destroy him and annihilate *griesha*. What did he want to do with it? "How long have you known about the crown?"

"My dearly departed wife has communicated her warnings to me."

Eh?

"I'm sorry. Your dead wife told you?"

He walked over to one of the walls filled with torture devices and grabbed a nasty looking set of pincers with hooks on the tips. "The Dark Arts can do many things. Reaching out to our loved ones is nothing. I've pored over Oberon's journals for years, but they never made sense to me. Just a bunch of mundane accounts of his life and the silly events leading up to The Rending. Yet my wife kept insisting the answers were there; that other races of Fae might know something. I've tortured countless individuals for answers, imprisoned others, mostly the offspring of royals. Paio and Grizelda were not the first or the last to have been kept here against their will. As far as where the diadem is located, I could not decipher the clues."

"But you knew we would be looking for the diadem."

"You would be seeking a way to destroy me. I knew that you would eventually come for the scrolls, but I'll admit to commissioning others in bringing you here."

"I'm aware of the deal you made with Queen Adris."

"I've made that same deal with plenty of Fae, but you eventually came to me either way."

"Jareth has the scrolls. He and my friends will find the diadem. Killing me to bring back your wife isn't going to work for you long-term. You'll still be stopped."

Moridan's smile chilled me to the bone. My words made little difference to him. He wasn't agitated by any of this, which meant he knew something I didn't. Were there really zero clues in those stupid scrolls? Had all of this been for nothing?

I thought back to the way we'd infiltrated the castle, the opposition we'd faced, the way Moridan knew where to find us in the end. The bloodletting spell. He'd been quite a few steps ahead of us all this time, knowing we would seek out the scrolls eventually. I felt supremely defeated, realizing I'd handed him the one thing he needed to enact his plan and bring back his dead wife.

And what would that do to the magical imbalance in the Fae realm?

I didn't want to find out.

I had zero mobility in my hands, but it didn't stop me from seeking out my magic. I visualized my core and reached for the colorful swirling threads. Every muscle in my body immediately seized up as my nerve endings lit with fire. I closed my eyes to focus on my core and pinpoint the source of the pain. I mentally shied away from pulling on it as I came in contact with fiery threads of what appeared to be magical barbed wire laced throughout my core.

"I'm afraid that isn't allowed, young lady," Moridan said. He tapped my bare foot with the tip of the hooked pincer. I bit my lip, but even that small reaction seemed to please him. "The chains that currently hold you are blocking your magic with a defensive spell of their own. Did you really think I'd simply stand here and grant you access to your core?"

I gave him one of my sickeningly sweet smiles. "I assumed you were just as stupid as you are insane."

Grizelda let out a muffled groan, mumbling something about royal egos and never knowing when to shut up.

"I'm going to overlook your insolence due to the celebratory mood I'm in."

King Moridan whispered something unintelligible under his breath. The sinking feeling in my stomach bottomed out as another stone altar rose from the ground, becoming level with Moridan's chest. There were several jars of body parts I didn't recognize.

"I thought it would be rude to exclude you from these proceedings, especially since your blood is so integral to bringing me my heart's greatest desire."

Yeah. Dread piled on top of dread, with a healthy dose of trepidation thrown in for good measure.

"You...can't be...serious," a small voice said. "Do you have any idea the added imbalance you will cause if you bring your wife back?"

My head slowly cranked to the right. I took in Chantara's pale face, her expression wracked with pain. I remembered any pain my body felt would be channeled into her.

"You need to release her from the spell that links us together," I said. "You have what you want. No need to hurt my friends."

"Unfortunately, the damage I've done to your body is quite extensive, and I don't want you to pass out...or die...when the fun is just beginning."

Moridan began chanting words I neither recognized nor cared to understand as he opened bottles and added ingredients into a large cauldron in the middle of the altar.

Really?

I mean, it just seemed so textbook supernatural. If he was going to bring back his dead wife wasn't there a cooler, more supernatural way of doing it than throwing witchy ingredients into an oversized cauldron? Cliché on every level.

Then he picked up some of the mixture in the cauldron with his bare hands and threw it against the stone wall. The stone peeled back, leaving a muddy, swirling vortex in its wake.

Okay, so maybe that's *not something you see every day.*

"You must stop this madness at once, Moridan," Chantara rasped. "That realm is forbidden. To open it goes against every law of nature. You will destroy us all."

Wow.

So all in all, this had been a really crappy week for us. I'd hoped for some good news and all I got was a dangerous vortex into another realm where I assumed Moridan planned to fetch his wife. If she got sent to this realm after her death then I didn't want to meet her.

Moridan reached for several vials of my blood. The vials levitated and uncorked themselves, swirling together and then migrating toward the black hole within the wall.

I kept my worried gaze on Chantara, expecting her to look defeated, but in all honesty, despite her wan, sweaty skin, her eyes were orbs of obsidian and the woman looked pissed.

Excellent.

If she had looked as discouraged as I felt, I might have truly given up all hope.

We needed as much fight in us as we could drum up because the dead queen of the Seelie Court was about to get resurrected, and I had no idea how to stop it.

Jareth

"It's been years since I've participated in a rescue mission," Queen Adris said.

I looked her over for a moment, deciding her euphoria was far more disturbing than her "resting witch face" as Crysta once put it. I tried to hold back some unmanly emotion at the thought of my fated mate and the pain she most likely endured at this very moment.

"I hate all this waiting," Nuallan said, shifting in his hammock-like cocoon. "The longer this takes us, the less time we have to prevent her death, and if your father hands her over to Rhoswen—"

I tuned Nuallan out for a moment, shifting in my own uncomfortable cocoon and wishing I could be cuddling close with Crysta in the leaves of this *reyun tree* rather than hiding out in their folds with Nuallan and Queen Adris.

"What activity can you see, Adris?" I asked. I tried to curb my impatience, but it had taken a full day to find the royal Hag within the tunnels. Then the three of us had spent the last several hours trying to get a read on the palace, the royals, and the Fae living in the outlier areas. We'd wasted a lot of time trying to figure out a way to breach the courtyard. We were several hundred yards out from the Seelie Palace and its wards, but Adris had the ability to commune with the shifting winds and could see what the wind could see.

Having an affinity with the weather was something I greatly coveted at the moment.

"I don't like it. The winds tell me there is little to no activity within the court or even the marketplace. Animals within the area are beginning to migrate further south, heading toward other kingdoms, and there is a dense cloud of Dark Magic hovering above one of the towers." She turned to me but gripped the top half of her cocoon as it jostled a bit. I reach out to steady her and clung to her gnarled hand. "Thank you. Our current, ah, hiding place leaves much to be desired."

"We're not hiding," Nuallan said rather defensively. "We're reconnoitering."

"Well, reconnoiter this, young assassin. Fae in your kingdom have either left in a mass exodus or they are hiding within their dwellings. That cloud of magic has grown in breadth and width, not to mention power, and it seems to be getting worse with every second."

"We've got to reach Crysta without tripping the wards," I said.

Adris made a satisfied sound in the back of her throat. "Those wards are no longer an issue."

"Beg your pardon?"

"Moridan is working a spell he doesn't have enough power to cast on his own. The power needed to maintain the wards has been drained. The fool has left his own kingdom weak and defenseless while he attempts only the goddess knows what—" The crows feet around her eyes deepened with worry as she paused for a moment to communicate with the elements. She muttered an ancient phrase that turned my stomach.

"What did you just say?" I asked, sincerely hoping I'd misheard.

"Your father is absolutely insane if he thinks he can pull off a spell like this and not create even more mayhem than he already has. I didn't think something like this to be possible." She leveled me with a look that made my very being shake. If Queen Adris felt afraid then we should all be terrified. "*Aiseiri*," she said. "He's accessed the Spirit realm. Any idea who he's attempting to bring back from the dead?"

"That is utterly impossible, Adris. There are no spells in existence that allow for this. My father is very powerful, but the strength this would take.

The risks to our realm. Why would he—" It hit me just as Nuallan blurted out the answer.

"Your mother. King Moridan is raising your mother."

"There will be consequences if he succeeds," Adris said.

"We apparate now." I grabbed Adris and Nuallan's hands, then I hesitated a moment. My magic had not been functioning properly due to Kheelan's sick addition to Crysta's core, and the last time I'd apparated I left Crysta behind. I knew this had more to do with her blood being in my father's possession, but I'd not risk losing Adris or Nuallan. We couldn't afford mistakes. "Will you do the honors, Queen Adris?"

"Absolutely."

I felt a sharp tug at my center, pulling me forward. Our leafy surroundings disintegrated, and soon we were standing within the Seelie Court, staring up at the most menacing visage of magic I had ever seen. The swirling clouds covered the entire palace and the outlying areas. Not a single servant stood within sight let alone a single member of the aristocracy.

"This is as close as I can get us. I've never been within the walls of the Seelie Palace."

"Where are they, Adris?" I asked.

She pointed to the tower at our right, but then her finger followed the high tower from its ground level until she gestured below us.

"They're underground?" I asked.

"I haven't seen much of the dungeons in my days, Jareth," Nuallan said. "I can't apparate us much closer than the entrance to level one."

"Do it now, Nuallan. Adris can lead us the rest of the way."

"What about her bio signature? Do you have a lock on that yet?"

I shook my head, a cloying anger building within my chest. "My father has taken every measure to cut me off from her. It's clear how blind he is to other variables, however. We can simply follow the trail of Dark Magic once we apparate."

"That dungeon is an absolute maze, Jareth."

I grabbed Nuallan and Adris again. "I've navigated much worse to get to Crysta. I'll allow nothing to keep me from her now. Take us to the dungeon, old friend."

The sharp tug at my center was all but forgotten as the entrance to the dungeons came into sharp focus. I sucked in a shocked breath. The walls were covered in red. Several of my father's guards had been slaughtered, lying outside the entrance and strewn about within the corridors. It was an absolute blood bath with no explanation as to what could have caused it.

Would my father have killed the dungeon guards?

I thought back on our arrival in the outer court and realized there hadn't been a single guard to stop or arrest us.

Had they all been killed?

Where were my brothers?

"We must hurry," Adris said, rushing ahead as if the gore didn't bother her one bit. "The power of the spell is building to a crescendo. I do not believe any of us should be in this area once that power bubbles over."

Nuallan and I rushed after her.

I'd never felt more terrified of losing Crysta than I did in that moment.

Crysta

*I*f I'd thought a portal into some kind of death realm was the most terrifying thing ever, it was only because I'd yet to see my blood smear itself across the surface of said portal. That's right. My blood just molded itself across the entire opening like some morbid Tupperware lid. For a moment nothing happened. I sincerely hoped that was the end of the show until the surface began to boil.

Ah dang!

In true *Alien* fashion, the outline of a face slowly appeared, pushing forward, covered in my blood. Soon the head began to emerge, and then the shoulders, until a womanly form emerged from the portal...*completely covered in my blood.*

There were sanitation laws about this sort of thing in the human realm. Blood transfusions were seen as sinful by some religions. Humans held all sorts of reservations and scruples when it came to sharing bodily fluids.

Rightly so.

Yet this female had willingly walked through several pints of my blood like it was the cure for anti-aging.

What the hell was wrong with these people?

"Rebirth," Chantara muttered. "Born from the womb and the blood of our mothers."

"I am *not* this woman's mother. No one is allowed access to my womb without my permission," I hissed, beginning to panic.

"It's symbolic," she said in a weak voice. "But it also goes against nature. He may get his wife back, but she won't be the same."

"Maybe that would be a good thing," I whispered. I watched in horror as the queen's skin absorbed the rest of my blood. Oh, the nightmares. I'd never sleep soundly again. "Moridan's wife doesn't seem all that wonderful if she was doing Dark Magic in her first life. Maybe this time around she'll be reborn a pacifist."

"Moridan must be mistaken. I knew his wife well, and she never practiced such things."

"Someone certainly did."

Moridan stepped forward as his wife lifted her hands and reached for him. Her skin continued to absorb my blood until she stood there in nothing but her birthday suit.

For real. The lady was completely naked and not a bit embarrassed by it.

Small potatoes, I guess. I probably wouldn't have been concerned about clothing after stepping through a portal that meant the difference between life and death. Her long silver hair fell down her back in perfectly structured waves. I was only getting a side profile here, but her delicate nose and high cheekbones looked slightly familiar. I couldn't recall ever seeing this woman before, but I felt an awful sense of foreboding as recognition set in.

Moridan fell to his knees, kissing his wife's hands and openly crying as she reached out to stroke his silver hair.

"My love, I cannot believe it is you."

"There, there, Moridan, my darling. You did so well. You finally acquired the necessary blood to set me free."

"Set you free? That doesn't sound like rebirth to me," I said. I hadn't realized I'd spoken until the woman's head swiveled sharply, taking me in. I nearly peed my pants when her shocking blue eyes locked with mine.

Holy crap.

Chantara gasped. "Mother? Is...is that you?"

The woman standing before us in all her naked glory was not the queen we had expected. Her gaze shot to Chantara where she studied her for a moment, quickly dismissed her, and then shifted back to me. Her interest in me was obvious. I didn't like the cold, calculating way she gazed at me, like a scientist eyeing an experiment, and there was something seriously wrong with her eyes. Despite the crystalline blue, she had some strange silver streaks zigzagging their way through the whole of them. Her eyes held a lightning storm within their midst.

The woman standing before us was not King Moridan's wife.

It was Queen Titania.

Jareth

"We have to double back again," Adris said.

Nuallan's groan of frustration echoed my own feelings, but there was no help for it. She was absolutely right. The dungeons were an endless maze of twists and turns. Certain corridors led us closer to Crysta's location, but many became dead ends. She could have been just beyond one of these walls, but we couldn't break through. We had to follow the correct path and circle back.

An infuriating waste of our time.

Several more minutes passed with Adris finding another corridor, taking us back in the direction of the Dark Magic, and following it until we hit another dead end.

Rinse. Repeat.

We were getting absolutely nowhere.

We trudged through more corridors leading to dead ends until we came to one that housed three dead guards, all lined up along the end of the tunnel.

"What in all the nine realms is this?" Nuallan asked.

"I'm not sure, but the Dark Magic is positively pulsing from this area," Adris said.

We approached the guards, surprised to find three Formage faeries. When Formage weren't creating shimmering mirages to protect themselves, their true appearance was always so startling. Violet hair, teal-colored skin, and pure white eyes. They covered themselves in thick clothing of neutral colors to protect their sensitive skin.

"What are these men doing here? There are no Formage in the King's guard," Nuallan said.

I studied the blue liquid leeching from several wounds along their chests, but the fluids were not falling according to the laws of gravity.

"Prince Jareth, look at this." Adris moved closer to the wall and pointed to a dark blue trail of Formage blood that crept along the stone wall, falling into the cracks and splintering outward. The lines of blood appeared sentient, slithering along the cracks and crevices like a host of parasitic worms. I'd never seen anything like it.

"What do you make of it?" I asked her.

"Your father did this, but I don't understand why. We have three Formage, murdered, and then left in upright positions against this wall where their blood is somehow defying gravity, intertwining to create a protective—"

"Wall," Nuallan and I said at the same time.

"Is it possible for Formage blood to work mirages even when the owners of said blood have been killed?" Nuallan asked.

"Sacrificed, you mean." Adris leveled us with a solemn look. "With Dark Magic, it is absolutely possible. We need to remove these faeries. Pull them away from the wall and lay them side-by-side."

Nuallan and I did as instructed. As a seasoned warrior and assassin, I was well acquainted with death, meting out justice when required, but I felt wholly sickened by the ruthlessness of their wounds, the obvious pain they'd endured as they bled out. I gently set the last one down on his back and carefully closed his eyes, committing all their faces to memory. These faeries had loved ones, families, of that I was certain. Formage had strong family units and protected their own at any cost. There would be much for me to make up for when it came to repairing the damage my father had wrought within this realm.

"It's still solid," Adris mumbled.

I stood as she slid her fingers along the cracks of the wall, not seeming to mind the Formage blood now coating her hands.

"So this isn't a mirage," I said.

"The Dark Magic is the strongest I have ever felt. It has to be here. If we double back again we will lose Crysta. We are missing something." Her sharp teeth bit into her bottom lip as she studied the wall, running her hands up and down the length of it and then the height. She pulled her hands back and stared at her palms.

I had no idea what she thought she could divine from this, but I was fresh out of solutions and panic had already impaired my ability to troubleshoot our current predicament. That I stood in this dungeon, a crown prince and an assassin, one of the most powerful faeries in this realm, yet couldn't locate and rescue my fated mate was like a heavy anchor wrapped around my neck, weighing me down in every way imaginable. My failings hammered at my usual confidence. Never once had I truly kept Crysta safe. It had been Crysta's determination, her tenacity in the face of insurmountable odds, that had pulled her through time and time again, despite my well-intentioned bumblings.

But I could not fail her now.

Not now.

Adris moved her gaze from her hands to the faeries laying at my feet.

"They're not truly dead."

"What?" Nuallan asked in disbelief. "They have to be. No pulse. All this blood loss. There is no sign of life within them."

"They are not alive, but they are not dead." Her hands trembled as she approached them. "Your father has suspended their spiritual entities; a limbo state. They can still feel everything their body is enduring. Their blood and their spiritual energies are linked together, looping back and forth, trapping them within their bodies. They cannot die, which means their blood is perfectly capable of powering this mirage to the extent that it not only looks real but feels real."

"But it's not real?"

"Depends on your version of reality and what dimension or realm you are working within, but for the sake of simplicity, I will state that this particular mirage is real and solid for us on this plane of existence. They are suffering, and the mirage is powered by their blood and their suffering. We need to set them free."

"How?"

"This is not what I signed up for," Adris said. She looked extremely uneasy as she continued to stare at the Formage. She closed her eyes and took in two deep breaths.

"Adris, how bad is it going to be?"

She dodged my questions and began barking out orders.

Which meant this was going to be very bad, indeed.

"I will need both of you to stand next to me. We must retrieve their hearts and destroy them. It must be done at the same time or there will be blow-back from Moridan's spell."

Astronomically bad.

"That's going to require a death spell, Adris. There will be consequences."

Magic, like anything else, required payment depending on the actions and the intent. Karma was not just a notion humans believed in. Spells such as these had a tendency to retaliate down the road, depending on what the result of such spells managed to accomplish.

"Let's just hope Nature understands the reasons for the extreme measures we must take. These men are suffering. There is no way to save them. We set them free, we get rid of the mirage, and we save the future queen of the Unseelie Court."

"I can work with those intentions," I said as I came up next to her and faced the fallen faeries.

"Just another day in the service of the Seelie Court," Nuallan said. He stood on Adris's other side, and then we waited for her signal.

"We say the words together at the same time. We don't say the last word of the incantation until I signal."

"Understood." I waited for her lead.

"*Cuireann an bás scaoileadh an anam éiríonn an spiorad ag dul suas.*"

We repeated the words with her, and the Formage began to arch and thrash.

"Stop," Adris said. She took in a labored breath and let it out. "We do this in English."

Nuallan and I gave her a questioning look.

"Your father is expecting the Irish tongue. There is no telling what types of traps he has set within this spell once it recognizes its counter spell. The moment we began in Irish, the Formage suffered. English will give us time to dismantle it and free the Formage, hopefully before we are met with any other tricks."

"In English, then?" I gave Nuallan a nod to make sure he followed. His scornful expression suggested I'd just offended his intelligence. It pleased me that some things between Nuallan and myself would never change.

"Everyone together," Adris said. "Death compels the soul's release. Spirit ascends and heartbeats cease."

"Death compels the soul's release. Spirit ascends and heartbeats cease." Nuallan and I repeated the spell over and over again, but the results of the spell were sickening to watch.

The sound of tearing flesh did in no way dispel the notion that we were somehow putting these faeries out of their misery. As their chest cavities opened wide, rivulets of blue blood began to levitate, slowly moving toward the wall behind us. We ignored the display and focused on the hearts, now rising before us in a row. There was an obsidian blade of magic running through all three, connecting the hearts together and preventing the souls from escape.

Our voices rose in volume and intensity as we continued to repeat the spell, focusing our combined power on the pulsating hearts and the black blade connecting them. The Formage began to writhe in pain again as the traps within the spell were finally tripped. We couldn't say the last word of the spell, however, not until Adris signaled. It was agonizing to watch the pain of the Formage while we focused our power and energy on destroying their hearts.

Sweat trickled down my temples, and my body shook with the force of the Dark Magic we were up against. Three fully powered faeries, two royals among us, and we struggled to maintain our focus and strength under this assault.

The power my father wielded truly terrified me.

Adris finally lifted her hand and signaled the last word of the spell.

"Freedom," we shouted.

The hearts pulsated for a moment longer before they exploded in a cloud of ash. The Formage lay still, their blood succumbing to gravity's pull. We turned to face the wall only to discover it missing. In its place was another long corridor leading to a flight of stairs.

"Goody," Nuallan said. "I haven't had my cardio for the day."

I rushed toward the bottom of the staircase with Nuallan and Adris following close at my heels. I didn't know what awaited me at the top of those steps, but if I found Crysta's lifeless form, there would be hell to pay.

And my father would be the one to pay it.

Crysta

Queen Titania's eyes narrowed, hyper-focused on me, the streaks of silver within them flashing in a way that deeply disturbed me. She raised a creamy white hand and pointed her finger. I flinched, assuming she was about to curse me or inflict some type of magical torture that Chantara would have to endure.

"We only need that one. Kill the other two."

Uh, excuse me?

"Your mama said what now?"

My attention moved to Chantara. I hoped she had some answers here since the resurrection or release—or whatever this was—of her mother had to make sense to *someone* in the room.

Chantara took the fight right out of me with her vulnerable expression. She no longer appeared ready to fight. Instead, she looked ready to absolutely lose her shiz in the worst way imaginable.

I'm talking some serious snot crying here.

So no help from that corner of the sacrificial altar.

Titania made her way toward Grizelda with murderous intent oozing from her aura.

"Now hold on just a second. Nobody moves," I said, feeling the last shreds of my fear dissipate as anger took over. Titania halted her movements and turned those emotionless eyes on me. "She's your daughter," I said, nudging my head in Chantara's direction. "I know you haven't seen her since she was a baby, but you must recognize her as your own on some level."

Titania's gaze moved to Chantara, showing the first real spark of emotion I'd seen since she'd morphed from a bloody blob to a faerie queen. She circled the foot of the altar and made her way to her daughter. Chantara looked too wasted to do anything other than stare at her mother with a resigned expression. It made me wonder if drawing attention to their familial connection had been a mistake. When Titania locked her eyes on you, it was with chilling intensity that bordered on predatory.

"This is my...*our* daughter?" she asked. She gave Moridan a questioning look. Not accusatory like I felt he deserved, and what did she mean "our daughter"?

I waited for Moridan to sputter or backpedal. How exactly was he going to explain himself to his *wife*—still mystified on that erroneous detail—when her daughter showed major evidence of torture at his hand?

Moridan didn't look right. Not that he ever looked right, but those crazy streaks of silver in Titania's eyes were now in his. The adoration in his expression as he addressed Titania looked fanatical. "Of course not, my queen. Don't you remember the faces of our children? This particular creature is a Siren, not fit to be considered one of us. She has been most valuable throughout this process, however. Incredibly strong when bearing the brunt of Crysta's pain. It has assisted in prolonging Crysta's life."

"He's been bewitched," Grizelda muttered under her breath.

At her words, sickening realization hit me. He had no idea who this woman truly was. Titania had somehow fried his brain, making him think he was talking to his dead wife. I had no idea what he saw when he looked at the scary queen, but it wasn't the same thing the rest of us saw.

Still, whether he knew it or not, he'd been torturing Titania's daughter, and that had to piss off the queen to some extent. My eyes moved to her royal highness, waiting for those crazy silver streaks to shoot out of her eyes and fry Moridan like so much crispy bacon. I fully believed she had the power to destroy him and solve all our problems.

Well, the problem that was Moridan.

"Excellent use of your resources, my darling, but I do believe it is time to put this unworthy Siren and this disgusting Goblin out of their misery."

Whaaaaaat?

Okay. I'd clearly read the room wrong.

Moridan was an evil monster, but he wasn't the one in charge. Not by a long shot. He was more of a pawn, a minion doing Titania's bidding. If Moridan was the puppet, then Titania was the sadistic puppeteer who held no qualms about killing one of her own.

And we had a whole new set of issues to deal with, providing I didn't die on this altar.

"So you're cool with killing your own daughter? You're brought back from—I don't know where, actually—and your first act is to murder your daughter and a Goblin royal?"

"I'm afraid she doesn't know what she is talking about, my queen," Moridan said.

"They are not necessary," Titania said. "And the purification of our realm will require sacrifice."

"Purification?" That did not sound good. "Why are you here?"

Metallic zigzags sparked within her eyes as a slow smile crept across her lips.

Chilling.

"To finish what I began so long ago. To restore order once and for all. To bring back what was lost. To avenge wrongdoings. To make him pay."

"That makes no sense. It also sounds like an abstract to-do list."

Her smile never wavered, and her eyes never left mine as she said, "Kill them, Moridan."

Jareth

"Kill them, Moridan."

I didn't recognize the voice, and I couldn't think of a single royal female who would have dared to bark out commands to the king of the Seelie Court, but I gave up all pretense of stealth upon hearing that order and raced up the remaining bit of staircase with Nuallan and Adris right at my heels. I barely made sense of the scene before me. The only thing that truly registered was Crysta secured to a crimson altar and my father's hand lifting as he prepared to follow through with the kill order.

"*Segmentum,*" I yelled. My Summer magic surged through my fingertips, barreling into my father's chest and flinging him against the wall where he slumped to the floor unconscious. I'd meant for my magic to cleave his hand off at the wrist, but this would do just as well.

"Jareth, look out," Crysta screamed.

I ducked low, feeling scorching heat lick the back of my neck. The spell meant for me exploded against the wall. Adris and Nuallan yelled out defensive spells behind me, protecting my flank. I roll toward the sound of Crysta's voice and came up on the side of an enormous altar covered in blood. I panicked, wondering if all this blood belonged to my fated mate. Then I saw her companions and had even more to worry about. Crysta lay chained between Chantara and Princess Grizelda.

Wonderful to have them all in one place.

Not so wonderful that their injuries would most certainly lead to death if we didn't get them out of here.

"I'm afraid we don't have time for this."

My eyes zeroed in on the source of the voice. I stared in stunned silence as I took in a faerie who perfectly resembled Queen Titania. A woman whose image I'd studied a thousand times over during my research of Fae history. Her eyes flashed lightning as she stared at Nuallan and Adris who held aloft threatening balls of light from their own core magics.

"Well met, Prince Jareth." She eyed Nuallan with approval, but her distaste for Adris was obvious. "I'm afraid I only approve of half of your entourage. Unfavorable company you keep."

"You're here working with my father. I'm afraid it is you who keeps unfavorable company. And why the hell are you naked?"

Her expression turned a tad condescending as she tsked in disapproval. "Your father mentioned there would be members of this family who would fail to fall in line. I do not wish to kill one of my own, but I'm afraid this quest for purification will require painful sacrifice."

"Who are you?" I bit out.

She appeared a bit indignant. "Your history books must be woefully lacking. I am Queen Titania, the true queen of this entire realm."

Adris sucked in a breath. "Your father didn't bring your mother back from the dead. He brought Titania back."

"You are not worthy to speak my name, Hag." Queen Titania's eyes narrowed in anger as she flicked a finger in Adris's direction. Nuallan's quick thinking blocked her spell as his Summer magic encircled Titania's, easily dissolving it before it could reach Adris.

Which truly puzzled me. Queen Titania was one of the most powerful faeries to have ever existed. Yet Nuallan easily subdued her spell. I inched toward the altar, but she threw out another spell which I deflected with one of my own.

She's not at full power yet.

Adris and Nuallan must have come to the same conclusion. They immediately began flinging spell after spell at her as I grabbed hold of the chains around Grizelda's wrists. I sensed their spelled essence immediately.

Nothing can ever be easy.

I focused my intent on the chains and prayed to the goddess my spell would behave correctly. "*Segmentum.*"

The shackles, rather than breaking in two, disintegrated into ash. Not the original plan, but the outcome worked for me. Unfortunately, the moment the chains disintegrated, Crysta began to writhe in pain, and the agonized scream that followed pierced me to the very center of my core. I looked up to see her broken body convulsing.

"She's feeling everything now," Chantara said.

An explosion just above my head brought my attention back to Adris and Nuallan who were doing their best to shield us from Titania's intense assault. With every spell they deflected, Titania appeared to grow stronger. I realized she was absorbing their magic. She didn't intend to hurt them yet. She wanted to draw out their fire so she could benefit from the effects.

"Get Crysta out of here now, Chantara. Apparate to the Unseelie palace," I said.

Grizelda and Chantara grabbed Crysta's hand to disapparate from the room.

But only Grizelda and Chantara disappeared.

Flaming pixie wands. Crysta's blood was everywhere, binding her to the castle, most likely binding her to the altar.

I crawled across the altar to get to my fated mate just as her eyes rolled back. I checked for a pulse, relieved to find one, but noting its weakness. Another explosion of rock hit the wall to my left.

We couldn't go on like this. Crysta didn't have much time left, and Titania was merely toying with us as she used the energy from Adris and Nuallan to fuel her own core.

We can't get her out of here until the blood is destroyed.

I focused my intent on the blood and called out, "*Uanescere.*" Rather than disintegrate, the blood on the altar sizzled, white smoke rising as the fluid evaporated. I closed my eyes and searched for her essence within the room, but I couldn't be sure I'd managed to destroy all the blood. Her bio signature was everywhere.

Time to try again.

I flung another spell at Titania just above her head, raining down more rock and debris. She stumbled to the floor, shrieking as she went. My next spell aimed at disorientation. It would only work for a moment (if it worked at all) before she absorbed the energy and gained even more power, but I needed to buy us some time.

"Adris, Nuallan, you're going to have to apparate with Crysta. Get to Roderick."

"What about you, Jareth?" Nuallan asked.

"I'm not leaving until I know you're able to apparate with Crysta."

They moved to her side and grabbed her hand just as Titania regained her footing.

"Now!"

Adris and Nuallan disappeared before my eyes, but Crysta remained on the altar.

Bloody hell!

Literally.

More blood. My father had more of Crysta's blood within the palace.

I cast my magic out again, directing my search in a meticulous sweep over the room as Titania stood to her full height and stared at me with unconcealed amusement.

"You're quite powerful, Prince Jareth. And your magic is intoxicating. Absorbing it has been a surprising treat."

"That's some dangerous Dark Magic you're practicing, absorbing magical energy from others. I'm surprised you would dabble in such things."

Her pale lips spread wide. Her smile did not give me what Crysta referred to as the "warm fuzzies".

"Dabble. How cute. You would make for a powerful ally in purging the land of impure blood."

"I'm afraid I don't understand what you're talking about. I don't know why you're here or why my father brought you back from the dead."

"I was never dead, Prince Jareth. I was trapped, and your father stumbled upon me in his quest to bring back your mother. He's been in my thrall ever since, believing everything I tell him, including the notion that I am his wife." She cocked her head, looking at my father slumped on the floor. "Poor Moridan. Some cores aren't meant to wield Dark Magic." She tapped her temple. "Messes with the mind, you see, although I suspect you've noticed your father's mental instability for some time now."

My father let out a low groan and shifted a bit, sending me a reading I hadn't picked up on before. I swept my energy over his body with clearer intent and identified a faint, yet familiar, signature.

"Now, as to why I'm here, I should think that obvious."

"And yet, I remain completely mystified."

I did a mental pull on the signature and noticed something moving within the pocket of my father's waistcoat.

It must be that vial of blood Paio mentioned. My father still has it.

"You did study your Fae history, yes?"

I gave her a vacant stare, hoping it would encourage her to talk more and attack less.

"Surely your books mentioned my reign as queen and the policies I enforced to purify our realm as I came to understand the power of the Dark Arts."

"Sorry. I'm afraid there was never any mention of Dark Arts or purification goals. You were murdered by Oberon after Puck worked Dark Magic on you, causing your child to be born the first mermaid."

She rolled her eyes. "Lies and half-truths. I'm most certainly here to make Puck pay for his part in my imprisonment, and the measures he took to mutate my daughter into something completely unrecognizable."

That grabbed my attention for a moment. "Make Puck pay for his part...Puck is dead. He and Oberon slew each other in one of the many wars between the Unseelie and Seelie Court."

Her eyes sparkled malice as her smile turned cruel. "Lies and half-truths, Prince Jareth. Those who dictate laws also dictate history. It is clear no one truly knows what happened between my husband, my lover, and I."

I glanced at Crysta, weighing my options.

"Escape won't help you in the long run, Prince. Crysta is more integral to my plans than you could possibly imagine."

"Are you saying you need Crysta alive?" I asked.

"Of course."

"Then I need to heal her. She doesn't have much time left."

Titania took a moment to study Crysta's still form. It pained me to see her chest barely rise and fall.

"By all means," she said, motioning me toward the altar.

I slowly inched toward Crysta, crawling backward on the altar and grabbing her arm.

Then I shot my hand toward my father and whispered, "*Recuperet.*" The vial of blood escaped the pocket of my father's waistcoat and flew to my hand.

I stared at Titania as she registered what I held. "Incendia," I said, causing the vial to burst into flames, destroying the last hold my father had over Crysta.

I expected Titania to attack me for my deception. Instead, the last thing I saw as Crysta and I disapparated from the palace was an enigmatic smile splintering across the cold, angular planes of the queen's face.

Jareth

The moment we apparated within the Unseelie courtyard, a bevy of familiar faces raced toward us, with King Roderick leading the charge and Kheelan, Adris, and Nuallan following closely behind.

Chuck had already swooped in, reaching Crysta before anyone else managed it. The poor thing squawked in alarm upon seeing Crysta's physical state.

"How did you get her out of there?" Roderick asked as he reached us and knelt next to her.

I didn't register his question at first. Instead, I pulled Crysta close to me as I sat haphazardly on the stone floor, assessing her injuries while Chuck nudged her head, making plaintive noises that damn near broke my heart. He breathed magic across her face, stabilizing her core temperature. I allowed him to do whatever he could as Kheelan knelt next to Roderick and reached for her hand.

Chuck hissed and bit at Kheelan's fingers.

"Easy, Lizard. I'm only trying to help." Kheelan swiftly pulled his hand back before Chuck could take a bite. His mother was injured, and he would attack anyone attempting to touch Crysta. I was surprised he hadn't attacked me.

"Chuck," I said in a calm tone, "we will need Kheelan's help. I will heal her, and so will you, but we can't save her without Kheelan."

Chuck looked between Crysta and my brother, scrunching up his snout in distaste, torn between protecting her and healing her. Finally, his common sense won the battle, and he gave Kheelan a reluctant snort to proceed.

I understood his sentiment. Kheelan was not my favorite at the moment, but we had no choice. As much as I hated to admit it, my brother was an accomplished healer, far superior to me, and already kneeling next to my beloved, looking horrified at the bloody scene before him. Compound fractures to both legs, multiple lacerations along her arms and chest, and internal bleeding that could end her life at any moment.

We didn't hesitate to use our combined magics to begin reparations to her system. The damage was so extensive, I could hardly stand it. I should have killed my father when I'd had the chance. Whether he had been in his right mind or not, there was simply no allowing him to live after this.

Kheelan and I wrestled for control as we attempted to heal her, but our magics were still behaving erratically due to his invasive spell hijacking my bond with Crysta and latching itself to her core. We did our best to work around the tangled mass of connected cords in her center, but I sensed Kheelan's own frustration at the hurtful side effects his reckless decisions had caused.

I didn't doubt his desire to protect her, but his own selfish needs had placed her in even more danger now that neither one of our magics behaved predictably.

Chuck continued to monitor her internal temperature and her vitals, regulating her heart rate as certain repairs put excess strain on her organs. Chuck's added magic proved a tremendous help.

After repairing the internal injuries and the damage done to her legs, I released hold of my core magic, recognizing that Kheelan could finish the job faster if my magic no longer interfered.

I stared at Crysta's wan and bloody face, feeling utterly broken.

I'm a prince of the Seelie Court. I'm one of the most feared assassins in our realm. I'm one of the most powerful faeries to have ever been born, and I have never felt more incapable or less competent in all my centuries of living.

It took one beautiful woman to bring me to my knees.

And yet this singular female had made me feel more invincible than I'd ever felt in my many decades of life. Love was the most powerful and most destructive force I'd ever encountered, more so than any spell or curse one might cast.

"Please, tell me she's going to make it," Roderick said in a hushed voice.

I finally took my focus off Crysta's face to stare at his grief-stricken expression.

"She'll be fine, Roderick."

Physically.

Psychologically, I wasn't so sure.

The Unseelie King let out a heavy breath and nearly burst into tears. I didn't blame him. It had taken me everything I had to maintain emotional control. I looked up to see more familiar faces crowded around us.

Paio and Chantara stood behind Roderick's kneeling form. Princess Grizelda and Adris were next to them, staring at Crysta with touching concern. Cedric flanked them all, shifting just enough for his wings to have unfolded, creating a protective semi-circle around our group. I didn't see Terise, Graul, or Lily, which caused me some concern.

"We have much to discuss," I said to King Roderick. "I need to update you on what we discovered when we rescued Crysta, and you need to tell me what's been going on in my absence."

"Chantara was trying to fill us in just as you apparated with Crysta. I'm not sure I follow much of it. Queen Titania back from the dead. Moridan a mere puppet in this massive conspiracy. I agree we have much to share."

"Well, let's share it in a large room where we can all discuss what the hell is going on while keeping an eye on Crysta," Kheelan said. "She's perfectly fine for now. We just need to wait for her to wake up. The strain of the trauma she endured may keep her unconscious for a while."

I looked at Chantara, remembering what she had suffered in Crysta's stead.

"Chantara, what about you? Please, what can we do for you?"

Her eyes glowed obsidian as she gazed from me to Crysta and back again. "We're going to find a way to annihilate my mother, no matter what it takes."

I made no more reference to her emotional state, completely understanding the need to focus on the task at hand rather than the fallout of what she'd endured.

She would process everything in due time.

"Let's get her inside the castle," Kheelan said. He reached for her, but Chuck snapped his jaws in defiance, nearly taking off my brother's hand.

I adored that scrawny Dragon.

"I am grateful for your help, Kheelan. Truly I am. Without your healing capabilities, Crysta would have perished, but Chuck and I can take it from here."

Chuck snorted in agreement and crawled on top of Crysta's torso, curling up just under her chin and letting out a satisfied grunt.

Kheelan's mouth turned up at the corner, giving us both a superior half-smile. Then he stood and backed away.

I gathered Crysta into my arms and got to my feet. As I began walking forward, Roderick stayed close to my side, and the rest of our group followed.

"How are Graul and Lily?" I asked.

"Kheelan was able to heal them both. His gift is quite remarkable," he said with grudging respect. "I sent them to follow up on a recent outbreak of *griesha* on a race that shouldn't be experiencing any symptoms. The Formage are powerful magic wielders."

"Formage? I wonder if there is any connection to this new outbreak and the Formage we encountered guarding the entrance to the tower," I mused.

"What was that?" he asked aghast.

"I'll explain everything once we get inside." As we hurried forward, I ran a mental head count of everyone with us, minus Lily and Graul. There was one person missing. "And Terise?" I asked. "Was Adris' daughter able to pull her out of the sleeping curse?"

Roderick appeared surprisingly angry. "Not only is Terise not awake, her illness has returned."

"Her illness? What do you mean?"

"About fifteen minutes ago, her skin began to develop red, splotchy sores, covering her entire body."

"Please tell me it isn't—"

"*Griesha*. She has *griesha* again."

Crysta

A faint buzzing noise made my ears feel like they'd been stuffed with cotton. Everything sounded a bit muffled around me. A familiar scent tickled my senses. It was a wholesome, comforting scent, like the earth after a spring rain. I shifted slightly and felt arms tighten round me, protecting me from the horrors I'd eventually face once I came to and dealt with more of Moridan's torture.

Except, didn't something go wrong with Moridan's plans?

The muffled sounds finally cleared, and I made out a few familiar voices.

"Let's start from the beginning. You say when you reached the tower to rescue Crysta, you found Queen Titania fighting on Moridan's side?" The voice sounded like my father, King Roderick.

I blinked my eyes open to verify the information, but I stared at the strong lines of Jareth's face as he cradled me in his arms.

Clarity returned...kind of. Jareth came to save me, but how he managed it was an absolute blank for me.

And now...

I felt a heaviness on my chest but figured I was just a little sore. I tilted my head to take in the room, but I didn't recognize the sterile environment. There were several beds lined up against the wall with a few occupants covered in red sores. My thoughts flashed to *griesha*. I was in a medical ward, and I didn't like it one bit.

"I don't understand it myself," Jareth said.

My eyes scanned the bodies of those faeries who suffered so needlessly. I saw a few Formage, a Nyad, and two Land Dwellers. Why on earth were they here with no Dark Elves in sight. Of course, no telling which races would be best suited for forming bonds with the Nyad and Formage races.

Then I remembered, whether they had found a suitable mate or not, they still needed me and Jareth to perform the spell.

Why the hell had everyone let me sleep?

I shifted a bit in Jareth's arms and then pushed completely out of them, nearly rolling off the bed. The heaviness on my chest squeaked in outrage.

"What in the...Crysta? What are you doing? You need to rest," Jareth said.

Then I recognized one of the Land Dwellers and nearly lost my shiz. Terise was in a bed across from me, and she still appeared to be suffering from Moridan's curse. I pulled against Jareth's restraining hand and yanked so hard I *did* go rolling off the bed this time.

Oof.

A very graceful landing.

More squeaking and squawking, though it sounded familiar.

I hurriedly stood, slapping away the hands trying to help me. "We've got faeries here suffering from *griesha*, Terise is still cursed, and you have me in a bed next to them, sleeping, of all things! We should be helping everyone in this room. Why are you letting me sleep?"

Dizziness overtook me, and the room blurred, making the many concerned faces surrounding me take second place to the one faerie I absolutely had to get my hands on. I remembered my own sleeping curse. It hadn't been pleasant. I didn't want Terise suffering a single moment longer than she had to.

A broad chest moved into my field of vision, and strong arms encircle me as I lost my footing and nearly had another graceless landing.

"Crysta," my father said. He chuckled a bit as he rubbed my back and kept me upright. "You have no idea how relieved I am to see you in one piece even though you can barely balance on your own two feet."

"That's crazy talk," I said, sinking into his embrace. "I'm a ballerina. I possess amazing balance."

That got more laughs from the group.

"Give it a moment, dear. Just wait until you regain your equilibrium."

I did as my father said, and took in a few deep breaths, steadying myself before pulling away from his embrace. Everyone circled us, taking their turn to give me a hug. I embraced Chantara and Paio, relieved to see them reunited. Graul and Lily stepped forward, and I flung myself into their arms.

"I was so certain I'd lost you both," I said, tears streaming down my face. "I can't believe you're standing in front of me healthy and whole."

Graul rubbed my back and placed a kiss on my head. "Kheelan heal us. Not like it much. He has cold hands."

"What Graul means," Lily said as she swatted him on the arm, "is we are very grateful to Kheelan for using his magic to save our lives."

Graul gave her a distasteful grunt. "Glad he save you. I was fine."

I turned as Kheelan approached, his expression a bit rueful as he opened his arms wide for a hug. I held out my hand.

"Thanks for saving my friends."

His rueful expression melted into amusement as he took a step back. "I'll hold out for the hug once you're ready to finally forgive me."

"Don't hold your breath," I muttered.

I ignored his hearty laugh as Cedric pushed his way through for a hug.

"I've kept Terise safe," he reassured me.

"I knew you would, Cedric. We'll wake her up soon. I promise you."

His watery smile tore at my heart. Nuallan was next, giving me a big bear hug after lifting me off my feet.

"Too many close calls, Crysta. I'd appreciate it if you and danger parted ways for a week or two. We all need a little vacation."

"Agreed," Adris said, getting in her turn. "You gave us quite a scare."

44

I relished her musty swamp scent. The fact that I was alive to smell it, made the awful odor that much more endearing.

Once she let me go, I turned to Jareth and took him in. I still had to suck in a breath every time I saw him. You'd think that at some point I'd get used to such raw perfection, but there were moments when I couldn't believe Jareth was real and that he loved me.

And perched upon his shoulder was my sweet little dragon, looking a bit miffed. I managed to walk toward them in a straight line—thank you—and threw myself in Jareth's arms. Chuck spread his little wings around our heads and licked our cheeks. The room grew silent as Jareth simply held me close and ran his fingers through my hair.

"I keep thinking I'll get used to the worry and the fear, but it never abates, Crysta. Not with you at risk. We need to get Titania's Diadem and end this madness as quickly as we can."

I pulled back to look at him, noticing the dark circles under his eyes and the strain around his mouth. The worry he must have felt once he had apparated and I hadn't. It sickened me to think about what that moment had done to him.

"You came for me," I said, reaching up to run my fingers through his hair.

He closed his eyes and let out a contented sigh. "Always."

When I didn't have the power to save myself, he saved me.

The damsel in distress once again, but this time it felt different. More like a partnership. There would be times I'd need saving and times Jareth would need saving. Moments when I would need his strength, and moments when he would need mine.

I didn't feel a hint of embarrassment as Jareth gave me a kiss so sweet and tender, my eyes burned with emotion. Once we ended the kiss and I turned in his arms, it was to see our motley crew of faeries, staring at us with soppy smiles on their faces...minus Kheelan of course. If he wasn't smug and above it all, he was usually scowling.

My father, Lily, Graul, Chantara, Kheelan, Paio, Cedric, Terise, Adris, and my sweet Chuck. As far as our group went, I was pretty sure we would all be saving each other in one form or another. That's what family did. We offered up our strengths to sustain us through our weaknesses.

"Kiss was good," Graul said. "Her eyes sparkle."

I chuckled, appreciating Graul's lack of tact or anything bordering on social niceties.

"Where's Grizelda?" I asked.

"We have her resting in her own quarters," my father said. "Her injuries were superficial, but she needed the rest and an opportunity to scry her parents in privacy."

"That reunion is long overdue," Chantara said. She gave Paio's arm a squeeze.

I couldn't imagine how she felt now that her son had been found.

Adris came forward then and lifted my chin, examining my eyes. It made me wonder if there was something more to what Graul had just said. She looked worried for a moment, but then she pasted a smile on her haggard face and stepped back.

"Will I live?" I asked.

"So far so good," she said, but she sounded troubled.

"Adris?"

"It will keep. Let's focus on the problem at hand."

Right. We had so many problems, but the most pressing one needed to be dealt with right away.

"I know we need to work out how Titania returned and why, but Terise is my number one priority right now. Did your daughter make any progress with her?" I asked Adris as I approached Terise's bedside. I stopped short as I took in her skin, covered in red, splotchy sores.

My eyes flicked to Kheelan's. "Did you break your bond with her?" I asked not bothering to hide my outrage.

His eyes flashed anger, but he kept silent as my father intervened.

"No, Crysta. This had nothing to do with Kheelan. It's a recent development. Her sores showed up a little before you were rescued."

I sat down next to Terise and took in the marks. They were awful. Not quite as bad as they had been the day she nearly died, but serious enough for me to worry.

It didn't make any sense.

Chuck landed next to her head and gave Terise's neck a sweet little nuzzle. Then he breathed magic across her face, but nothing in her condition changed, and I hadn't expected it to. His gaze, when he looked at me, was filled with remorse. I got the impression he'd tried to revive her multiple times during my absence.

"This is not your fault, Chuck. Your magic can't fix this. Only the diadem can."

He hung his head and fluttered into my lap, clearly feeling as if he had failed me.

"Not your fault," I whispered, kissing him on the head. He nodded, but still appeared defeated. I turned my attention to the group. "Are other bonded Land Dwellers suffering from a return of the disease?"

"No," Kheelan said. "The moment Terise's condition changed, I contacted King Ordin to report the health of the Land Dwellers bonded to his people. Not a single one has experienced a relapse in health."

"Then it's you," I said.

Kheelan appeared confused. "What's me?"

"I told you, messing with the bond between Jareth and I would have major consequences. I need you and Jareth to touch me and Terise at the same time so I can try and figure out what is happening within her core."

Kheelan simply nodded. He tried to mask the look of remorse, but I knew he felt guilty. The idiot couldn't feel anything less than guilt and shame considering the callous way he'd handled things with Terise, but he could have had the decency to own it instead of behaving proud and indifferent to the situation.

With all four of us connected, I closed my eyes and pulled on my core. I saw our cores and the threads of magic intertwined between them.

Unfortunately, the threads that should have been forming an infinity ring between Terise's core and Kheelan's were now split. The infinity rings were still present, but the thread feeding magic back to Terise's core looked frayed and damaged, with tendrils leaking magic in their wake.

"It's no longer an infinite loop feeding magic back and forth. There's a leak, Kheelan, and the longer it's there, the worse she gets. If you don't sever the threads of magic you have linked to my core, you will lose her."

Kheelan shook his head. "It's not that simple. My spell is designed to complete itself with your core once Jareth's threads are removed."

"That can't happen. We're fated mates."

"That's how it must be," Kheelan said.

"Then at the very least, find a way to remove your bond to Terise."

"I can't. You are the only one who can complete this infinity ring between us and remove both Jareth and Terise from the equation."

I grabbed Kheelan by the shirt and shook him. "She will die if you don't let this go."

I pulled back in surprise as a slow tear trickled down Kheelan's cheek.

"Crysta, I honestly did try, the moment she became sick again, I was willing to break my bond with you and win you another way. I know I'm heartless and deceitful, stubborn, and selfish, but I'm not so horrible as to watch one of your friends suffer and die if I can save them. My spell within your core was designed to work without any other bonds interfering. I hadn't counted on Terise's core being bonded to mine, and I now have zero control over the way this spell behaves. Jareth and I barely have control over our magic. I can't undo what I've done even though I've tried. Only you can."

"How?"

"You must remove your bond with Jareth and allow my bond to take its place. Only then will Terise be free of me. Only then can you bond her with someone else...someone like...Cedric." He swallowed hard, like Cedric's name tasted foul.

"You know I can't do that," I said. "I'm not giving up Jareth."

"Then Terise will die."

"There has to be another way."

"There is always another way when it comes to magic," Adris said, placing a hand on my shoulder to calm me down. "If you can create a spell, not to mention the many things that can go wrong with a spell, then you can troubleshoot the issue, although it will take some time."

"Does Terise have that kind of time?" Cedric asked.

Adris bent down and touched Terise, closing her eyes in meditation for a moment. After a few seconds her eyes popped open. "She does if we keep her cursed." Her expression held sympathy as she turned to me. "I know this is not something you want to hear. You and I both understand what it is like to be trapped in a sleeping curse. It might be tolerable for her, but it might not. However, the magic keeping her in this dream state will also slow the disease down as *griesha* latches on to Moridan's magic fueling the curse."

"That's not a permanent solution," Cedric said, kneeling on the floor next to Terise's bed.

"No. It is not, but it does grant us a brief reprieve. And maybe with the diadem, we'll have more answers."

I didn't like it, but I saw the wisdom in putting our focus on what we had been working so hard to achieve. I couldn't save a single soul without the diadem.

"How long was I gone?" I asked Jareth.

"Two days."

"Please tell me you guys searched the scrolls and found the locations we're looking for."

"Your father and I have been tirelessly pouring over the scrolls. I don't think you will like what we've managed to come up with."

More bad news. "Why? What did you find?"

"Nothing," my father said.

"Nothing." It sounded hollow to my ears. We'd gone through hell and back again only to grab scrolls that did *not* contain the information we needed?

"We can't access the information because it is spelled," Kheelan said, rushing to explain.

Spelled. I rubbed my temples and then my neck, feeling hot tears of defeat burn behind my eyes. "Why does everything in this realm have to be cursed, spelled, or enchanted? Why can't you folks just use a damn lock and key every once in a while?"

My father wrapped an arm around my shoulder and drew me in close.

"We can talk about this in a more private location."

"Wait. I need to heal the rest of these people."

"Crysta, you've suffered a lot of strain, and my magic is not exactly performing as it should," Jareth said. "I agree we need to help them, but we don't have volunteers for bondings at the moment, and we have no idea who will match best with the Nyads and Formage. I think we need to focus on our main objective here."

My father gestured toward the door leading from the room. "Let's take this discussion back to my study where we can look at the scrolls and go over Queen Titania's sudden arrival within our realm."

Right.

Queen Titania.

I'd forgotten about that old cow.

Crysta

I stared at the scrolls of Oberon—heads up, it didn't look like scrolls at all. Just a big, black book inside a big, black case. The idea that this book had nearly cost me my life, not to mention the lives of my dear friends, made me want to shy away from it.

Illogical.

Stupid.

Chuck must have sensed my mood. He perched himself upon my shoulder and gave me a comforting nudge.

That's right, Chuck. Back to work.

"Tell me about the spell," I said to Kheelan as the rest of our group circled round the large room. The smell of leather and spice within the study comforted me, reminding me of my father and the fact that I was safe. For now, anyway. "What part of the book do you not have access to?"

"We have access to all of it. That's not the issue. This journal is exactly that, a journaling of events throughout Oberon's life, including The Rending and the attempts made to restore balance by using children with abilities similar to yours and offering them the diadem."

"Then what is the issue?"

"There is no mention of the diadem's location. Not because it isn't in there, but because the journaling itself is the spell."

I said nothing for a moment, taking in the consternation and bewilderment of everyone else in the room. "I'm confused."

"You weren't the only one," my father said. "All these centuries, and not a single faerie— none of our historians—picked up on the fact that the writings of Oberon are an illusion, a mirage. The true events of what took place are hidden beneath the mirage."

"How did you miraculously discover this when no one else ever has?" Jareth asked.

Kheelan looked a bit sheepish. "I'd like to say I managed to see through the spell due to my own perceptive powers, but the truth of the matter is your father and I had spent several frustrating hours on the scrolls, discovering nothing about the location, and I...er...became slightly agitated, accidentally spilling my wine over the pages."

"You mean you threw your glass, *full of wine*, at the book," my father corrected.

"You..." My mouth opened and closed like a fish out of water. I couldn't believe he'd done something like that.

Nope.

Wait.

This was Kheelan. Of course, I could believe it. "You threw a tantrum and dumped alcohol on an ancient journal that contains the very key to this realm's survival?"

Kheelan refused to meet my gaze as he nonchalantly folded his arms across his chest and leaned against the table.

"To coin a human phrase, I was ticked."

My father rubbed his tired eyes and walked over to a corner of the room where a small shelf held a few bottles of wine. He grabbed a thin bottle and brought it back to the table where he proceeded to open the book and pour the red substance directly onto its pages. The moment the liquid hit the material, it split in the middle, as if Moses were present and parting the Red Sea. It never touched the actual pages but ran down the sides. The words on the page shimmered for a moment, like raw heat in a sweltering desert, before reverting back to their original form and remaining still.

I touched the page, noticing the thick parchment feel to it and the complete lack of moisture.

"What type of spell is this, and how do we break it?" I asked.

"It's a spell woven by a Formage, and it is powerful. I would hazard a guess that the Formage who willingly worked such an intricate spell on Oberon's behalf—a spell capable of being completely undetected by powerful faeries over the centuries—paid a significant price. This spell was created with blood magic."

That had an effect on most of the group, but I didn't understand the significance.

"Blood magic. I take it, this is bad."

"You talked about locks and keys. Consider this the ultimate magical lock, needing a very specific magical key. It's Dark Magic, and there are only two ways for the spell to be broken," Jareth said. "The exact spell that was used, reconstructed into a counterspell, or the right type of blood."

Nuallan rapped his knuckles on the table. "And it isn't Type A, B, or O that we're talking about here. Every faerie that has ever existed has a unique blood type that is influenced by their magic. And the Formage who created this spell had to have known the identity of the person whose blood would be needed for the key."

My shoulders slumped in defeat. "We have no way of knowing who that particular faerie is or if that faerie is even alive."

"Which is why a counterspell is the only option," Kheelan said.

"We don't have time for counterspells." I bit my lip, panic punching me in the gut. I wasn't safe. None of us were safe. We had to solve this problem now or we'd all end up back in Moridan's dungeon, tortured and killed.

Or worse. Just tortured...forever.

"We don't have time to sit in the library, studying all the various types of spells that could have been used to create this particular mirage," I said.

"It's quite literally our only option." My father pushed the book toward me. "Before your dramatic escape and subsequent arrival to the court, Kheelan and I were doing just that. And believe me when I tell you, it hasn't been pleasant. I've lost a few more wine glasses due to this one's temper."

"It relieves stress," Kheelan said. "And your library is woefully inadequate. We haven't found a damn thing."

I grabbed the book with both hands and stared at the pages before me. The random paragraph my eyes landed on contained an innocuous account of Oberon's lunch that day. Not a single interesting or helpful fact concerning the diadem.

I glanced around the room, looking at the faces of my weary friends. All eyes were on me at the moment, like I might have an answer for this, some miraculous epiphany that would solve this riddle and save us all.

I had to know *something*. Moridan certainly thought I did.

"King Moridan already went through this and found absolutely nothing, but he never let on that he knew about the spell," I said.

My father leaned against the desk. "*Does* he know? Does he think we know how to solve this? Does Titania?"

"That might explain why Titania didn't seem too perturbed by my escaping with Crysta. Perhaps she thinks we can solve this spell and lead them to her crown," Jareth said.

"Speaking of, can we please discuss the impossibility of Moridan bringing Titania back from death?" Cedric asked.

Chantara moved to my side and ran a finger down one of the pages, scrutinizing the text in a way that made me feel somewhat hopeful. She was Oberon's daughter, after all. Maybe she could see through the spell. Unfortunately, her angry expression dashed that hope to smithereens.

"He accessed the Netherworld, the realm of the dead, but there are two parts to this realm. Some are in a type of spiritual prison and some are in paradise," Chantara explained. "He used Crysta's blood to bring my mother back to life."

"Not according to your mother," I said. "Her exact words were that he freed her. I guess being brought back from the dead could be considered a type of freedom, but she made it sound like she'd been imprisoned there."

"That's true. And why did Moridan behave as if my mother was his wife?"

"Bewitched," I said, repeating Grizelda's explanation when we were in the tower.

Jareth nodded his head in agreement. "Titania was more than forthcoming on that score. She said father went looking for mother using the Dark Arts, and by the time he stumbled upon Titania in the Netherworld, he had already lost his mind. It wasn't hard for her to take advantage of the situation and convince him she was his wife."

"But why? Titania is a beloved queen, the first of our realm. Why would she wish to return, and by such nefarious means?" my father asked.

"More troubling is her partnership with my father. It seemed as if she not only used him but was in collusion *with* him. She said that father mentioned some of us wouldn't fall in line with their plans," Jareth said.

"Which are?" Kheelan asked.

"Something about purification, but I don't remember much about that conversation," I said, feeling frustrated.

"That's right. I completely forgot. I was so focused on distracting her so I could get Crysta out of there. She said our Fae history is filled with half-truths and lies. According to her, she has returned to finish what she started. She claimed to have been using the Dark Arts all along to purify the realm, and she's returned to continue her plans. She also mentioned something about making Puck pay for the part he played in her imprisonment."

"Puck? But he's dead," my father said, confusion lacing his words.

"Imprisonment? How very interesting she used the word imprisonment instead of death."

I glanced at Chantara, wondering what she meant and noticed her eyes had remained their obsidian color. Man, but she was pissed. I didn't blame her at all, but I'd never seen Chantara this emotional before.

"What are you thinking?" I asked.

"What if she didn't die? What if she was banished?"

You could have heard a pin drop in the room after Chantara delivered that bomb. Unfortunately, I had no idea why that distinction seemed so significant to everyone else.

"Why do you guys look like the end of the world has just come to pass?"

My father let out low groan as he sat down in his high-backed chair. "For a person to be imprisoned in the Netherworld, or Death realm, some heinous crimes must be committed, and it takes tremendous power for banishment into the prison section of that realm to be enforced. The spell is not easy, and Dark Magic must be wielded since the normal pathway to any part of the Netherworld is death."

"So Puck must have sent her to prison, right? That's why she wants revenge...on a dead dude," I said.

"Again, none of this makes sense," Nuallan stated. "We're assuming, based on Titania's crazed ravings, that she was evil all along and was banished, rather than killed by Oberon in a jealous rage. Have you all forgotten that bringing someone back from the dead, whether from prison or paradise, creates insanity? It goes against the natural order of things. The loved one you bring back is not the loved one you lost."

"So she could just be a crazy version of Titania brought back from the dead," I said. That explanation still didn't gel for me.

"Normally I would agree with you, Nuallan, but that doesn't explain why or how she was able to convince my father to bring her back. It's clear my father is mad, but if Titania had been resting peacefully within paradise, she never would have pretended to be my mother. My father would have found my mother instead. No. Our history is wrong. We need to figure out what really happened between Oberon, Titania, and Puck."

"We have to undo the spell cast on these scrolls," Adris said. "All our answers are hidden beneath that Mirage spell."

"We don't know how long that will take, and we need to figure out her end game now. What exactly does she mean by purification? What is she trying to purify?" Chantara said.

Jareth shifted, looking uncomfortable as he said, "Impure blood."

"What?"

I followed his gaze to where Adris stood. "The way Titania looked at you, Highness, as if you were beneath her."

Adris's tone was dry when she said, "I'm quite accustomed to the disdain, Prince Jareth. Not surprising in the least."

Jareth walked around the table, his eyes going a bit distant while his mouth pinched in dismay.

"Jareth?"

"She's going to wipe out any race she deems less than worthy." He slammed his hands on the table. "Impure blood."

"Purify the realm," I said.

"Not possible. Too much power needed," Graul said. "Logistics too complicated."

"Agreed." Nuallan tapped a knuckle on the desk as a sudden thought hit him. "Unless she has something that can magnify and channel magic. An object with which she is already very much familiar."

"The diadem." Jareth pointed a finger at the scrolls. "Whatever power she intends to wield, she can do so with the diadem, magnifying the extent of this genocide and even specifying which races are wiped out."

A heavy silence descended on our group as the magnitude of what Jareth suggested began to sink in.

"Everything points back to the diadem. It's the only way to collect and store Moridan's magic and then transfer it to the rightful heir. It's the only way to magnify the bond Jareth and I are forging between couples to save them from *griesha*, and it's quite literally the only weapon Titania can use to accomplish *her* goal."

"We have to get to it before they do, but Moridan didn't seemed to know the scrolls were spelled. Do you think that buys us some time?" I asked.

Before anyone could answer, a thunderous boom set my ears to ringing, making the floor shake. Books toppled from the shelves, and my father's massive table shifted. I steadied Chantara while anchoring myself to the wall.

Did the Fae realm experience earthquakes?

The moment the tremors stopped, Roderick and Jareth moved toward the door.

"What the hell was that?" I called after them.

"Mountain trolls," Roderick said. "They're trying to break the wards down. Nuallan, stay here and protect our females. I'll need the rest of you to follow me."

Protect our females?

I gave the females in the room a, *is he on drugs,* look before grabbing the scrolls, handing them to Chantara for safekeeping, shoving my way past Nuallan, and following the menfolk out of the study. Chuck let out a trumpeting noise and wiggled his haunches, getting ready for battle. I didn't have to glance behind me to know that Adris, Lily, and Chantara were right on my heels.

"It's like these idiots don't know you at all, Crysta," Nuallan said as he sidled up next to me. His jovial wink and amused expression bolstered my confidence. "Do me a solid and promise to stay by my side. After all, the King of the Unseelie Court just put your safety in my hands."

Do me a solid? The slang dictionary strikes again.

"I'll never leave your side." My demure little smile said it all. I'd do exactly what needed to be done.

"Ah, Crysta. You are a law unto yourself." Nuallan chuckled and then helped to steady me as another tremor rocked the court.

Well, what I lacked in polish and skill, I made up for in loyalty and determination.

No way I was letting anyone fight these battles without me. We were all going to face down these trolls together.

That was simply how this newfound family of mine rolled.

5

Crysta

he outer courtyards were filled with panicked faeries, racing to
file into the security of the palace, which made filing out to
face down the Mountain Trolls a little tricky. After clearing the
palace walls and zipping down the stone steps, I came to an abrupt halt at
the sight of five enormous trolls spread out before us just beyond the outer
courtyards and the wards of the palace. The troll in the middle held a large
wooden club covered in spikes. He raised it high above his head and
brought the full force of his swing down upon the wards.

Another shattering boom brought me to my knees. The pressure within
the wards popped, as did the pressure in my ears. Ahead of me, Jareth,
Kheelan, and my father were approaching the trolls, attempting to speak with
them.

"There's no reasoning with a Mountain Troll once it's been given an
assignment," Adris said, coming to stand next to me. Chantara stood on my
other side, joined by Lily.

"An assignment? You think someone sent them here?"

"King Moridan tasked me to curse you and deliver you to him. He did
that to countless faeries, promising them a multitude of rewards. These trolls
have no way of knowing Moridan already got what he wanted. We'll have

more faeries coming out of the woodwork, ready to curse, kidnap, and deliver you back to him."

"He got his wife back. Well...sort of. What makes him think I'm of any use to him now?"

"You're a threat, Crysta." Chantara's obsidian eyes were filled with fury. "You're alive and capable of wielding something only Titania was ever able to safely wield. He will never stop coming for you."

Chilling thought.

I turned my attention back to my father who had actually managed to get the Mountain Trolls' attention.

"Gilbraith, explain the meaning of this. Your attack on this court is tantamount to a declaration of war. I assure you, the Unseelie Court will show no mercy for your kind if you continue your assault."

The Mountain Troll's voice resonated deep and rough in the back of his throat. "We will leave as soon as you give us what we came for."

"And that is?"

Gilbraith lifted his club and pointed it in my direction. "The Princess. Our Mistress demands it."

Titania was now their mistress?

She hadn't wasted much time.

"You tell Titania, my daughter is none of her concern. Now leave here immediately or you will feel the full force of this court upon your kind."

"I do not know who this Titania is. I speak on behalf of Lady Rhoswen."

Eh?

And just as if speaking her name had summoned the saucy wench, Rhoswen apparated right in front of Gilbraith. The sight of her in all her pink, frothy glory, quivering with rage, her height barely reaching the middle of the Mountain Trolls' ankles sent me doubling over in a fit of laughter. I had to grab Chantara's arm, I was laughing so hard. Once I could stand upright and wipe the mirth from my eyes, I noticed that everyone, including my father and Jareth were staring at me like I'd lost my marbles.

Yes. I probably had.

"Did you enjoy your bath, Rhoswen?" I choked back another laugh as I thought about the smelly water I'd trapped her in. Rhoswen's color changed to a furious shade of red. Without a word, she raised her hands and shot a bolt of fire in my direction, which harmlessly hit the wards and then evaporated on contact.

"You are nothing. Do you understand me? I'll see you dead by the end of this day."

"Rhoswen," Jareth barked. The cold steel lacing his tone pulled her crazed eyes to his. They softened for a moment as she composed her expression and smoothed down the ruffles of her dress. "Are you out of your mind? You've brought your own army to attack the Unseelie Court and assassinate its princess. You've quite literally signed your own death warrant."

"She's still trapped you under her spell, but I'll set you free, Jareth. Then nothing will come between us."

I didn't like the fanatical look in her eye as her gaze landed on me and she slowly placed her hand on the wards.

"Jareth, what is she doing?" I asked.

He looked just as confused as the rest of us until she started chanting a spell in Latin. Then he was dashing forward, a panicked look on his face.

Things happened pretty fast after that.

"Rhoswen, stop!" Jareth shouted.

"Get to the palace." Roderick was already running toward us with Kheelan fast approaching, but Jareth had almost reached Rhoswen, and all I could think was how wrong this picture appeared. Everyone ran away from danger I couldn't quite wrap my head around, yet Jareth ran toward it.

Just as he neared the wards, Rhoswen's eyes flashed open, glowing blood red. "Obliviate," she screamed.

Wine-colored cracks appeared along the wards, starting at the middle of her hand and spreading out fast, then the ward exploded, sending us all flying backward. I landed hard on my side, the sound of flesh tearing accompanied by waves of pain. I didn't know what kind of damage had been done to me, and I didn't care. Jareth had been right by the ward when it exploded.

And how the hell had a single faerie done that?

I shoved myself to my feet and assessed the damage. The Mountain Trolls were no longer contained, and they were pissed, wreaking havoc on the outlier buildings, homes, and any faerie who had been stupid enough to *not* take refuge within the palace.

Our group was already flinging spells at the interlopers. Chantara channeled water into a Mountain Troll's mouth, causing him to gag and choke. Kheelan and Nuallan were flinging containment spells to bind and entrap another troll.

Chuck had managed to attack one of the trolls, using his claws to scratch at the giant creature's eyes.

I blinked my own bleary eyes, searching for Jareth and spotted him on the ground unconscious, with Rhoswen leaning over him, caressing his face, a concerned expression on hers. The sight of her touching him, especially after she had hurt him, filled me with a rage I'd never experienced before. I instinctively reached within my core, called upon all three magics, and shot raw power straight at her head. What was normally threads of magic became battering rams as they pummeled into her, sending her toppling head over foot until she made an ungraceful landing several feet away from my fated mate.

To her credit, she recovered fast, shot to her feet, and flung her own fiery Summer magic at me.

I mentally constructed my shield, just as Adris had taught me, and it was fueled with all the hatred and loathing I held for this pitiful woman. Rhoswen's power hit my shield, barely jarring me, and that's when I knew. I just knew she was no match for me.

And then I ran. I held my shield in place with one hand and used the other to wield a ball of Winter magic.

I threw it at her chest, but she managed to construct a shield just as it landed.

She retaliated, encompassing me in a ball of fire that ate at my skin and singed my hair before I could use my Winter magic to neutralize the spell. I ignored the pain, flicking my wrist at an angle and using my Spring magic to call forth ropes of vines, tangling her arms and legs together.

She laughed and the vines exploded, showering down upon her. Then she launched a full assault, barreling into my shield with everything she had. I fought against it for a moment before noticing something strange about the exchange. Kheelan's Summer magic attached to my core wanted to absorb Rhoswen's and latch on to its energetic properties. I allowed it what it wanted, sucking up Rhoswen's magic and feeding it into the strange loop between me, Kheelan, and Jareth.

My entire body began to tingle. I closed my eyes and let the Summer magic wash through me, recognizing it couldn't stay forever. It was simply too much power and energy absorbed all at once, but it could be channeled out. And that was exactly what my core wanted to do. Magnify my own magic and expel it from my system.

My eyes flew open, zeroing in on Rhoswen as I visualized my intent.

I had her magic, and I was going to use it against her.

I headed straight for her, and the look of terror on her face was a thing of beauty. I reached for my core, pulled on everything I could, sensing a blue sphere of magic building around me, getting brighter and brighter as I demanded more from it. Then I sent it, with all of my focused intention, barreling toward her. The blue sphere engulfed her, smothering her screams, and then the icy threads of magic penetrated her skin. The magic entered her veins like a toxic entity, freezing her cells, transforming her skin, creating icy spots along her arms. Her face was covered in spidery, blue veins, her eyes white as glass. Her body levitated from the ground as she screamed out her pain.

"Crysta, I don't know how you're doing this, but you must stop now!" Jareth said.

Jareth?

I kept my hands raised, but my focus was now split. Jareth stood by me, blood trickling down the side of his face. He stared at me in horror for a moment and then reached a hand up to touch my cheek.

"Your eyes, Crysta. They're filled with lightning."

Lightning? What was he talking about?

The wind around us kicked up, the clouds overhead grew dark with malice. The smell of ozone made my nose crinkle as I stared at Rhoswen and felt nothing other than an intense desire to destroy her where she floated, limp and helpless.

"Crysta, this isn't you," he yelled above the din. "It's one thing to protect, defend, and punish, but this is torture. Rhoswen will be punished, but you need to stop what you're doing."

I studied Rhoswen like I would if I were dissecting a frog in a science experiment. Her body pulsed with a turquoise glow, her skin deepened into a frosty blue.

She looked dead to me.

Had I killed her? Was I a killer now?

I abruptly pulled back and released my core, releasing Rhoswen in the process. She slumped to the ground, the color returning to her face, but she wasn't conscious, and I wasn't sure she was breathing.

I wasn't sure I cared.

Nuallan raced toward Rhoswen, knelt beside her, and checked for a pulse.

He grimaced. "Unfortunately, she will live."

The look of relief on Jareth's face hurt me. On the one hand, I didn't want to be a murderer, I didn't want to enjoy it, but she had tried to kill me multiple times, and he still had a soft spot for her. He still cared for her.

It had been self-defense, either way you looked at it, even if I had enjoyed it a little, teensy weensy bit.

I turned away from him, unable to look him in the eye, feeling like a monster, like an impostor, and confused at my own behavior and abilities.

"It's not like that, Crysta." Jareth came up behind me and placed his hands on my shoulder. "I know what you're thinking, and I care nothing for Rhoswen. Any kind feelings I might have had for her ended when she tried to kill you. But I know you. I know your sensitive heart, and if you had killed her like this, tortured her and taken her life, it would have slowly eaten away at you. The guilt would have undercut your confidence and your self-worth."

Maybe.

I supposed he knew me pretty well.

I allowed a tear to steal slowly down my face. He was forever looking out for me, preventing me from making mistakes he knew I would regret. I wouldn't have hesitated to kill Rhoswen to defend myself and my loved ones, but he was right. What I'd done was inhumane, cruel, and sadistic. There were better ways to deal with Rhoswen.

He turned me to face him and pulled me into his arms.

"I love you," he said. "And I can't lose you, so please stop inserting yourself into the fight. Stop taking these risks."

"I couldn't just stand there and let her hurt you. This is my fight, Jareth, and whether you like it or not, I am Princess of this court. I need to be the most powerful and the most competent. I need my enemies to fear me and my subjects to love me. None of that is possible if I stand back and cower behind everyone else. I have power. I am going to use it to defend this realm and the faeries who live in it, and goddess help whoever stands in my way."

He studied my expression for a moment, weighing my words with his feelings before swallowing down his protests and giving me a rueful smile.

"You're right. You're exactly right. I've never seen anything so powerful as what you managed to do with Rhoswen's magic, turning it against her like that. We just need to make sure you don't lose focus or control. Your emotion played too big a part. I don't blame you, but it will get you killed if you can't compartmentalize what you feel in relation to what you must do."

"Understood."

He raked his gaze over my face and arms, grimacing at my battle wounds. "Now then, can we please get you to Kheelan. I can't stand seeing you like this."

"Like..." I looked down at my arms and noticed burn marks along my skin. The skin on my face felt stretched and tight, and my side, the area where I had been stabbed by Moridan's bloodletting spell, had reopened and was leaking fluid.

"Huh. I didn't even feel the pain."

Until now.

Interesting how acknowledging injuries sent pain signals to your brain. Chuck had already started repairing some of the burns with his breathy magic. It felt cool to the touch and eased the tight feeling on my skin.

"Thanks, buddy," I said.

He chirped an answer and landed on my shoulder as I turned, taking stock of our situation amidst the aftermath of the attack while Jareth went in search of Kheelan. The Mountain Trolls had been neutralized, unconscious and sprawled out in the outer courtyard, encased in different containment spells. Adris and Chantara looked to have a few scrapes, but nothing major. Graul was already lecturing a disgruntled Lily on putting herself in danger.

Been there. Done that. Males were so predictable.

I'd never seen Lily anything but sweet with him, so I chuckled in delight as she pointed an angry finger in his face, said a few sharp words, and walked away. Too bad she was dealing with a cave man. Graul let her get about two feet ahead of him before he went after her, grabbed her, and kissed her senseless.

Yummy.

The rest of our group had a few superficial injuries but nothing major.

I seemed to be the most badly hurt.

Whatever. Battle scars. I was one tough Unseelie Court Princess...who...felt slightly dizzy.

I awkwardly slumped to the ground and put my head between my knees, taking measured breaths to dispel my sudden nausea.

The scent of swamp water hit my nose, but it didn't bother me since I knew who stood next to me. "I've never seen anything quite like what you did to Rhoswen," Adris said as she sat down with a grunt. "It was extremely satisfying to watch."

I let out a surprised laugh and immediately cursed myself for the pain it caused my side.

"Not sure how I managed it. I just knew I could absorb the energy and then send it back ten-fold."

Adris scrutinized my eyes for a moment. "Yep. Very interesting."

"This is the second time you've looked at my eyes with worry. What is it, Adris?"

"There's just something in them I've never seen before. Doesn't show up all the time, and I didn't see it until after we got you back."

"What?"

"I'm not sure what it is, but I don't like it."

Chantara hurried to my side and sat next to me, handing me the scrolls and then examining my side.

"This wound wreaks of magic. Is this the bloodletting injury?"

"Yes," I said. I stared down at the scrolls, noticing some blood on my hands had dripped onto the leather cover. "I'm getting it all over this thing."

With a shaking hand, I lifted the cover and tried to rub it off, but I clumsily smeared it instead and dripped more blood onto the first page.

I expected the blood to part, much like the wine did when it hit the pages of the scrolls. Instead, the page absorbed it, drinking it in like a thirsty vampire.

"What in the name of Danu is this?" Chantara muttered.

The words on the page levitated, scrambling to rearrange themselves and then returning to the thin parchment paper. Chantara and Adris gripped my arms in disbelief. The language looked unfamiliar to me. I couldn't read it.

"Do either one of you understand this?"

Chantara read the words on the page.

"I, Oberon, King of all faeries, must confess a grievous sin, a sin made necessary to save the Fae realm from the sinister and crazed delusions of a woman I still love with all of my being. This is the true and full account of events leading up to and following The Rending."

"Flaming faerie wands, how is this possible?" Adris said. "How did the Formage who cast this spell have access to your blood, Crysta?"

"There's only one answer," Jareth said.

I startled, looking up and noticing the rest of our group had gathered around us while I'd been so engrossed in the scrolls.

"What?"

"Crysta is a direct descendant of the individual whose blood was used to create this spell."

"Like she needed another reason for that target on her back," Kheelan said. "The bullseye just grew in radius."

Well, hell.

Crysta

Kheelan did his best to cauterize the bloodletting wound again—ouch—but it did not wish to cooperate, not interested in healing properly. The rest of my burns were gone, but we were going to have to keep an eye on my wound. It did close up, but it looked infected.

Roderick quelled the chaos by delegating various tasks to his staff, including the imprisonment of Lady Rhoswen and her Mountain Trolls. They got to join dear old dad, or rather, my fake dad who was actually my uncle, in the dungeons.

I thought about Rodri and felt a hollow pain in my chest. He'd only been father to me for a few months, but I found that, despite what he had done, I still held love in my heart for him to some extent.

Couldn't say I was too bothered by the vision of Rhoswen surrounded by bars. If I'd been more petty, I would have made plans to visit her in her cell and gloat.

All right, I was seriously considering it.

While my father finished overseeing clean-up, we gathered back inside the palace in a more private banquet area where we could freely discuss our next move and eat. Defending an entire court against Mountain Trolls was hungry work. Plus, I was currently pricking my finger and rubbing blood on every single page of the scrolls. That's right. The spell required blood on every page.

Sadistic faeries.

"I wish I had an idea of who Oberon used to create this spell," I said.

"I've got a feeling we'll have all the answers we need once you finish bleeding all over the scrolls." Nuallan flopped down at the table and dug into his enormous salad. "Also, what happened to sticking by my side when we faced off with the Mountain Trolls?"

"I remember a disembodied voice giving out vague commands," I said. I looked at my friendly Hag, queen of the Annis, sitting across the table. She dug into something resembling live worms. "Queen Adris, do you remember Nuallan throwing out that order?"

She swallowed and wiped her thin mouth with her gnarled fist. "Can't say that I do. You'll have to speak up next time, young assassin. This old woman is hard of hearing."

"Your ears. They are hard? They are broken?" Graul looked at Adris in concern. "Kheelan heal it."

Adris reached over and patted his arm. "Very sweet of you to suggest, but he has cold hands."

Graul grunted in agreement while Kheelan looked between them in annoyance.

"Such animosity," he said. "It's truly getting old."

"Then sever your bond with Crysta so we can fix Terise," Cedric shot back.

"Listen bird brain, I've already told you I can't do that."

"Can't or won't?"

Kheelan and Cedric shot to their feet. I wasn't surprised that things were about to get physical. This feud between them had been building for a while now. Chantara kicked Cedric behind the legs, forcing him into his chair before sitting down next to him. Chuck let out a soft little chuckle by my ear. I guess the idea of Kheelan getting a whooping at the hand of Cedric pleased him.

"If you two are done wasting our time, we need to focus on getting the diadem. If it has the power to channel Crysta and Jareth's bonding spell, then maybe it can help us undo what Kheelan has done."

I'd never considered that, but it definitely made sense.

"Okay, last page. My finger may never recover."

The blood drops absorbed into the paper, and the words levitated and reassembled themselves just as they had on every other page. I flipped to the beginning of the scrolls and handed them to Chantara.

"I think it only right that you be the one to read this. It's your father's journal, after all."

Chantara smile gratefully and cleared her throat. She then started where she had left off. *"I first discovered my wife's involvement with the Dark Arts while she was pregnant with our daughter, Chantara."* She paused for so long I wondered if she was okay.

I stared at her, noticing the tears welling in her eyes.

"What is it? Do you need someone else to read this?"

"I'm just so confused. He never once acknowledged me as his daughter after I was born, and he clearly wrote this many years after The Rending." She wiped away her tears and cleared her throat, continuing to read. *"My brother, Puck, introduced her to this magic without my knowledge or permission. Puck's dabblings with Dark Magic had happened many years previous, but I had assumed, foolishly, that he'd learnt the error of his ways and turned from his dark practices. Unfortunately, that was not the case, and we have all suffered for it."*

Chantara read late into the evening as we listened to every horrifying detail.

Several thousand years ago, there had been an uprising among the Fae, where certain species of Fae believed they deserved to rule the realm. Goblins, Formage, Dark Elves, Stargis, etc. were involved in the uprising, claiming they were underrepresented. Oberon had quickly squashed the uprising, but in the skirmish, two of Oberon and Titania's sons were killed.

It completely devastated Titania. According to Oberon, *"She was never quite the same. Her loving nature and happy disposition gone forever."*

"So Puck used Titania's grief to press his own agenda," Jareth said.

Indeed he had.

He'd essentially brainwashed Titania into not only believing the Dark Arts were ethical and safe to work, but that the magic was necessary to protect themselves and their loved ones from the greedy, evil machinations of those he dubbed "lesser Fae", a phrase coined by him.

He indoctrinated her into the very racist, sociopathic beliefs he held. He wished for a pure society where only the strongest Fae remained. Those Fae he deemed less magical, less powerful, or less beneficial to the realm and the society he wished to create were of no use to them, a dangerous nuisance, and one hundred percent expendable.

"Sweet Danu," Adris said. "She and Puck believed it was best to purify the realm and get rid of all the lesser Fae. Oberon may have loved Titania, but it sounds to me as if her grief, and her intense hatred of the faeries involved in the uprising, slowly drove her to madness."

Couldn't argue with that. Not if Oberon's accounting of events held any merit, and I suspected they did. Not exactly the history everyone had been taught, though. The shell-shocked expressions around the room no doubt mirrored my own.

"She became cruel and cold, unfeeling and completely without mercy," Chantara read. *"She delighted in the pain of our enemies and oversaw the torture of our prisoners from the uprising. It sickened me to watch someone so beautiful and kind become twisted by her grief and rage."*

Chantara paused for a moment to collect herself. Jeez, this had to be so difficult for her.

"She saw herself as a goddess among unfit subjects and desired to surround herself with the very best of the best. It didn't take much for Puck to bring her over to his side. I strongly disagreed and forbade them from pursuing purification and the Dark Arts. I had hoped that Titania would see reason, and after forbidding her to align herself with my brother or his views, the unstable behavior abated, and the old Titania returned. At least, I thought she had."

Chantara's eyes misted over, but she kept reading. Dogged and determined, she continued to reveal every painful, unpleasant detail her father had to offer. I felt horrible to have given her this task, but it was clear she needed and wanted it. She had to know the truth. We all did.

Titania played her part for a while, but behind the scenes she and Puck continued to work their Dark Magic, creating a spell so powerful, so destructive, it would slowly wipe out less powerful faeries.

"I first became aware of this magical disease when a few of my subjects could not be healed by the most powerful of healers within the realm. Red sores broke out upon the victims' skin, fevers raged, their minds were lost, and magical powers of any kind were drained from the individual. Eventually, the sores bled and became so numerous, the faeries quickly succumbed to the disease."

"Wait a second," I said. "Is he talking about *griesha?*"

"Flaming hobgoblins, it certainly sounds like it," Cedric said.

Jareth's expression was thunderstruck. "It makes sense. *Griesha* has slowly gained ground over the last several months due to my father's persistent handling of the Dark Arts."

"Yes, but he has been doing them for over eighteen years," I said. "Why didn't *griesha* show up sooner?"

"It did," Chantara replied. "Your mother was very ill, Crysta."

"But she was the only one at the time, and she was an incredibly powerful faerie. Are we sure it was *griesha* she had?" I looked at my father for confirmation.

"She never confided in me that she was sick, and I never saw any physical signs of it."

Adris let out a grunt of disagreement. "I thought *griesha* took hold of its victims due to the lack of a fated mate bond and low levels of magical ability. Weren't fated mates a given back then?"

"They were, but not everyone had found their fated mate," Chantara said. She hesitated for a moment before continuing. "We also have no idea if the disease was more powerful back then. Oberon states the illness caused insanity. We've yet to see that symptom."

"A variation, then? A more benign form of the illness is what we're seeing now? We know a fated mate bond is the cure, but I don't think Oberon knew. I wonder if he made the connection, found similarities in who became sick and who didn't," Jareth said.

I tapped my foot. "It's linked to Titania in some way. Keep reading, Chantara. Maybe there's an explanation in Oberon's scrolls."

She shifted in her seat and turned the page. *"As the epidemic grew, I began my own investigations, noticing the illness held magical properties. I traced these properties back to the original source and couldn't deny the owner of its signature. My wife, Titania, had created the disease."*

Not only had Titania created the disease, she'd gone a step further and targeted the races who had led the uprising.

The Formage.

"When I confronted her, she claimed no knowledge of the disease, and blamed Puck for everything. She declared that he had used her magic to create something abominable, and she didn't know how to stop it."

"I believed her for a time, banishing Puck from the realm and attempting to eradicate the disease now that the one who had created it had been stopped. Unfortunately, unbeknownst to me, Titania was still targeting her enemies, and the disease continued to spread."

Oberon finally caught on after Titania gave birth to a race of Fae never before seen.

"My wife's use of the Dark Arts poisoned her body, mutating our only daughter into a new race of Fae. After the birth of Chantara, I confronted her again, accusing her of hurting our child, of never once considering the risks to Chantara's health and safety. Of sentencing our daughter to an existence where she might never be allowed her own fated mate, the petition process taking hundreds of years."

"Hold up," I said. "Never *allowed* her own fated mate? Petition process?" I gave Chantara a questioning look, but she appeared just as mystified. "That sounds different than never finding a fated mate due to the fact that mermaids were an entirely new species." I glanced around the room, hoping someone had a few answers. "Were the lower social classes and races of Fae not allowed to be bonded to their fated mates unless they petitioned for it?"

"That might account for this uprising that led to the deaths of two of their sons," Adris said. "Consider the gift and blessing of a fated mate bond. Consider how much more powerful faeries are when bonded together; what their magics can do to support and strengthen one another. When it comes to any monarchy, total power is key. The books are so flawed in our history, does it surprise anyone that the ruling classes would have limited power to the lesser classes? Does it surprise anyone that Fae would fight for the right to be bonded to their loved ones?"

"If what you're saying is true, and I'm horrified to think that it is, Oberon and Titania led a society of privileged races filled with fated mates while the lower classes knew their fated mates and were never allowed a bonding," Jareth said. "I can't imagine the sorrow this caused so many individuals."

"It made them easy targets for Titania's disease," I said. "No fated mate bonds. What happened after Oberon confronted your mother, Chantara?"

Chantara's eyes went black as she stared at the pages. "I think it's safe to say she was never my mother, especially when you hear this next bit." She continued to read.

"Titania claimed there was an easy solution for what Chantara had become. We would simply kill our daughter. She was an abomination in my wife's eyes. That's when I knew, Titania had gone completely insane."

Oberon did his best to imprison his wife, believing her to be a danger to herself, to Chantara, and every other Fae in the realm. He didn't have the heart to hurt her, so Titania spent several weeks magically imprisoned in a tower within the palace while Oberon did all he could to work with the healers to reverse the madness within her.

Can't cure crazy, I thought. *She was nuts before the Dark Arts. Her grief and anger saw to that.*

Oberon was unaware that Titania managed to get a message to Puck, and the idiot came rushing in to save her. I wasn't sure why Puck was willing to risk everything for Titania when he'd already been banished. Maybe some of the lore behind their history was correct. Puck had a thing for Titania, the only scenario that made sense.

Didn't end well for any of them.

Puck released her from her imprisonment. Titania, instead of taking advantage of the out Puck had given her, immediately headed for Chantara's room and attempted to murder her baby girl. Oberon stopped her before she could kill their baby, and there was a brutal battle between hc and Puck, where Puck quite literally abandoned Titania to save himself.

"She begged me to kill our child and allow her magical disease to avenge the death of our sons. There was simply no reasoning with her, and no other options left to me. She was the true originator of the illness, and to get rid of it meant getting rid of her. But I could not kill her."

Chantara read a few more passages before my father's angry scoff cut her off.

"He imprisoned her and the disease tied to her," he said, sounding a bit frustrated. "I understand the dilemma he found himself in, but he should have killed her instead of banishing her to the Netherworld. From the way he describes it, the process was pretty traumatizing."

Jareth nodded. "Their fated mate bond broke during the spell casting. I don't understand the logistics of that, but there is no denying the repercussions."

Chantara continued reading. *"I was unaware that banishment would have such devastating consequences. The disease may be gone, but The Rending was our alternative. Bonds were severed. Magics stripped from all of us. Most of us only capable of wielding one magical element. It was a heavy price to pay, but the disease would have wiped out more than half of the Fae population."*

"It's *griesha* for certain," Lily said. It was the first time she'd spoken in hours. I studied her features, noticing the drawn expression and the dark circles under her eyes. I recognized that look.

Trauma.

The things she had suffered at the hands of Moridan's soldiers, and then witnessing Graul's torture. She had always seemed so fragile to me, but staring at her as she gazed off, not truly focused on anything, I realized she wasn't doing very well.

It hurt me. Waves of guilt buried me at the sight of my sweet, kind friend altered so much by these experiences.

I wanted my Lily back.

"If father has been using the Dark Arts for a while, reaching into the Netherworld to find our mother, it isn't too far-fetched to assume that the disease Oberon banished to the Netherworld with Titania has leaked into ours via Moridan," Kheelan said, looking shaken. "And to think we'd all been blaming Crysta's fated mate bond with Jareth."

"You did the blaming. Some of us had more faith in our bond than that," Jareth said.

It surprised me that Kheelan had actually referred to my bond with Jareth as a fated mate bond. Usually, he was drowning in denial. But this Kheelan looked like he'd had a major wake-up call and didn't like what he'd discovered about himself.

"Nor is it too far-fetched to assume that this recent influx of *griesha* is due to her return to our realm," Jareth said.

"We've got to send her back. Preferably dead." Adris grabbed the book and scanned her eyes over the pages. "Any thoughts on how to make that happen?"

"This all circles back to the diadem. The fact that she and Moridan want it makes it imperative that we get it before they do. It's clearly the damn key to pretty much everything," Nuallan said.

Lily leaned her head against Graul's shoulder. "I just want this to be over."

Graul's arms tightened around her, holding her with a ferocious protectiveness that made me love him all the more.

His intense gaze when he made eye contact with me spoke volumes. "Read more. Find stone and diadem locations. We do this now."

"Yes." I did the best I could to convey as much reassurance as possible. "We do this now."

Jareth

I studied Crysta as she listened to Chantara read the scrolls. She still had blood stains on her tunic, a grisly reminder of a wound that wasn't healing properly. My worry for her was endless. The constant fear of losing her nearly paralyzed me at times. Yet she had made such an important point when I forbade her from putting herself in harm's way. She was a princess and would eventually be queen. That position, as I well knew, demanded absolute power and respect.

I wanted to protect her and hide her away, but she was meant to rule, meant to shine, meant to come into her own, and completely within her rights to sacrifice her safety for the sake of her subjects. Not many royals had done so in the past, but this was Crysta, and she had changed absolutely everything.

Including me.

I could attempt to shield her from this realm, or I could stand by her side and help her better it. This fear would never abate, but neither would my love, respect, and admiration. She deserved this chance to find her place, discover herself, and fulfill her destiny.

I gazed at our motley crew, with its varied races and diverse backgrounds. Crysta had done this. She had brought us all together, fighting for a common cause and battling against a common enemy. It startled me to realize I considered every single person within this room, not to mention Terise, family. We were all family here. Everyone equal and just as important as the next, everyone contributing something valuable. Everyone willing to sacrifice to save our realm.

The barriers between races meant nothing to Crysta, and they now meant nothing to me. I would follow her anywhere, and so would her subjects.

She was most definitely coming into her own.

"Jareth?"

I took my gaze from Crysta, who stared at me with a quizzical expression, and turned to address Nuallan.

"Yes?"

Nuallan rolled his eyes, a very human gesture, and patted my shoulder. "If you're done staring lovingly at your fated mate, we'd so appreciate your weighing in on this next bit of text."

I smiled, happy to have been caught staring at her. "Of course. Read it again."

"Because we haven't already gone through it three times." Kheelan leaned back against his chair. "We've got an idea of where the stone and diadem might be."

That certainly grabbed my attention.

"Where?"

Crysta pointed to the middle of the page. "Oberon says he placed one in a mountain and one in a lake. Not sure which one went where, though."

"That's not very specific. Lakes and mountains abound in our realm, as they do in most. What makes you think you know where to look?"

Chantara picked up the book and read the text again. *"There were two of my subjects I trusted more than most to hide the stone and diadem. They had witnessed firsthand the diadem's ability to channel power and its very destructive nature—"*

"Wait a moment. Destructive due to what occurred to the few children who had more than one magical element?"

Crysta rubbed her forehead, clearly looking exasperated. "Jareth, just how long did you zone out?"

Zone out? That was some new slang I would file away for future reference.

"Start back to where Titania was banished."

Everyone in the room either groaned or chuckled. Graul simply gave me a pitying look.

"You not focus. Kiss Crysta, then we move on."

The entire room erupted into laughter. The boyish smile on my face could not be helped, and I certainly didn't need an invitation to kiss my fated mate. I quickly reached for her, pulled her into my arms, and brought the full force of my love to bear upon her sweet, soft lips. As they melded to mine, my core magic vibrated, sending waves of energy through my system and into hers. It was what I needed so badly. I always needed some kind of contact with Crysta, and it always felt as if too much time passed in between kisses.

Her body molded to mine as she wrapped her arms around my shoulders. I swear if we hadn't had an audience, a few inappropriate things may have taken place.

"Please be finished soon," Kheelan said. "The connection I have with Crysta makes both of your energies a bit unbearable."

I ended the kiss, feeling satisfied at the dazed look in her eyes.

"Kheelan, any discomfort you feel is warranted," I said.

"Be that as it may, it's important you understand what the diadem can do. It would seem that not only were the children mentally damaged as they tried to repair The Rending and fated mate bonds, but strange things occurred when anyone attempted to use it."

"Such as?"

"Anyone wielding it lost control. At one point, one of the children attacked Chantara, and one child caught the disease. It was an isolated case, but Oberon was convinced that Titania still had some kind of connection to the diadem despite her banishment. Oberon dismantled it, fearing Titania's powers even beyond this realm."

"You're telling me there's a possibility that Titania's magic tainted this diadem? What will happen to Crysta if she wields it?"

"Only one way to find out," she said. "We put it back together, and I wear the dang thing. We'll start out with a simple bonding between a couple and see how that goes. Then we can attempt a few more bondings at once. We'll just have to experiment."

I bit back an angry retort, recognizing my fear for what it was, and also acknowledging that as Princess and a royal she had every right to do what needed to be done. She waited, gaging my reaction, and preparing for battle. I could see it in her eyes. She wasn't going to back down, and she wouldn't appreciate any coddling.

By the goddess, it killed me to ignore my protective instincts toward my fated mate, but I wouldn't alienate her or do her the disservice of doubting her in front of others. I'd done that far too many times in the past.

"Okay. We take it slow. We run some experiments. Just remember, we can't save this realm or its people without you. So we must be very careful."

Her appreciative smile was so glorious and bright, my knees felt week. She lifted herself up on her tiptoes and kissed my cheek.

"Thank you, Jareth." She took a step back to look at the scrolls, but I felt the absence of her warmth like a cold breeze across my neck. "Oberon states that these two subjects he trusted were royals of their own races. One was a Goblin, the other was a Drac."

"Then it would be natural to assume that Goblin Mountain and the Lake of Beatha are our hiding places."

"Correct," Kheelan said. "What isn't clear is where these items were hidden within the lake and the mountain."

"I wonder if Grizelda would know," I said. "Don't you find it suspicious that my father had her imprisoned and wouldn't release her?"

"You're right," Crysta said. "I can't believe I didn't put it all together. Paio, didn't you mention that Moridan had you trapped because he wanted you to find the crown? Did he mean the diadem?"

"I have no way of knowing. Half of his ravings made little sense to me," he said. "He kept interrogating me for information about my home and its artifacts, but I didn't tell him anything. And I'm not a Drac."

"No, but your home is in the Lake of Beatha."

"But how did Moridan know where the stone and diadem were located if he couldn't read the scrolls?" Nuallan asked. "It doesn't add up."

"It does if Titania has known all along," Crysta said. "If she is connected to the stone and diadem as Oberon feared, then she must have had some vague idea as to where they would be, and Moridan imprisoned the faeries he thought capable of giving him leads."

"Which means they are several steps ahead of us and don't even need these scrolls. The whole thing was a set-up. A way to lure Crysta to the palace so he could use her to bring back Titania."

"Then we need to get moving immediately," I said. "We still have the advantage. Titania is not yet powerful enough to leave the palace, and I doubt Moridan will be willing to leave her side. Let's pack some provisions, update Grizelda, and return her to her father. From there, we can discuss this scenario with the Goblin King. We will need his permission and his insight if we are to search that entire mountain."

"Like finding a tiny stone amidst a stack of boulders," Kheelan said.

"You mangled that phrase a bit." Crysta's eyes sparkled as she smiled. "Look on the bright side, Kheelan. We don't know if we'll find the stone or the diadem."

"That's your bright side?" Kheelan stood with the rest of the group.

"Crysta has same side. Not look too bright to me." Graul guided Lily in front of him while Kheelan slapped a hand over his weary eyes.

"Will someone please give Graul a slang dictionary? I'm fairly certain the Stargis is only ever understanding half of what is discussed."

Crysta let out a low chuckle and slipped her arm in mine as Chuck perched himself atop my shoulder. Her touch was electric, creating a warmth within me I never wanted to lose. As we left the dining room, I had only one thing on my mind.

Protect my fated mate, no matter the sacrifice.

Crysta

While our group finished up last minute preparations, I decided to go check on Terise. It killed me to think of her trapped in that sleeping curse with no way out. I didn't know if the world she remained trapped in was filled with pleasant dreams or if Moridan had managed to taint the spell. What if she was sequestered in a never-ending mental hell?

We had to break the curse, and I had a few ideas of how to do it. The caveat? If I was successful, then *griesha* would run its course at an accelerated rate. There were no good choices here.

As I entered the healing quarters, I was shocked to see several more faeries of varying races being tended to. All of them covered in red, angry sores. I approached one of the healers, a woman who looked like an Elf, but not like a Dark Elf. Her eyes were not red, and her skin was the color of ivory. Her hair shone in ebony waves along her back.

When she saw me enter, she hurried over to assist me, giving me a low bow that made me feel super uncomfortable.

"You don't need to do that," I said. I touched her arm to bring her out of her curtsy. She looked a bit surprised by my touch. I linked my arm with hers and walked her toward Terise, which earned me an uneasy glance. "It seems like more and more people are becoming ill."

"Yes, Princess," she said, steadying herself. "The disease has escalated. We do what we can, but without a permanent solution, all we can do is keep them hydrated and comfortable."

I bit my bottom lip, feeling a strong urge to cry as I saw a little girl, a Land Dweller, curled up next to an older woman who looked human. The human was fine, but the little girl was covered in sores.

She was too young for a fated mate bond, but she wouldn't last very long. I could have stopped and attempted to find mates for most everyone in the room, but it would have taken up too much time, and at this point our goal had to be the diadem. I could save everyone at once if I had the crown. One-by-one was no longer an option.

"How is Terise doing?" I asked. I stopped short when I spotted Kheelan sitting next to my friend, holding her hand and placing a cool compress on her brow.

"You should ask Master Kheelan," she said. "Or Master Cedric. Those two always come to check on Terise."

"Thank you."

She gave me a curtsy and went about her business. I walked toward Kheelan and took a seat on the other side of Terise. He blinked in surprise, a small grimace fighting for supremacy.

"I thought you didn't care about Terise," I said. I didn't say it accusingly. I was genuinely curious as to what his motivation might be.

He reached for Terise's hand, taking care not to aggravate the swollen, red areas. "This curse was meant for me," he said. "My father once cast this very curse on me when I was much younger, as a way to punish me for some mischief I'd spearheaded. I can't even remember the details now, but I remember the fear, the pain, and the confusion. I knew I was dreaming, but it was all unpleasant, made up of my worst fears and insecurities. I know Terise is suffering, and she suffers because of me."

I wept for his childhood. When I considered some of the abuse he'd had to bear, it helped me understand why he was so screwed up.

However, Kheelan's countenance had changed over the last few days. I honestly didn't feel as if I recognized him anymore. That smug surliness and arrogance of his peeked out every now and then, but what I saw more consistently was humility and remorse.

"She made a choice, Kheelan. She instinctively chose to protect her fated mate. It's what any fated mate would have done."

"Except for me. Not me."

His bottom lip quivered, and when he looked at me there were actual tears in his eyes. I was so surprised by the show of emotion, I couldn't help but grip his hand and offer him some comfort.

"I felt something for her the moment you brought her to my cell, and I was furious, so angry that I recognized a depth of feeling and connection to her that I had never felt with you, even though I love you."

"You can love many people in your life. I believe that. I think our hearts have zero limits when it comes to affection. It's simply a matter of who will be our better half? Who is best suited to walk by our side throughout our lives? Why were you angry to discover that woman was probably Terise?"

Kheelan blinked, allowing the tears to flow.

"Because I love you, and it felt unfaithful. It felt like cheating. If my love couldn't stand the test of anything and everything, then what was the point? It also felt like losing. I'll admit to petty competition on my part, wanting what my brother had, fearing that I would never have what has always come so easy to Jareth."

"And what's that?"

"Contentment."

I stared at him in wide-eyed disbelief.

"No matter Jareth's lot in life, he has always made the best of it. I've never been able to manage that. I thought you were the key on so many levels, but I've been a damn fool, and now Terise is paying for it."

"You refused to accept it or believe it before. You refused to accept *her*. What's changed?"

"Me. I've changed because of her." He took a deep breath as tears slowly streamed down his face. "I belittled her, I insulted her, I did everything I damn well could to push her away from me because her very presence, her very existence, threatened to be my undoing, and I had already set my course and chosen you. Yet despite my horrible treatment of her, she threw herself in front of me. She saved me, and I didn't deserve it."

I reached for a lock of Terise's hair, running my fingers through it and studying her sallow complexion.

"No, you didn't deserve it, but that doesn't mean you can't become exactly what *she* deserves. Once we bring Terise back—"

"Once we bring Terise back, we will find a way to sever my bond with you and her, and she will be bonded to Cedric."

"Kheelan, what are you saying?"

His eyes were filled with so much pain and loathing it pinched my heart, quite literally taking my breath away. I could feel his pain, his torment, his own chastisement at not being there to protect and cherish Terise.

"If we can't find a way to get rid of our link to one another so she can have a bond that isn't tainted, she will die. My link to you has made her susceptible to *griesha* again. This never should have happened. You all warned me, but I remained obstinate and selfish. A fated mate is a gift, someone you cherish and place above all others, and I haven't done that a single moment I've been bonded to her." His shoulders shook as he held back a sob.

Alarmed, I reached over and placed a hand on his arm, trying to soothe him, but knowing the pain, guilt, and shame he felt were necessary. These consequences and their burdens were his to shoulder.

"When and if we figure this all out, you must bond her to Cedric. He is far more deserving of her than I am. He will make her happy in a way I will never be able to. I don't deserve her. I don't."

"What if she chooses you? You do realize she has the final say in this. Once she knows how you feel, once you apologize and show her how you've changed, I'm willing to bet she would give you a chance."

Kheelan wiped his eyes, retreating from my attempts to comfort him. He quickly stood and adjusted his tunic. "That's just it. She'll have no reason to choose me if she never knows how I truly feel." A sardonic smile reached his lips. "After all, I'm just a pompous, selfish prince who would risk the entire realm for a single night with you, Crysta. That's the version she'll see when she wakes up. She'll have no alternative but to choose Cedric."

"Kheelan," I warned. "Don't destroy your own happiness and hers. Give this a chance. Do what is best for Terise."

The smug smile returned, the cocky arrogance coming out with the tiny lift of his chin. "Why, my darling Crysta, that's exactly what I intend to do."

Crysta

a pparating to the foot of Goblin Mountain felt a bit surreal. I just kept having flashbacks of Kheelan and Rodri. I felt slightly guilty that most of my time spent with them had been pleasant, even if it *had* been steeped in lies.

"Any chance we can save some time and apparate straight to your father's doorstep?" Nuallan asked Grizelda.

She shook her head. "That's not really how the wards here work. Don't worry. My father will recognize me soon enough. Remember to stay on the path."

Yeah. No problem. My last experience with a Yanrath, though congenial, was not something I wanted to repeat.

Being dragged underground.

Not my favorite.

I'd definitely stick to the path.

As we filed into a single line behind Grizelda—we thought it best she be the first thing any Goblin scout saw when spying on us—I took a moment to appreciate the scenery once again. The lime green trees and neon yellow leaves adorning them paved a narrow path. We were warned to avoid touching anything unless we wanted to slowly be transformed into a Goblin.

That idea still fascinated me. I really wanted to understand the magical properties behind that.

I'd put a pin in it. Study it another day when the Fae realm didn't need so much saving.

I'd expected at least one hour of travel before we were spotted, but Grizelda's signature must have been recognized. It only took about ten minutes of uphill climbing before the path shimmered ahead. Grizelda was already stumbling toward the disturbance, flinging her arms around her father the moment he apparated. The joy on the Goblin King's face as he held his daughter close brought tears to my eyes.

And then I realized he was still naked, as was every other Goblin who magically appeared. Grizelda always had clothes on, but I got the feeling that the clothes were for everyone else's benefit. On their mountain, in their domain, naked was the end all be all.

It was a damn nudist colony over here.

I kept my eyes glued to their filmy yellow ones.

The rest of our group hung back for two reasons. One, we really wanted to give them a little privacy and two, we really didn't want to give them a reason to think we were hostile. Not interested in any magical battles taking place. Our position wasn't ideal. We were more or less boxed in with Goblins apparating around us.

"King Roderick, well met. I hadn't expected our ruler to personally deliver my daughter," the Goblin King said.

My father walked forward and grasped his outstretched hand.

"I only wish I could have done so a bit sooner, and while I'd like to take credit for her rescue, I'm afraid you owe her release to Queen Adris, Prince Jareth, and Nuallan."

The Goblin King's expression of disbelief brought a smile to my face. I'm sure their involvement on any level would have been a surprise to most faeries. Things were certainly changing around here.

Jareth squeezed my shoulder and stepped past me. He bowed his head in a show of respect, further surprising the Goblin, if his wide eyes were any indication.

"King Lothe, I can't tell you how sorry I am for the part my father played in this."

"He wanted the stone."

Wow. So we were getting right to it. The stone was hidden here. I slowly moved forward so the king could see me. "He kidnapped Grizelda so you would hand over Titania's stone?"

His gravelly voice was a little hard to understand since English was clearly not something he was used to speaking. "I don't know anything about Titania. Moridan believes in a legend passed down from generation to generation among my race. The first Goblin King was entrusted with the safekeeping of a dangerous stone by Oberon himself."

"Do you have any idea where that stone might be hidden?" Nuallan asked.

King Lothe stared at him for a moment, and then he turned his eyes back to me. "You believe the stone exists, just as Moridan does. You believe in the myth."

"It's no myth," I said. "It's the only thing that will save this realm and heal your people." I looked pointedly at the sores upon his body.

"If I could give it to you, I would. I would have handed it over to Moridan the moment he took my daughter, but it is simply a myth. We were never given its exact location. The story has never made much sense to us, but perhaps you will understand the first Goblin King's writings."

"This myth was written down?" Jareth asked. "And you'll let us read it?"

"Yes. You have returned my daughter to me, and you are offering to heal my people. If this stone exists, then you may have access to the writings. We will guide you there."

I assumed he'd just start climbing up the mountain and we would follow. Instead, the Goblins approached us. One slowly reached for my arm, lightly touching my shoulder. I had to grab hold of Chuck in case my dragon decided to take a chunk out of the Goblin's hand. A quick pulling sensation, followed by the scenery melting away, meant we were apparating to a new location. The scenery took shape once again, forming into an enormous clearing filled with an assembly of Goblins who seemed to be waiting for our arrival. The moment Grizelda appeared, arm-in-arm with her father, a large female broke from the group and raced toward her.

Must be her mother.

It warmed my heart to see that reunion. I didn't remember being held in my mother's arms, but I imagined it to be a wonderful feeling.

Jareth came up beside me and held me close.

"We did a good thing today," he said.

"I think you, Adris, and Nuallan get to take credit for that."

King Lothe motioned us forward. "Come," he said. "We welcome you to our home."

Home? I looked around the clearing, not seeing any buildings. The clearing was surrounded by the same lime green trees that lined the mountain path.

King Lothe turned with his entourage of family and attendants and headed toward the very back of the clearing. He made a chopping motion with his hand. The trees ahead of us shook, uprooting themselves from the ground and shuffling to either side, revealing an enormous village filled with small cottages made out of gold.

At least, I thought the material looked like gold. A main path led directly down the middle of this village, heading straight toward a golden palace just beyond. We followed the king down this path while Goblins on either side rushed out of their homes to see what the commotion was all about. When everyone got a good look at their king, and us trailing behind them, they immediately bowed in deference as we passed. I studied the cottages and shops, fascinated with the idea of buildings made out of gold.

"Goblins adore shiny metals and precious gems, but their favorite metal is gold. They like to hoard it for their own and have been known to make deals with those who possess it," Jareth said.

Cool.

I glanced behind me to check on the rest of our group. The only two who seemed as fascinated by the scenery were Paio and Lilly.

Poor guy. Paio had been imprisoned for far too long. He needed to get out more.

Lily clung to Graul, but her curiosity and wide-eyed wonder gave me a little hope that she would recover from the trauma she'd endured.

"More writings to read and interpret," Kheelan muttered as he came to my other side. "How forthcoming do you think this text will be?"

"If the Goblin King couldn't retrieve the stone, despite clear motivation to do so, I'm worried the text is going to be very obscure indeed," Jareth said.

"Yeah. I was afraid of that. Any bright sides to this, Crysta?"

"We actually have text to interpret?"

Kheelan let out a dissatisfied grunt.

"Hey," I said, "the Goblin King could have said, 'Good luck searching the entire mountain.'"

"Well, depending on what we read, we may be doing just that."

"Your pessimism is annoying."

"Just keeping it real."

I quirked a brow at his playful smile. "Keeping it real?"

Jareth chuckled. "Better than zoning out."

∞ ∞ ∞

I thought the decor would be different within the palace. I was sorely mistaken. Every surface within view was covered in gold. The walls, the vaulted ceilings, even the furniture, though soft to the touch, were covered in a dusty gold substance. The effect was stunning, although the presence of naked, green Goblins seemed a bit out of place. I had a lot of preconceived notion of the type of home this race would abide in. It shamed me a bit that I'd assumed they lived in poverty due to their grimy, unappealing appearance.

Then again, what I thought was beautiful wouldn't be the same for someone else. I looked at Graul, remembering my initial impressions of him were that of a skeleton with washed out green skin. His union with Lily would have shocked me once upon a time. Now, I didn't see a foreign species when I looked at Graul. I saw family, and he was absolutely beautiful to me.

I had a feeling the more time I spent with Goblins, the more beautiful they would be to me as well.

King Lothe led us into a large, circular room filled with sparkling chandeliers. I'd never seen so many in all my life. They covered the entire ceiling. As I peered up at the dazzling stones, I realized that none of them were crystal. They were gems of varying color and grade.

"The stones will protect us from prying eyes and magical attacks," King Lothe said.

"Why don't we have this at the Unseelie Court?" I asked my father.

He gazed at the ceiling in amazement. "Mining the amount of precious gems, imbuing them with defensive powers, and then fusing them within these chandeliers would be nigh impossible to achieve. Only Goblins are capable of such metal work. I didn't even know something like this could exist, but it doesn't surprise me. They share a close alliance with the sprites in the sprite mine."

A large table of pure gold stood in the center of the room. "Please be seated. I'll have the text brought in for your viewing." The Goblin King sent a servant off to retrieve the text just as another servant came rushing in. He frantically whispered something to the king whose solemn countenance turned grim.

"Others have breached our mountain," he said. "There is a unit of Formage making their way up the path, bearing the crest of Moridan."

"The Formage? That doesn't make any sense. Their allegiance is to the Unseelie Court," I said.

"There is a very good chance they've been enchanted." Adris rubbed her weary eyes, as if she'd been expecting this. Her unruly hair fell across her lined cheeks. "When Jareth, Nuallan, and I came to rescue you, Moridan had Formage guarding the entrance. Dark Magic had been used to not only destroy them, but to create a powerful spell of illusion so believable it actually became solid."

"You think he's using my subjects against me? Putting faeries of the Unseelie Court at risk?" my father asked. He directed his gaze to King Lothe. "How much time before they breach the clearing?"

"We can keep them occupied for as long as necessary, but their illusions will be difficult to defend against if they've been enchanted."

A large scroll, an actual scroll, with gold handles on either end, was quickly brought in and spread across the table. We hovered over it as the Goblin King ran his finger along the indecipherable writings, landing in the middle. He proceeded to read the strange text.

"Oberon has entrusted me with the Stone of Destiny, a stone so powerful we fear it falling into the wrong hands. Destroying it would have been our best option, but it appears invincible. Nothing we do has succeeded in blotting it out of existence. So hide it, we must. I shall take it to our great mountain where it will be safe within the skies of our kingdom and the fires of Zelres."

King Lothe stopped reading. "That is all the text offers in the way of location. Does this help you?"

Not exactly. Womp womp.

But I'd never heard anyone refer to the stone as the Stone of Destiny. Giving it a name helped identify it. Maybe it would help in locating it. Did that mean the diadem had a different name as well?

"You don't have any idea what this means? Zelres or the skies of your kingdom?" I asked.

"It could be a reference to certain landmarks on this mountain, but I can't think of anything that would match such vague descriptions," the Goblin King said. "I would have rescued Grizelda long ago if I had known where to look."

"Zelres isn't a location. It's a creature. I remember vague accounts of a dragon named Zelres," Chantara said. "The dragon lived within the Goblin kingdom, protecting the Goblin's precious gems and metals. Though there is no way of knowing if that dragon is alive today."

"Fascinating," King Lothe said, looking at Chantara as if he would like to peer into her memories and hoard them for himself. "There is no mention of a dragon in our histories."

"I get the feeling quite a bit of history was changed by the first Goblin King." Jareth took a step back and paced a bit. "They needed to protect the stone. I'm surprised he would even write about this."

"He wrote about it because it was determined that someone worthy would one day come to lay claim to it, reversing The Rending," King Lothe said.

"It says that in the text?" I asked in surprise.

"Yes. In our legend, a queen returns to right The Rending using this very stone."

"Why doesn't anyone else know about this legend?" I asked.

"The races stick to each other. Most don't offer up secrets, histories, spells, or personal information that might allow other races to target or weaken them," my father said. "We've never really been united, though many races live under one court."

"It seems to me that needs to end. Everyone has scattered bits of information, little pieces to the puzzle," Cedric muttered.

"Chantara, do you know anything else about this Zelres?" I asked.

She cocked her head to the side, her brows knitted in concentration. I noted her eyes were back to their beautiful lavender color, but the obsidian had definitely been popping up more frequently.

"Just that he guards the Goblin treasure within an inactive volcano. Honestly, I thought it just a scary story my nanny told me to keep me from misbehaving."

"Does a volcano ring any bells?" I asked the Goblin King.

"I'm sorry." He rubbed his hand against his bald head in agitation. "There are no volcanoes, inactive or otherwise, on this mountain."

"We need to speak with someone who was alive during the time of The Rending," Nuallan said. "Chantara's memories, while helpful, are also a bit incomplete. We can't expect her to know what the text refers to when she was just a child at the time."

"That would take a while, and it's time we don't really have." Jareth directed his gaze at King Lothe.

Shoulders slumped around the table, most of us feeling a little defeated that the answer was here, but impossible to interpret.

"How much time do we have before the Formage reach your village?"

King Lothe's eyes went vacant for a moment, as if looking at an entirely different scene. He blinked a few times and began shouting orders to his guards in a gravelly language I didn't understand.

"Well, that's not great," Adris said.

"What's happening?" I asked.

"The Formage have managed to find their way to the village. I think King Lothe assumed the magical wards meant to trick, distract, and deceive would keep them circling the mountain. It seems they've made their way directly toward us."

"It's impossible," King Lothe said. "I don't understand how they have managed this."

"We can't leave until we've found the stone. We have to locate it before Moridan's minions do."

"The Fates," Kheelan said. "By the gods, we should have gone directly to them. They'll know exactly what this bit of text means."

"Then let's get going," Lily said. "Before the Formage get here."

I took one look at her terrified expression and realized the Formage had most likely been used in the torture and torment of Lily and Graul. I didn't want her coming undone in the face of her nightmares, but I wasn't going to leave the Goblins to fight a battle we'd quite literally brought to their doorstep.

"Graul, have you ever been to the top of this mountain?" I asked.

"Never been. Can't apparate there."

"I will take you," Grizelda said, grabbing hold of Lily's trembling hand and giving it a squeeze.

"Thank you, Grizelda." I turned my attention to our group. "The rest of us aren't leaving until we take care of the Formage."

The Goblin King appeared agitated. "It isn't necessary, Princess. It is our duty to protect the Unseelie Court and its royals."

I reached across the table and grabbed his hand, noting it to be rough and calloused. "We're not leaving you. Formage are formidable, and these particular faeries are not in their right mind. We stay."

I looked around the room, noting the determination on Adris's face, the proud look on my father's face, and the out of place excitement oozing from the rest of the group, minus Jareth. Not surprising since he didn't want me anywhere near a battle.

"Let's move," I said, heading out of the room. "We take the fight to them."

Crysta

areth was already by my side as we gathered in the outer courtyard of the palace. Battles in outer courtyards seemed to be the theme for the day.

A group of ten Formage came marching through the village. I noticed they barely spared a glance for any of the Goblins scattered on either side. They only had eyes for me. When they were about ten yards away they stopped, fanned out in a straight line, and then froze in place. Their eyes were vacant, except for the Formage in the middle. His contained creepy streaks of silver, like lightning.

"We do not intend to harm anyone. Moridan merely requests you hand over the stone."

"We haven't found the stone," I said. "We didn't have much time to go looking before you barreled in here without an invitation."

The Formage exhibited no emotion. Nothing to indicate whether my snarky tone upset him. He simply remained still for a moment as his eyes went completely white. After a few seconds, the pale color slowly leached back in, along with the silver streaks. When he spoke again, his voice didn't sound like his own. It sounded like Titania.

"I sense the stone is near, but I believe you do not yet have it. I will allow you the opportunity to retrieve what is mine. Go quickly and return with the stone. If you should find it and flee, your Goblin friends will suffer."

She wanted me to retrieve it even though she had ten soldiers here to do her bidding. I thought that was *very* interesting. "If you can sense it, why not have the Formage grab it?"

"You have one hour, Crysta. Then I kill your friends."

For whatever reason, she couldn't force the Formage to retrieve the stone. I didn't understand why she needed me, but it didn't matter. I was done with the threats. I was done with the abuse of power.

I motioned Adris closer to me and lowered my voice. "You mentioned the other Formage you dealt with were already dead. Is that what we're dealing with here? Are these Formage merely shells being used by Dark Magic?"

Adris gazed upon the Formage, anger and outrage already creasing the lines of her face. "Their hearts are linked together much like the other three were. It will make their mirages powerful and lethal, but to answer your question, yes, they are already dead, in a sense. There is no saving them, other than to free them from Titania."

"Then let's put them out of their misery."

I stepped forward and quickly pulled from my core, utilizing the three elements within and sending them like a tidal wave toward the soldiers. Either Titania hadn't expected my bold move or she simply couldn't mobilize ten men at once. The magic wrapped around the guards, weaving in and out of their limbs and anchoring them to the ground.

"How do we unlink their hearts?" I asked Adris.

Before she could answer, a trembling shook the ground. Just behind the Formage, a large hole opened up, an arm punching through the soil. More arms punched the terrain around us as the ground shook and Goblins fled.

"Yanrath," Jareth shouted. "Watch your flank." He pointed toward Cedric where a Yanrath slowly pulled himself out of the ground.

"No, the Yanrath are on our side," I said. At least I thought they were, until the one next to Cedric grabbed hold of him and attempted to drag him through the large hole in the ground. Paio went to his aid, shooting water from his hand and spraying the Yanrath in the face. The Yanrath disintegrated right before our eyes ,and Cedric fell backward toward the group.

Paio looked at his hand in astonishment while more Yanrath continued punching holes upward through the ground, reaching for more victims.

"That's never happened before. I didn't mean to kill him." Paio said.

"It's a mirage," Jareth yelled. "Keep throwing spells at the Yanrath. Give Crysta and Adris the time they need."

Utter chaos ensued after that. The cries of Goblins being dragged underground tore at my heart as my group circled our backs, keeping the Yanrath at bay. The Goblin King and his guards joined the frey, heading toward the village and firing off their own magical spells that quite literally disintegrated the Yanrath on contact.

"Let's do this, Adris. Tell me what to do."

We huddled together, but another hand shot right in front of us. I directed my magic at the hand, but it effectively blocked it, not disintegrating in the slightest. The hole grew wider when a very familiar face peeked up at me.

"Langren?" I shouted in disbelief. His other arm broke through, and he swiftly pulled himself to his feet, blocking a magical blow from Jareth in the process.

"It's okay," I yelled. "He's on our side."

Langren's wide smile sent a jolt of adrenaline through my system. We were so winning this battle. The white crescents under his eyes were just as I remembered them.

"You know this Yanrath?" Adris eyed him in disbelief.

He focused his attention on me.

"Well met, Princess. I believe you are in need of our assistance."

"You have no idea."

"My people will attack the mirages while protecting your friends."

"What will you do?"

He took a step to my right, stamping down on a hand that had just emerged from the ground right next to my foot. The hand disintegrated, and he turned to give me another glorious smile.

"I will protect you."

I looked out across the village, noticing Yanrath fighting against Yanrath and saving Goblins dragged underground. I didn't know how the Yanrath could tell mirage from reality, but I was grateful for their help.

"Adris, let's save these Formage."

Just then, a large shadow covered the sky, zooming above us and sending faeries flying in every direction.

I looked up and stared in horror at the biggest bat-like creature I had ever seen.

"This is not good," Langren said. "You continue. I will take care of this mirage."

The bat-like creature opened its mouth wide, its spiky teeth jutting forward as it hung suspended in the air. Then it made a choking sound and expelled a river of green liquid from its mouth. Langren jumped in front of Adris and I, presenting a large shield that burned as the liquid made contact.

"By the goddess, Titania just had to summon a Bordesh," Adris said.

My attention was distracted by a jerk at my ankle. Another Yanrath had hold of me. I sent a blade of ice through its arm and watched it disintegrate with satisfaction. Unfortunately, the Bordesh wasn't letting up. It continued its acidic assault on Langren, who valiantly held his shield, but it wasn't going to last much longer.

Adris and I needed to concentrate, and this madness did not help. I pulled from my core, backed up a few paces so I wouldn't hit Langren, and then I shot my hands upward toward the Bordesh, aiming at its furry brown wings. I coated them with ice, fully expecting it to disintegrate like the rest. Instead, the Bordesh screeched in pain, lost altitude, and plummeted to the earth. The sound it made when it hit the ground almost caused me to vomit. I heard bone crunching and an agonized wail.

It's just a mirage, Crysta. You didn't really hurt the dang thing.

I focused my attention on the Formage before us, noticing the silver sparks in the middle guard's eyes flashed with more frequency, which gave me an idea. I lifted my hand, bringing two fingers to bear, and pointing them directly at his eyes.

"*Inanis exstinctique.*"

A thick, icy film covered the Formage's peepers, blinding him to everything. The moment I rendered his sight useless, Yanrath everywhere began to disappear.

"Adris, quickly. What do we do?"

"It won't be pretty. Repeat after me, and when I tell you to, say freedom," she said. "Death compels the soul's release. Spirit ascends and heartbeats cease."

Langren and I repeated that with her, lifting our hands toward the Formage as she lifted hers. I had no idea what this spell was or what it would do, but it took lots of power to maintain it. My core heated as energy shot from my hands and spread across all ten Formage.

I nearly lost the contents of my stomach as an awful tearing noise rent the air and their rib cages expanded, breaking open to reveal their hearts.

"Holy hell," I said.

"Stay focused. Continue repeating the words."

Jareth came up next to us, lifting his hand and adding his magical strength to our efforts. They had done this with three guards back at the Seelie palace, but we were looking at ten. Even with Jareth's assistance, we couldn't get their hearts to leave their chest cavities.

"Nuallan," Jareth shouted.

"You rang?" Nuallan appeared at Jareth's side, covered in sweaty grime and blood spatters. He looked like death but wore an exhilarated expression.

Goddess save me from thrill-seeking faeries.

He lifted his hand, adding his voice to the incantation, and the hearts ripped from their chest cavities. The black blade linking them together hung long and thick. Adris kept shaking her head, indicating we didn't have enough power yet. Too many Formage, and Titania was working the spell with Moridan's help.

Suddenly, I felt an influx of power and saw my father, King Lothe, and the rest of our group lining up to help, throwing their magic toward the Formage and reciting the incantation. Within seconds the black blade began to crack.

"Now," Adris said.

Like a mighty battle cry we roared in unison, "Freedom."

All ten hearts exploded in a cloud of ash, and the Formage fell to the ground.

I stared at their mangled bodies in dismay, praying they hadn't felt any pain throughout that goddess-awful spell.

"That is by far the worst thing I have ever been witness to," Cedric said, staring at the Formage and looking a little nauseated.

"Is everyone okay? No one injured?" I asked.

"A few scrapes and bruises, but I think we'll all survive," Kheelan said.

"I'm going below to see if any Goblins were dragged under," Langren said. "But before I do, will you have need of anything else, Princess?"

I responded by reaching out and pulling him into a hug. So what if he was naked. Everyone on this mountain was naked.

I decided to embrace the naked.

Literally.

His response was hesitant at first, but then he hugged me back, tucking my head just under his and letting out a soft chuckle. "You are a different sort of person, Crysta. I think it is a good thing."

He released me and stepped back, taking in our wide-eyed group. It occurred to me that none of them had ever seen a Yanrath before. They went from staring at him in fascination to staring at me in disbelief.

"Prince Jareth, I understand she is your fated mate," Langren said.

Jareth gave me a warm smile and put his arm around me. "She is."

"I am relieved. I did not like the other suitor she had." He pointed to Kheelan who gave him an annoyed look. Nuallan burst into laughter, causing everyone else to let off some steam.

Langren reached out to shake Kheelan's hand. It looked a bit like a peace offering. "Well met, Prince Kheelan. Thank you for your aid in protecting our Princess."

Kheelan gave him a reluctant smile but returned his handshake. "I will always do so."

Langren nodded one last time, and then the ground he stood upon crumbled, swallowing him up.

It. Was. Disturbing.

"Just when, exactly, did you have time to make friends with a Yanrath?" Jareth asked.

"When I was here on Goblin mountain with Kheelan and my fake father. We had a nice little chat while Kheelan and Rodri napped."

Kheelan groaned. "She'd befriend a Mountain Troll if she thought it even remotely possible."

"Or a Bordesh," Nuallan said.

"Speaking of...did you see the way that Bordesh didn't disintegrate?" I cast my gaze out across the village and spotted a large, brown lump the size of a large boulder. I headed toward it, wondering why the Yanrath mirages had disappeared but this mirage hadn't.

A firm hand on my arm held me back. "It's not a mirage, Crysta. It was drawn to the magical battle here. Bordesh are a confrontational species, and they absorb magics much like Chuck does, only they hoard magic the way dragons hoard treasure."

"Are you telling me I really hurt that creature?"

I slipped from Jareth's grasp and raced toward the mangled animal.

"Crysta, Bordesh are dangerous."

But I didn't listen—surprise, surprise—mainly because I could hear another voice in my head, one begging for mercy and death.

I reached the Bordesh, noting the odd angle of its wings and the large gash along the back of its bullet shaped head. Its ears were bat-like, and its snout looked exactly like that of a pig's. Its bottom fangs had broken through its top lip, and one of its legs bent at an odd angle. He stared at me with pain and pleading in his eyes. I rested my hand on his head and heard his voice within my own thoughts.

"*Kill me.*"

"Not today," I said.

Jareth and Kheelan were already at my side, along with the rest of the group.

"He's suffering. We need to put him out of his misery," Jareth said.

"No. We need to heal him. Kheelan, can you use your magic on him?"

Kheelan looked exasperated by my request. "Crysta, this is a dangerous animal. They spit acid at their victims and use it to absorb their victim's magic. If I heal this creature, it will attack."

"*Please, kill me.*"

I didn't sense any animosity or malice from this creature. Instead, I felt a kinship and connection to it just as I had to the Cù-Sith in Moridan's dungeons.

"If you won't heal him then I'm going to try, and that could end up making things worse. It's not my gift. I don't understand how healing works. So please give it a go, Kheelan."

He shared a look with Jareth who finally gave him a terse nod.

"Fine, but you will stand back."

Jareth pulled me into his arms and drew us several feet away as Kheelan worked his healing gifts on the Bordesh. The slow knitting of bone and sinew did not sound pleasant, and the creature cried and shrieked until Kheelan got his pain under control. Soon, however, the healing ended, and the Bordesh breathed slow and steady. It climbed upon it's clawed feet as Kheelan scrambled back and lifted up his hand, forming a shield.

"*Your healer need not fear me. I would thank him for his help.*"

"Kheelan, he says he won't hurt you. He wants to thank you instead."

Kheelan shook his head. "How do you even know—right, telepathic. I forgot." He cautiously lowered his shield and waited for the Bordesh to make his move. The creature slunk lower, folding its wings slowly around Kheelan.

"Crysta?" Kheelan said, sounding a bit alarmed.

"He wants to give you something," I said, already seeing the gift from the telepathic link I shared with the Bordesh.

The creature slowly rested its forehead against Kheelan's for a moment in thanks. Then he lifted his head, opened his mouth, and coughed up a green stone into Kheelan's palm.

Kheelan just stared at it in surprise, and then looked up at the Bordesh in wonder. "He just gave me his heart stone," he said.

"What's that?" I asked.

"It means I'm his master. He gave me a way to summon him whenever there is need."

"*Thank you,*" I said to the Bordesh.

The creature smiled wide, revealing sharp fangs. Then he bowed his head toward me, stepped back a few paces, and shot into the air, flapping his now healed wings, becoming a small speck on the horizon.

Kheelan stared at the stone in his hand, turning it over and over, clearly not believing his good fortune.

"I'm not deserving of this," he said.

Jareth walked toward him and slapped him on the shoulder. "It would appear that the Bordesh thought you were, and since we know Bordesh have the power to assess one's soul, it looks as if you're not nearly half as bad as you always make yourself out to be."

"I disagree. I think the Bordesh must have hit its head rather hard to consider Kheelan his master," Nuallan said in a teasing tone.

"You are all worthy faeries. You stayed to fight with us when you should have left to find the stone," the Goblin King said. "My people and I will always be indebted to you for this."

Roderick grasped his arm. "I think we just agree to help each other whenever necessary. It's what we should be doing anyway."

King Lothe's smile transformed his face into something I thought profoundly beautiful.

"We need to get you to the Fates," he said. "Let's help you find that stone before Titania sends more Formage."

Agreed. The sooner we found the stone and got off this mountain, the less chance of our Goblins being targeted and attacked again.

Crysta

*A*fter that harrowing adventure, our group was pretty eager to get to the top of the mountain. We apparated to the entrance where a hint of lavender and rose hit me square in the nose. The garden looked every bit as beautiful as I remembered it. A smooth path widened into a flat plain where an immaculate garden sat, surrounded by gurgling streams. In the middle of the garden I saw the same marble altar with a wooden pillar standing just to its right. It held that same bowl and curved dagger meant for blood offerings to The Fates.

Such a serene setting for such an unpleasant task.

Lily rushed to me the moment we arrived.

"Oh, I was so worried. Graul kept trying to reassure me. He said there was nothing you guys couldn't handle, but I hated not knowing how you were. I was ready to go back there and fight with you."

Her loyalty was touching, but I could see how the thought of it really freaked her out.

"Your job? Stay safe. Best thing for Crysta...you stay safe," Graul said.

"I couldn't agree with you more, Graul."

He came up behind Lily to wrap his comforting arms around her, but I could see the worry in his eyes. She still hadn't recovered, and he didn't know how to help her. It was something we would need to address as soon as we could. In fact, as much as I wanted them with me, I almost wondered if it would be better to send Lily and Graul to a safe location until this was all over. I just wasn't sure how much more of this she could take. I squeezed her hand to reassure her and then took in our location.

I stared at the rich purples, reds, and pinks of the garden and figured it best to just get on with the summoning. Without hesitation, I headed toward the altar, grabbing the curved dagger.

"Now wait just a moment," Jareth said, stilling my hand just before I sliced my palm open. "If a blood sacrifice is necessary, why don't you let me make it?"

"Because I'm the one who is going to be asking the questions." I stepped back and carved a nice gash in my palm before he could stop me.

It took me everything I had not to let out a girlie whimper. It was one thing to see folks slice their hand up in the movies, but reality stung.

"Stubborn," I heard him mutter under his breath.

I quickly moved my hand over the silver bowl and squeezed. I knew it wouldn't take much for The Fates to be summoned once the blood hit the bowl. The moment I finished, it vibrated, building up a powerful energy that erupted into light, shooting high into the sky and summoning The Fates who appeared by degrees, descending next to the altar.

Their greedy swallows as they imbibed my blood made me grimace. Yuck.

"Crysta, you have summoned us again," said the one in the middle. "I see you have come into your own since last we spoke."

"Yeah. Quite a few things have happened lately. It's why we're here."

"Zelres will not appreciate being disturbed," the Fate on the left said.

"How did you know that we came—stupid question. Disregard," Jareth said.

"So Zelres is alive?" I asked.

"Last time we checked," the Fate on the right said in a dry tone. "If you wish to secure the stone, you'll have to convince him. He had very specific instructions by the first Goblin King to hold on to it unless certain criteria were met."

"What criteria?"

"You'll have to discover that for yourself."

"Okay, how we do we find Zelres?" Nuallan asked.

"You'll have to enter the mouth of the volcano..." said the Fate in the middle.

"...and descend below," the other two said in unison.

"Where is the volcano?" I asked.

The Fates raised their right arms and pointed toward the sky.

Silence prevailed for a few moments as we all directed our attention to the heavens, waiting for some kind of explanation.

"Is this a metaphor we need to untangle?" Kheelan said.

"You do not see Zelres' kingdom?" the Fate in the middle asked. She lowered her head and gave us all an amused look.

I stared up at the sky again, noticing a few clouds...and nothing else.

"Is this kingdom invisible?" I asked.

The Fate in the middle gave me a knowing look. "Crysta, you cannot see it with your eyes. You must see it with your magic."

My magic. Did I have a magical third eye or something?

Actually, that thought wasn't half bad. I kept my face turned upward and closed my eyes, focusing on my core magic to guide me. At first, there was only darkness behind my lids, but as I tugged on my core to light the way, a vision opened up to me, and I could see a huge land mass floating several hundred feet above us. I tugged on the magical cords within my core, thinning them out and increasing the light and energy diverted to my eyes, more specifically, my third eye.

My sight zoomed in, pulling me up and over the land mass as if I was having an out of body experience. I spotted an enormous castle that rivaled Sleeping Beauty's. Rivers crisscrossed the land, meadows of green dotted with colorful vegetation gave the landscape depth and texture. And smack dab in the middle of this enormous land mass, a large crater in the ground, easily the circumference of the base of the castle, broke up the otherwise flawless green. Smoke lazily rose above the surface, only to be whisked away by the soft breeze.

I need to go there. Right at the lip of that volcano.

The moment I thought it, a sharp tug pulled at my center. I heard an alarmed cry from Jareth and a few others from my group.

Am I apparating?

The smells and sounds of The Fates' garden were swept away by the unpleasant aroma of sulpher. I blinked my eyes open and nearly lost my balance when I realized I had landed exactly where my thoughts had led, right at the lip of Zelres' volcano. My arms flailed as I over-corrected and fell backward, landing hard on my rump.

Jareth

One moment she was there, the next, she had disappeared. My heart nearly jumped out of my chest as I let out a desperate shout. I wasn't the only one freaking out. It seemed our entire group rushed the last spot she had stood. I turned to The Fates. It took me everything I had not to smack the satisfied smiles from their faces.

"She is a quick study," the Fate in the middle said, staring up at the sky.

"Where is she?" I demanded.

"Exactly where she should be."

"Not exactly specific. I'd appreciate it if you would dispense with riddles. My fated mate needs me."

All three Fates held up their hands in protest. "Your fated mate is the only one who can do this."

"This has been foretold. Your father knew of her before she was born," said the one on the left.

"Enough of these riddles, Fates. This realm is dangerous. My daughter cannot last on her own," Roderick said.

"I would have to agree. She has showed incredible potential, but she lacks the training," Nuallan said.

Chantara came up beside me and placed a comforting hand on my arm. "I believe the Fates understand this better than we do." She turned her gaze on the three trolls. "What exactly was foretold?"

"Many things pertaining to Crysta and her role here in this realm. Moridan's Seer saw only a fraction of what Crysta was meant to achieve, and his interpretation, along with his Seer, was flawed and corrupt."

"I need to follow her," I said, feeling a tightness coil around my heart, and the distance between us grew. "She shouldn't have to do this alone."

To my surprise the Fate in the middle reached over and gently placed a hand on mine, patting it in a grandmotherly fashion. Her skin felt like thin sheets of sandpaper, but I took comfort in it anyway.

"You must have faith in her abilities. If she cannot do this alone, she cannot do anything. The baby bird must leap from the nest. This is how she becomes."

"Becomes what?" I asked.

"What she was meant to become."

Kheelan let out an annoyed sigh. "Go to the Fates, they said. You'll find answers, they said. Obscure and abstract should be the theme of the day."

"We hold on to Fates," Graul said. "When they go, we go with them."

Graul's idea wasn't half bad, but the Fates were making quite a bit of sense to me. Crysta had to do this on her own. The thought of her facing down a Dragon made every protective instinct I felt for her rage in defiance, but I'd promised myself I was going to give her the room she needed to grow. She had to be strong.

If the heir to the Unseelie throne was incapable of ruling all her subjects, anarchy would soon follow, and we had seen plenty of that with my own father. She had to find her footing. I simply wished I had her flank. I didn't know what she would be facing there without my assistance.

"Looks like we're letting go and letting God," Kheelan said.

"This human phrase, yes?" Graul asked.

"Correct, my skeletal comrade."

"Not like it."

I didn't either.

Crysta

The volcano may have been inactive, but the heat rising from the lip of the large crater-like hole was humid and uninviting. The sharp smell of sulfur was so pungent, it made my eyes water and the back of my throat burn. I gingerly crawled toward the edge, sticking my head over and staring down at the bottomless depths below.

"Well, hell," I said. "How am I supposed to get down there? I can't even see the bottom."

So no apparating since I couldn't visualize what I was apparating to. I cast my gaze around the lip, looking for a staircase, a rope ladder, or a nice little sign that said, "Descend the volcano here."

Nothing.

Heaven forbid any part of this journey be a cakewalk.

I took in my surroundings, wondering if I could cut down hundreds of vines and tie them together. The scattered trees were several hundred yards away. Any other vegetation around the area wasn't exactly rope ladder material. Besides, I had no way of knowing how long I would need to make it, and I didn't have the upper body strength to pull myself back up if I needed to.

I stared at the way the sides of the volcano held deep grooves, almost like footholds, and it gave me an idea. Pulling on my core, I formed a large block of ice in my hand and sent it levitating over the lip of the cave, within moments it began to melt, so I added Spring magic to the structure, the threads of Spring wove together, creating a block of green twigs and debris that looked solid enough to step on. Moving my hand toward the edge, I fastened threads around it and anchored it to the volcano's craggy insides where it held fast once finished. I bent over the lip of the volcano and pressed my hand down upon it to see if it could bear some weight. It remained sturdy, as if it had always been part of the volcano.

As quickly as I could, I created another heavy block, using the same process I had with the first one, and attached it to the inside of the volcano, just a step down from the first.

This was my version of a staircase. I imagined any other faerie would have known exactly how to navigate this scenario, but this was about all I could come up with so I'd roll with it. I made five stairs, attaching them to the side of the volcano before finding the courage to actually try them out. I placed my foot on the first stair and then stood with both feet planted on its surface, ready to reach for the cliff's edge if I felt even the tiniest hint of give. It remained completely immovable.

Very reassuring. I took a step down and held still for a moment as I waited for the stair to break away or disintegrate.

Nothing.

It wasn't going anywhere.

Feeling triumphant, I took another step and then another.

That's right. This princess knows how to troubleshoot.

As I continued down my makeshift staircase, I continued to add more and more blocks, descending the volcano in a circular pattern as I added steps to its circumference and spiraled down. I did my best to pull on the right amounts of energy, expending only what I needed to expend. I had no way of knowing how many steps would be needed, and I didn't want to burn out and get stuck with hundreds of feet left to go.

My hair stuck to my sweaty neck. The rest of my clothing felt damp and scratchy on my skin. The deeper I went, the more the atmosphere turned into a sauna. I was in my own personal hell as I dealt with temperatures outside my comfort zone. After about fifteen minutes of my continued efforts, I noticed the ice I created didn't have the same solid structure it needed. I paused for a moment to consider what I could do with Autumn and Spring magic combined since my Winter magic wasn't working as well.

I pulled Autumn threads from my core and watched as they manifested above my hands. I visualized fall leaves as they landed on the ground and became mulch over time. The fall leaves formed above my hand and then bunched together. I added mud, dirt, and branches to create a more solid, temperature-resistant structure before warping Spring magic around it and encasing it in wood.

Once finished, I attached it to the wall just a step below me and put my weight on it. It took me a moment for the cracking sound to register, and a panicked moment for me to realize it hadn't come from the step I currently stood upon. Something whistled past my face, nearly smacking me in the process. I lost my balance and fell backward, landing on the step above.

Another crack with another object flying past me, only to make a distant crashing noise below. At least I knew this thing had a bottom, but it looked like my icy staircase above had lost ground to the heat and humidity of the volcano. I hurriedly stood, constructed a shield above my head with one hand and utilized my new formula for stairs with another. It took a little more time with one hand, but it couldn't be helped. An occasional stair would land just above my head, and without the shield, I knew I'd be injured and thrown off the part of my staircase that was actually stable.

I really had to hurry, though. I had no way of knowing if my new formula for stairs was going to last as long as my ice stairs had. I formed them as quickly as I could, gingerly stepping down, down, down. Another bang to my shield actually rocked my energy, throwing me off balance. I dropped my magic as I flung my arms out to steady myself, but I toppled over anyway. With a shriek, I reached out to grab hold of the last step. My fingers found purchase, but my arm popped out of its socket as it bore the full brunt of my weight. I screamed in agony as searing pain gripped my shoulder, tearing at my ligaments.

My other hand grabbed hold of the volcano's bumpy surface. I dug my fingers into some nicks and grooves to take some weight off my injured arm.

"Why don't you just let go?" said a voice from below. It sounded cultured with a bit of a hiss at the end of its sentence.

"Uh...what...do what?" I asked. I gritted my teeth as the burn in my shoulder intensified.

"Let go. You're literally three feet from the bottom, child. Just a small jump and you'll be fine."

"I...you...really? Who are you?"

The voice ignored my question. "Clever, though. What you did with that staircase. I've never had anyone attempt that before." There was a moment of silence before the voice said, "Are you going to let go?"

"Honestly, no. I have no way of knowing if you're telling the truth. You could be luring me to my death."

An impatient snort filled the silence. I felt a momentary increase in heat near my ankles. "My dear child, there's no need to lure you to your death. If I wanted you dead, I would simply eat you and be done with it."

"Good point." My arm demanded I let go, and since I couldn't create any other stairs in this position, I figured I didn't have much to lose.

"Okay. I'm letting go now."

"Wonderful."

I really wanted to let go. I did, but I still couldn't see the bottom.

"This will require movement on your part," said the disembodied voice.

"Yeah. I'm working on it."

I said a silent prayer to any god or goddess who might care, and then I released my hold.

Unfortunately, the fall was a little farther than three feet. I screamed all the way down, until I landed on something soft and bouncy. The impact wouldn't have hurt at all if my right shoulder hadn't been so messed up.

"That was not three feet," I shouted into the dark abyss.

There was a low chuckle to my left. "Princess, would you have been willing to jump if I had told you the truth."

"Not a chance."

"Human psychology. Strange that I should have need of it with the heir to the Unseelie Court." Heavy footfalls sounded. The movement of a very large creature shook the ground.

"You know who I am?" I asked as I tried to shift on the fuzzy, squishy...whatever it was I had fallen on.

"Allow me to make introductions." A loud swoosh of air, followed by blinding light, caused my eyes to squint and tear up. Torches lit along a very wide, high corridor before me, and at its center stood a fire red Dragon about the size of a school bus.

Sweet Danu, he was enormous.

He peered at me from intelligent, curious eyes that glowed yellow in the torchlight. He had a bright red beard that jutted from the bottom of his pointed chin, and his mane of red hair flared out wild and free behind his long, pointed ears. His hair and ears ended in gold tips, as did his five-fingered claws on hands and feet.

"Zelres?" I asked. I felt relieved and wary. I needed to find him, but he was freaking terrifying.

Long, narrow snout filled with bone crushing teeth?

Check.

A scaly body covered in armored plates and spikes?

Check.

The kind of creature who could swallow me whole?

Check and check.

The Fae realm was a little scary.

He must have accurately interpreted my terrified expression. He shifted lower and sat on his haunches, then he rested his clawed fingers before him and cradled his head between them near the ground. "The first time can be rather intimidating, but I'm quite friendly...until I'm not."

"That does *not* instill confidence."

"I assume you're here to collect the Stone of Destiny?"

"That is correct." I shifted a little, attempting to scoot my bootie toward the side of the large cushion I'd landed on. It looked like a cat cushion, if the cat you owned happened to be the size of a haul truck. I forgot about my arm and put too much weight on it. Hissing in pain, I shifted to my other arm to bear my weight so I could get enough leverage to crawl off. After several awkward moments, I opted for lying down and rolling off the dang thing.

Totally worked.

And then I landed on my arm.

"Son of a...really?"

"You're quite fragile. Can't you use your magic to heal what ails you?"

I looked above me, seeing Zelres' head peering over me, wearing what looked like an amused expression, though who could really tell if a dragon smiled. And why did most Fae creatures look a little creepy when they tried?

"I don't have much of a gift for healing," I said. I groaned as I propped myself up on my good arm and finally moved into a seated position. "I'm barely figuring out what I can do with the magic I have."

"So an untrained faerie dares to enter my domain? You're either incredibly smart or incredibly stupid."

"I'd prefer the former, but I'm inclined to think the latter." I took in a deep breath and let it out slowly, all the while Zelres hunkered down, staring at me with curious, yellow eyes. His pupils were slitted, and his brow ridge was lined with bumpy scales, ending in a single spike at the corner of each brow ridge. "Those look sharp." I nodded toward his head.

He snorted, fanning me with his warm breath. "Useful for tearing apart flesh, sinew, and bone."

"Oh, the things I'll never unhear." I gingerly moved my injured arm, but the pain was intense. So bad, in fact, I had trouble concentrating. I probably should have been more terrified to be seated right in front of Zelres' enormous jaws, but I hurt too much to care.

He let out an exasperated sigh. "You'll never manage if you continue on in this fashion." He opened his mouth wide, displaying teeth in which I never *ever* wanted to find myself ensconced.

In my current fog of pain, I prepped myself to be snatched up and crushed between those massive jaws. Instead, a hard blast of hot air hit me square in the face, burning my nerve endings from head to foot and back again. I opened my mouth to scream, but nothing came out.

For a moment an unbearable burning suffused my skin, and then the temperature returned to that of a normal, humid sauna, complete with the choking smell of sulfur, zero exit plan, and a man-eating dragon whose snout was two inches from my face. I raised my arm to shield myself from being grilled, barbecued, and/or roasted, when I realized I was using my injured arm.

And it felt just fine.

I rolled my shoulder around a bit. "How did you do that?"

"All Dragons have the ability to heal with their breath. Surely your little sidekick has helped you out before."

"You know about Chuck?" I placed my hand on his snout and scooted back a bit. Being this close to him made me go cross-eyed.

His slitted pupils widened in surprise, and then he let out a low laugh. "You touch my snout when most would run. I like you, Princess. Perhaps you will not get eaten after all, no matter the outcome of this little visit." In a graceful movement I wasn't prepared for, Zelres rose to his hind quarters and stretched his forelegs upward. "I can smell your little Dragon on you. His charms of protection, not to mention his bold claim on you, is a difficult scent to dismiss. He truly believes you to be his mother. I find that curious."

"Why?"

"Dragons, no matter the subspecies, are not prone to leaving their kind. Perhaps you'll share how that came about later. At the moment, we have work to do."

He lowered his head to my eye level. "Please, allow me to carry you."

I gave his scaly cranium a dubious look. "I'm good, thanks."

"You have tiny legs. It will take you much too long to get where we need to be going, and I am not a patient Dragon. You may sit atop my head, or I will have dinner a little earlier than scheduled."

"Your head looks so inviting," I said.

I quickly moved forward, grabbing hold of the spike on the left side of his brow ridge and placing my foot on his snout. Climbing to the top of his head was a lot like climbing a rock wall with jutting stalactites. Spikes everywhere. I positioned myself on the left side of his head where I could grab hold of one of his devil horns and cling to it for all I was worth.

"Do hold on," he said. He quickly raised himself, sending my stomach through my liver. Motion sickness wasn't a thing for me, but the heat and the smell of this place had done me in. He turned around and headed down the enormous corridor. The torches continued to light our way, going out just as soon as we passed them.

"Why do you live down here, separate from the rest of the realm?"

"Dragons seek out their own solitude. I find most faeries rather trying."

"So you don't have a wife or a girlfriend?" The minute it was out, I knew it was stupid.

"We mate to procreate. We do not mate for life. At least, my particular species doesn't. Too much jealousy when it comes to treasures and trinkets."

"Really? That seems a bit petty when you consider lifelong companionship with someone you love."

"Love. It's always been a fascinating concept. Rather abstract, really. Don't your humans declare that love conquers all?"

"I seem to remember something along those lines," I hedged. I gripped his horn a little tighter as he picked up the pace. "Not a fan of...love...are you?" I squeezed hard, grateful he didn't have any nerve endings in his horn.

"I neither condone it nor condemn it. I simply wonder about the purpose it serves."

"It makes people happy."

"No one should depend on another for their happiness."

"I agree, but a person can be independent and still seek out love and companionship. It's meant to be fulfilling." I squealed as Zelres began to trot, his long gait and jerky movements nearly succeeded in bouncing me right off his head.

"Would you like to know what I find fulfilling?"

"I assume this question is rhetorical."

"This."

Zelres broke into a full-blown sprint that elicited another embarrassing squeal from me. Up ahead I saw the end of the corridor opening into a vast space of nothing.

"Where's the rest of the corridor?" I screamed.

"Where we're going, we don't need corridors."

"Was that a *Back To The Future* reference?"

"Haven't a clue as to what you're referring to."

"No...no...nooooooooo," I screeched. I wrapped both arms and legs around his horn and held on like a desperate child on an out-of-control merry-go-round. Zelres unleashed his leathery wings, picked up even more speed, and jumped into the abyss.

His wings caught some air, pulling us up and backward. The sharp flapping of his wings as he steadied out and headed straight rumbled like thunder next to my ears. I didn't even bother talking to him at this point. I couldn't hear a dang thing, and I was too terrified to move a muscle let alone my jaw muscle.

I had no idea how he navigated in the dark, but I knew better than to think he had no idea where he flew. I wasn't worried about us running into a wall either. I was more concerned that he would pull some crazy spiral stunt and flip me right off his head.

"Relax, Princess," he shouted. "We're nearly there."

"Where is there?" I muttered.

"The castle. Surely you noticed it when you apparated at the lip of my volcano."

"This leads to the castle?"

"Of course. I fly underground to get where I need to go. The castle holds an enormous cavern below it where I protect my treasures. We will go there, and after you assess the situation, you will decide if you wish to continue."

Huh.

That sounded ominous.

11

Crysta

"Nice," I said. "How long did it take you to collect all of this?"

I waved my hand around the pillared cavern, and by pillared I meant there were towering structures holding up the base of the castle, spanning about a hundred feet in length. I tilted my head back, trying to take in the gigantic space. I could have fit several two-story houses within this Dragon's keep. I could have fed thousands of starving children with the treasures he possessed.

I could have hidden the entire Fae population in this castle just to see if that miraculously rid them of *griesha*.

Aside from the entrance and pillars, I hardly saw much else in regards to structure. Everything was covered in gold, jewels, gems, and other priceless things that had probably been stolen over the centuries.

I took a peek at Zelres, noticing the satisfied gleam in his slitted eye.

"Fulfilling on so many levels," he said.

"Well, if you're happy, I'm happy." I took a step toward a sparse path, barely visible. "Does this lead anywhere important? Like, to the stone?"

Zelres let out a heated snort and proceeded to throw his humongous body atop one of his piles of treasure. The ground shook on impact while Zelres rolled around in his gold like a puppy testing out his new bed.

"Are you sure you wish to attempt this so soon? I'm growing rather fond of your company. You don't stink of fear, and your conversation is stimulating."

"You're lonely," I said.

"Not at all."

"That's a lie, oh solitary one. You feel lonely. You need to get out more. Come hang out with us faeries down below for a change. I'll introduce you to Jareth, and you can meet Chuck."

Zelres rolled over on his side and brought his face close to mine, eyeing me as he considered my offer.

"Who would guard my treasure?"

"Is there anyone else on this land mass?"

"No."

"Then it will be here when you get back. Although, I think it's super weird to have a castle here with no other inhabitants. Not a damn soul even knows this place exists. It's not recorded in anything."

"Then how did you find me?"

"The Fates told—"

"The Fates!" He puffed out a heated breath, only this time tendrils of black smoke escaped between his lips and nostrils. Then he let his head drop with a weary sigh, blowing out one last puff. "I hate those old biddies."

"What?" I said, choking down some laughter.

"They're very unsettling."

"*You* think *they're* unsettling?" I shook my head in disbelief. "Pot meet kettle."

"I don't understand."

"There seems to be a lot of that going around." I rubbed my temples, taking another step along the path.

"You don't know where you are going or what must be done."

"Then tell me. I need to find this stone."

"And what will you do with it once you find it?"

"Save the Fae realm."

Zelres' leathery lids blinked once as he considered me. "I wasn't aware it was in need of saving."

"By your own admission, you don't get out much." I tapped my foot, feeling more than a little impatient. "We gonna do this or what?"

"Considering this is the realm I live in, I suppose saving it is reason enough to secure the stone, but you will have to do it, and I will be unable to assist you. I can only give you instruction and watch your progress."

"Fine."

He lumbered to his feet and swept his tail along the path behind him, clearing away more treasure and giving me a sure trail to traverse.

"Follow me."

Zelres took the path at a much slower rate so I wouldn't have such a difficult time keeping up. He seemed more at ease and a lot less rushed. Then I caught him gazing longingly at his shiny treasure and smothered a chuckle. The Fae realm and all its inhabitants were under attack, but Zelres was more interested in rolling around in his piles of stolen property.

We all had priorities, some less understandable than others.

I steered clear of his sweeping tail, grateful that he continued to create a path for me, but wary of being swept aside with a hundred pounds of gold nuggets. Near the end of this humongous room was a large opening. Zelres moved through it, and I quickly followed. He stopped a couple dragon paces in which gave me ample room to move to his side and stand next to his left foreleg.

The walls were made of marble with swirling creamy whites and browns. It was a stark contrast from Zelres' treasured lair. The pillars were still present but made of the same marble as the walls. The flooring was also made of marble but that was where the similarities ended. Deep grooves lined the floor, making it look like a massive checkerboard, minus the black and white squares. Within each marbled segment, a tiny design had been carved in the middle. I spotted one a few feet ahead that bore a circle with a dot on either side.

"What are these symbols?" I asked, moving forward so I could bend down and run my fingers along the carved designs.

"Princess, not yet," Zelres said.

Before I could turn to him and ask for an explanation, the large square I had just stepped on opened downward like a trap door. My whole body shot through the hole in the floor and landed on a slippery slide. Water splashed over me, the force of it sending me down the slick chute. I shot my hands out, scraping my fingers against the wall as I tried to grip something to stop my momentum, but the walls were just as slick. I finally cleared the chute only to be catapulted high in the air. I was surrounded by massive waterfalls, churning crystal clear water in an icy lake below.

I free-fell, heading down toward the middle of the lake where some leathery looking serpents lazily awaited my arrival. I threw my hands in front of me and shot icy air from my fingertips as a panicked response to my situation. The propulsion of that blast sent me flying upward for a moment before gravity took effect and pulled me back down.

I shot the icy air out again with the same result. Straightening my position, I placed my hands palms down on either side of me and shot a continuous stream of freezing cold air that allowed me to levitate. I assessed my location, noting there didn't seem to be any other openings aside from the large holes where liquid fed the massive waterfalls. I pictured the marble room and attempted to apparate, but nothing happened.

Wards. Wards within a watery cavern of death.

This never would have happened in San Diego.

My only option: return to the chute and climb back up. I spotted the hole in the wall where I had unceremoniously been dumped and tried to figure out how to steer myself over there.

"Come on, Crysta. What would Iron Man do?"

I kept my body stiff but allowed myself to tilt forward at an angle which propelled me toward my intended destination. Unfortunately, I ended up giving it a little too much gas and slammed into the wall before I could get the right angle for reentry. My magic sputtered and then stopped, and I plummeted again, letting out a shriek as I placed my hands on either side of my thighs and shot myself upward with a jerk. I evened out the power enough to simply levitate in one place as I took stock of my situation. A glance down provided a horrifying glimpse of the painful death that awaited me.

Five serpents lazily observed me from below. They looked a bit peckish. One of them opened its massive jaws and snapped them shut like it was taunting me.

"Nice teeth," I said.

I glanced around, searching for the chute and realized it was about fifteen feet above me. I slowly added a little more power to my propulsion system and began to inch my way upward. Once I levitated eye level to the chute, the next maneuver became tricky. I had to magically propel myself up at a diagonal. I moved back a bit to give myself some room to tilt, then with a silent prayer I added more power to my magic and inched my way into the hole.

An outraged shriek distracted me for a moment. I looked down to see the serpents, who I assumed couldn't reach me, begin to rise to their full height.

Freaking scary. Since slow and steady seemed to be out of the question, I gave it more juice and shot up through the chute as fast as I could, not caring when I misjudged the angle here and there and banged my head against the wall.

"Princess!" Zelres voice sounded urgent.

"I'm coming," I screamed.

I saw light at the end of the chute. I kicked up the power a notch and burst forward. Just as my head reached the surface, something wrapped around my ankle and yanked me back.

"What the—"

I drew on my core with everything I had, pulling against whatever had wrapped around my leg, but exhaustion leeched the power from my core, and I knew I wouldn't be able to keep this up for much longer.

My eyes cleared the chute, and I saw Zelres staring at me in amazement. "Something has my ankle," I screamed.

"Cover yourself in ice, Crysta," he said.

Was he serious? Why would I do that?

He opened his mouth wide, his rows of teeth glinting in the light. His chest expanded several inches before it finally occurred to me what he had in mind. I diverted some power to forming a shield of ice around me, holding my breath as the shield creeped over my shoulder and covered my neck and head. The only thing not covered in ice were the palms of my hands. I still had to use my magic to keep me levitating.

Unfortunately, the thing wrapped around my leg was also encased in ice, and the creature attached to it was getting stronger by the minute.

Zelres made a strange coughing sound in the back of his throat. A roaring rush of fire exploded from his mouth, completely engulfing me, rushing past me and down the chute. A muted shriek reverberated from the slick tube, and then the thing wrapped around my leg broke away. I flew upward like a slingshot and crashed into Zelres' large torso before hitting the ground in front of him and shattering my ice shield.

Sitting up, I took stock of my situation, noting a painful ringing in my ears. I fished out the remaining pieces of ice and noted the stinging sensation on my palms. Red, but not blistered. I figured I had minor burns. I tilted my gaze where I got an upside-down view of Zelres studying me.

"By the way," he said, "I don't recommend stepping on the marble floor just yet."

"Ya think?"

"There's a certain way of doing so without falling to your death."

"I kind of hate you." I coughed up some moisture and leaned against his foreleg, feeling absolutely worn out.

"That was some impressive work, Princess. I thought for certain you'd become fodder for the Bakunawa."

"Is that what those snake things were?"

"Not very intelligent creatures, but always determined to catch their prey. Good thing you have such magnificent instincts. To use magic to levitate. I've never seen one of your race manage something like that."

"Yep. I'm just full of surprises." I slowly pulled myself to my feet and assessed everything. Other than the slight burns on my palms, I seemed to be okay. My side ached a bit from that wound that had never quite healed, and my energy was drained, but I was alive and kicking.

Scrappy little Crysta for the win.

I studied the symbols carved in the squares, making sure I kept to the rough stone where we currently stood.

"What are the symbols on the floor?"

"Glyphs," he said.

"Glyphs. Okay. And I fell through the one with the scorch marks surrounding it?"

I noticed the trap door had closed. The glyph on it looked like half an infinity symbol with a dot housed in each curve.

"That glyph represents water," he said.

"How nice. Nothing in that glyph about what's hiding *in* the water. Do you know what we call that in the human realm?"

"Haven't a clue."

"False advertising."

His lips curled back in delight. The creepy equivalent of a Dragon highly amused.

"I wish you would stay."

"I wish you would leave your solitary island and come visit me at court."

He nodded. "I do believe I will, provided you save us all, that is."

I shook my head. "No pressure. So what are the rest of these symbols?" I gestured toward the massive chessboard.

"Other glyphs represent moon cycles, elements, and royalty."

"Okay. I assume I'm supposed to somehow get across this floor to be able to leave this place." I looked around the room, noticing a wide door on the other side near the corner."

"Is that my destination?"

"Not unless you wish to visit a different realm."

I snapped my eyes back to his in astonishment.

"Are you serious? You can travel to any realm you like?"

"Yes, but I don't recommend it. The Dragon who guards that gate between the voids is a bit mischievous. And always hungry."

"Then what am I supposed to do to get to the stone?"

"You must step on these glyphs in the correct order. The very last glyph will transport you to the next step in your journey."

"The next step? This isn't the last step?"

Zelres snorted as if to say, *bless your heart you sweet, simple faerie.*

"How am I supposed to figure out which order they go in? Furthermore, am I supposed to use all of them or only some of them?"

"You are the one to decide."

I slapped him on his leg, giving him my best glare. My attempt at intimidation was minimized due to the fact that his skin was hard as granite, and I had to glare *up* at him. If only I'd been fifteen feet taller. "You're supposed to guide me."

"I just did. Try not to fall through any other trap doors."

"You are not my favorite."

Zelres showed me his gleaming teeth. "And yet, Princess, you are quickly becoming mine."

After some negotiating, which involved agreeing to various deals that would no doubt come back to haunt me, Zelres finally told me what the rest of the glyphs represented. There were twenty-four squares in a four-by-six pattern. The elements and moon glyphs were scattered. Then there were glyphs for fear, hope, power, blood, energy, balance, etc. Even a random one for crown.

I had my eye on that one since I needed to get the stone for the diadem, but it seemed a little obvious. Also, at what point was I supposed to step on it and how? It was in a corner on the other side of the room, closely located next to the door I *wasn't* supposed to go through.

The squares were large, large enough for two people to fall through them, which meant I might be hopping from one square on one side of the room to another square on the other side. How was I going to leap across the room like that? When I mentioned this to Zelres, he snorted in derision.

"You just flew out of a watery chute, avoiding a torturous death, and used your magical flying abilities to best a Bakunawa. Just propel yourself up and over to the next square."

"Oh."

Work smarter, not harder.

Even Dragons understood that concept.

After debating for a moment, I decided it would be best to randomly choose a square, hover over it, and go from there.

I tried the glyph that represented air: two upright, curved lines running next to each other, with a dot on either side. Assuming my iron man position (that was going to be my new thing now), I pulled on my Winter magic and slowly began to levitate.

"So entertaining," I heard Zelres say in a lazy tone. "A bit primitive as far as flying goes, but creative, nonetheless. If only you possessed wings."

I ignored his side commentary and tilted forward a bit, gliding over to the air glyph that sat at the first column in front of me, row two. I straightened and hovered above its center.

Now what?

I didn't want to put my full weight on it, but I'd have to touch it, either way. I lowered myself to just an inch above, allowing my foot to scrape against the glyph's surface. The trap door flew open, and a gust of wind blasted me in the face, throwing me backward with enough force to clear the floor and crash into Zelres' side.

The chuckle that burst forth, followed by his full-blown laughter, was super irritating. He rolled over on his side, blowing out occasional puffs of fire as he tried to get his laughter under control.

"I've decided...you're not worth...you...not worth eating. Far too valuable...entertainment. I'm really...so very...what a delight you are."

"Are you finished?" I said. I placed my hands on his leathery side and gave him a good shove which only elicited more laughter from him.

"This is so stupid," I said. "I don't have time for this."

I flipped my palm up, pulled on my core, and created a solid sphere of ice the size of a golf ball. Then I chucked it at the waxing moon glyph, column one, row three. The ice landed with a thud, and the trap door flew open, revealing pale moonlight. After a few moments the trap snapped shut, and the pale light disappeared.

"Huh. What would have happened if I had fallen through *that* trap?" I asked.

"I do believe you would have teleported to outer space, and what an exciting adventure, no? Not sure how you would have found your way back from that one. Nice trick with the ice, however. A little less risky for you, don't you think?"

"I think most of you faeries are sadists," I muttered under my breath.

"Beg pardon?"

"I think my only option is to throw ice at a glyph, wait a few minutes, and then throw ice at another glyph. At some point I'll be able to figure out which glyph comes first."

"Process of elimination. It's definitely a plan, but it will take time. I think a better bet is to consider what Oberon was thinking when he created these little tests."

"Why?"

Zelres' lids fluttered for a moment, and I could have sworn I saw an irritated eye roll in the movement.

"Oberon only wanted this stone found by the one who was meant to wield its power and wear the diadem that went with it. If that is you, consider what the Fates must have told him concerning your arrival into this world."

"The Fates knew I would be coming."

"They knew *someone* would be coming. Whether that is you or not, only tests will tell."

"Tests will tell," I repeated. I thought back to the scrolls and what had been required to get past the mirage spell. Oberon's spell had to identify the right individual.

With blood.

My blood.

I searched for the glyph that represented blood, a straight line with a curve running through it, and underneath the curve two dots resting side-by-side. I found it in column three, row three. Without hesitation, I levitated up and over, hovering just above the glyph. Then I lowered myself down until my foot lightly scraped the surface. When nothing happened, I put my full weight on it, waiting for the trap door to spring.

"Blood. Excellent choice, Princess. Blood will tell, as the saying goes."

"Pretty sure the saying is 'blood will out', but I'm used to you faeries mangling human colloquialisms."

I studied the crown glyph next to me, a detached triangle shaped with two dots in the middle. I considered putting my foot on it next but realized I wasn't done yet. Blood had been required to undo the spell on the scrolls. Was blood required here as well? I pulled forth a tiny thread of Winter magic, formed it into a needle, and pricked my finger. I squeezed until enough blood oozed from the tiny wound. Then I reached down and wiped the blood on the glyph, tracing the outline until the glyph gleamed red. It shimmered for a moment, turning a faint gold until the imprint of the glyph rose into the air.

"Zelres," I said in alarm. "What's happening?"

His look was knowing as he bowed his head in reverence and said, "What was meant to happen, Highness. The Princess of the Fae realm has finally come home."

The golden imprint hovered before me and then rushed at me, colliding with my chest where my core immediately absorbed its power. The initial impact felt like a tickle, and then it burned within me, flowing through my veins and filling me with a rightness concerning myself, something I hadn't felt in a long time.

Other golden imprints of glyphs rose from their positions, floating toward me in a beautiful dance of light and magic. The next glyph to merge with my core was the glyph of life, followed by light, hope, balance, energy, and power. With each new imprint, I felt a rush of warmth fill me. It was as if every part of this realm and the energy it contained joyfully greeted me, welcoming me home. The tears came unbidden as air, water, earth, and fire merged next. The crown glyph rose up afterward, shining more brightly than the others.

"Close your eyes, Princess." Zelres' voice came out as a soothing rumble. "Focus on your core and accept your birthright."

The crown gently glided in a beautiful dance of homecoming. I could have sworn it skipped, giddy with emotion. I closed my eyes just as it reached me and welcomed the lighthearted feeling its energy evoked.

My body glowed with the power of the glyphs. I lifted my hands to look at them, taking it in.

I stared at Zelres who wore a contented smile. "The glyphs have identified you just as Oberon wished. Long live Crystiana Tuadhe d'Anu, Princess of the Unseelie Court, Princess of the Seelie Court, and Ruler of the Fae realm."

White light engulfed me, growing so bright I had to close my eyes and simply feel the energy around me.

When I opened my eyes again, it was to see Zelres next to the forbidden door.

"Come, Princess."

"I thought we weren't supposed to use that door."

"We won't be going through it. I must guide you as you peer into it."

Confusion blossomed within my chest as I levitated again and floated over to his side, landing on a stone ledge and facing the door with Zelres towering behind me.

"You must pass through one more test, Princess, and I am afraid you will not enjoy it."

The door shimmered as an image blinked into focus like a movie on a projector screen. My mother stood in the center of an ornate room, a look of stark terror on her face as a figure raced toward her.

My heart seized in my chest as I watched the figure move with superhuman speed and attack my mother, going for her throat and ripping into it.

A scream froze within me. I stepped forward to stop the events from unfolding, but there was nothing to be done, no one to call out to for help, nothing I could do since this was the past and the past could not be changed. I watched as the life drained from her eyes, her blood running down the front of her ornate gown as her attacker slowly lowered her body to the floor.

The image froze. I couldn't pull my eyes from it.

"How does this make you feel?"

"Are you serious? How do you think...how?" Loss, grief, pain, anger, a serious sense of disconnect, helplessness, a total lack of control, and underlying all of that, a cold flash of...

"Vengeance," I said.

"What was that?"

"I want to kill this vampire. I want to kill all the vampires. Every single one of them should die for what they did to my mother."

Zelres let out a sigh that sounded close to commiseration. "Yes. I understand. And now *you* understand."

I ripped my eyes from the heinous sight of my mother's murderer and tilted my head back to look at him. His blurry features made me realize tears were streaming down my face.

"Understand what?"

"Not what. Who. Now you understand Queen Titania."

"I understand..."

I stared back at the door, at the image of my mother lying dead on the floor. "No. I am nothing like Titania."

"Yet your initial reaction upon seeing your mother murdered by a vampire was to eradicate the entire race of vampires in defense of your loved ones, to assuage your grief, to bring to pass a reckoning of sorts. Is this not accurate, Princess?"

I swallowed hard, realization dawning.

"That is accurate."

One large claw softly landed on my shoulder.

"Princess," he said in a comforting tone, "your feelings are not shameful, they are universal. We all experience a wide spectrum of emotions due to life and the variety of scenarios it has to offer, but the way we process such stimuli and experience will mold us into the Good we wish to perpetuate or the Evil that Good will fight. You must understand all creatures have a propensity for both good and bad. You must see that we are not born evil, we are a product of how we internalize our experiences and how we choose to react to them. Oberon understood that his wife's grief over their sons' deaths opened a doorway to her undoing, but it didn't have to be that way.

He did not kill her because he believed there was something left of her worth saving, and he wants you to save her."

"By understanding her pain," I said.

"Yes. That would be a good start."

I shook my head. "It won't undo all the destruction she has caused or the lives stolen by her actions. It won't undo the consequences of her decisions or the punishment in store for her."

"No."

"I can't save her."

"No, you can't. Not in the way you imagine."

"I don't understand."

"You will, eventually. Now look."

I stared at the image of my mother and watched as the vampire lovingly caressed her hair, closing her terrified eyes. Then he laid his head against her chest and began to weep.

"Why is he crying?" I asked in shock.

"Do you believe all evil is wrought by evil people?"

"Are you saying this vampire isn't evil?"

"I'm saying our circumstances dictate our choices at times. Moridan held this vampire's eldest son hostage, threatening to kill him if this vampire did not assassinate your mother. He made his choice, sacrificing your mother for his son, but I wonder if you can sympathize with his impossible situation."

I remained silent for a moment, staring at the vampire's shaking shoulders, taking in the grief he felt at the choice he'd had to make.

The answer was suddenly very clear to me. "I can."

"Killing an entire race of vampires to avenge your mother's death is not quite as clear cut as it originally appeared."

"You're right."

And he was. I felt sorry for the vampire as he clung to my mother and sobbed into her dress. I ached for him, the horrible choice he'd had to make, the decision to kill for his own son's safety. Had he been able to save his son?

Was he able to live with himself afterward?

I wanted to see him. I wanted him to know I understood.

I wanted to forgive him.

"This is important, Crysta. Titania's grief prevented her from seeing that the faeries who killed her sons were acting on orders, protecting their own loved ones. What motivates a specific course of action is never quite so black and white, yet we see it as such when seeking revenge and justifying our own actions. Oberon was not capable of helping Titania see."

I took a deep breath and slowly let it out, cleansing myself of my own self-righteous anger. "She has to see."

"Much like you just did."

I reached out and gently touched the image of the vampire who cried over my mother.

"Is he okay? This vampire. Will he be okay?"

"Do you wish for him to be okay?"

"Yes."

"Then you may have the stone."

When I opened my eyes again, I stood in the middle of the garden, before the altar of The Fates, with all of my loved ones kneeling in a semi-circle. I felt a tingling sensation in my right hand and looked down. A soft glow peaked through my clenched fingers. I opened my hand, shocked to discover I held a stone filled with swirling energy the color of sapphire.

"Long live Princess Crystiana Tuadhe d'Anu, Princess of the Fae realm," The Fates intoned.

Jareth looked up at me, awe, reverence, and love in his expression. I blinked moisture from my eyes and cleared my throat.

"I really wish you guys would stop kneeling like that. You'll get grass stains," I said.

Shared laughter ensued as everyone got to their feet.

"At least we know power won't go to Crysta's head," Kheelan said.

"Was there ever any doubt?" Nuallan asked.

"Never." Jareth came toward me and wrapped me in his warm embrace. "Never a single doubt in my mind."

I leaned into Jareth, suddenly feeling a bit weak now that the adrenaline had worn off. I'd learned more than I'd bargained for. Zelres has given me a lot to think about. Chuck flapped his wings next to me, making an alarmed squawking noise next to my side.

As I pulled back to ask him what was wrong, I felt a sticky substance coat my side and a sharp pain lance through the same area. I gripped my lower abdomen, pulling back a shaky hand coated in blood.

"What..."

"Kheelan," Jareth said in an urgent tone as he knelt next to me and pulled up my tunic. Blood gushed from that same wound that hadn't healed properly. Jareth used his sleeve to wipe away some of it, only to reveal blackened flesh around the laceration.

"Flaming pixie dung, the Dark Magic within the bloodletting spell is getting worse," Kheelan said. "We need to get her back to the castle. It will take more magic healers than I to stop the spell's progress."

Without a word, Jareth lifted me in his arms, careful of my side, and apparated us back to the palace.

Crysta

*areth apparated us straight to the medical ward, but the place was packed. He cradled me in his arms as I stared at the patients. Every available bed was in use. There were even patients spread out on cots, moaning in pain and begging for assistance. Faeries of familiar species and some not so familiar were there, seeking medical attention for none other than *griesha*. Since Titania's return, the illness had become a full-blown epidemic.

One of the healers spotted us and rushed to give us aid.

"What has happened to the Princess?" she asked. Then she spotted the blood coating my side and quickly pulled us through the madness of the sick room.

"We keep receiving more and more faeries suffering from *griesha*. It's impossible to keep up. We'll need to treat you elsewhere."

"Where is Terise?" Kheelan and Cedric asked at the same time.

"We moved her to the Princess's quarters as beds began to fill up. We thought it safer there. I will take you to her."

"Have there been any deaths since we've been gone?" I asked, feeling guilty already.

Her shoulders tensed as we rounded a corner and headed down a long corridor. Several healers ran past us, looking frazzled and exhausted. "We've lost ten patients in the past hour."

Ten?

I tried to wiggle my way out of Jareth's hold. He held me fast as he continued to follow the healer. I looked behind us to see our group on our heels. A sharp pain in my hand registered. I looked down to see I'd been squeezing the stone like a stress ball.

"We need to get back to the med ward and start bonding those people to compatible partners."

Nuallan drew closer to us and shook his head. I rested my chin on Jareth's shoulder, still looking behind us at Nuallan who grabbed my hand and gave it a squeeze.

"Your heart is as compassionate as ever, Crysta, but you're bleeding out. You can't help anyone until you get help yourself."

"I'm fine," I said, even though my eyelids fought against gravity. I moved my gaze to the rest of the group and found their gazes fixed on me, their expressions grim.

"You'll be the death of yourself if you don't let us take care of you."

I gave Nuallan a reluctant nod and tried to push the images of those sick faeries out of my thoughts. I couldn't help them if I couldn't stand. So no more bleeding. That was a priority. Chuck stayed at my side, breathing healing magic on my wound as we entered my quarters.

Seeing Terise's sleeping form on my bed gave me a measure of peace, although the red sores on her body were now climbing toward her face.

It looked as if the sleeping curse had definitely held back the progress of *griesha*, but I worried she didn't have much time left.

Jareth gently set me down next to her, guiding me to my uninjured side so they could better assess the damage. As I lifted my hand to wipe the worry from his face, I nearly choked in shock. Tiny, red spots had broken out all over my hand, covering the back of it right up to my fingernails.

"Jareth," I said, in a strangled whisper.

I flipped my hand around to show him the damage and watched as his face drained of color.

"No. No that's impossible," he said.

He knelt down next to me as Kheelan and the other healer began checking me for *griesha* on my arms and legs.

"It's only on her hand," the healer said, sounding greatly relieved.

"It shouldn't be there at all," Jareth said, giving Kheelan a death stare. "She is one of the most powerful faeries in this realm. How could *griesha* have taken hold?"

Kheelan's expression held a remorse as he looked from my hand to me. "I think the complications from our convoluted fated mate bond and the Dark Magic poisoning her wound has made it impossible for her to not only heal but remain immune to the disease."

"She is part of the cure, Kheelan," Jareth shouted. "This can't be happening."

I reached over and touched Jareth's face. He leaned into my caress, kissing my hand as a few tears rolled down his cheeks. "I'm so tired of always being on the brink of losing you. I will not let this happen."

"Just do your best to fix my side so we can go find the diadem." I brought his face closer to mine and gave him a soft kiss. "This is not going to beat me, Jareth. Don't you know how much I'm willing to fight to stay with you?"

He kissed me again, gripping my hand in his. "We need to find a temporary fix for the Dark Magic spreading along your wound."

Kheelan and the healer did their best to clean the wounded area, but the skin surrounding it did *not* look pretty.

"I've just never seen a bloodletting spell take a turn like this. It's not normally a simple fix by any means, but Dark Magic has never been involved," the healer said, turning to Kheelan. "I think our best bet is to trap the Dark Magic to this single area and then use a different spell to cauterize the wound."

"I opt for unconsciousness," I said, remembering how it felt the last time Kheelan and Jareth cauterized the wound.

"You won't feel a thing," she said, running her hands along my body. Slowly, a heavy numbness settled into my limbs. I blinked in surprise and gave Kheelan an accusatory glare.

"Why didn't you do that the last time?"

He looked a bit sheepish. "We were a bit panicked, seeing you bleeding out everywhere, and we didn't have much time."

"Fair enough."

My entire body felt numb, including my hands. I had a difficult time holding onto the precious stone, so I offered it to Jareth, knowing I was in no shape to guard it.

"You are the only one I trust to protect this stinking thing."

He chuckled as he took it. He whispered a soft spell under his breath and the stone disappeared.

"Where did it go?" I asked.

"I've hidden it in an enchanted pouch on my person. Invisible to the naked eye and impossible to remove from my body. It will be safe, Crysta. Be at ease and let us heal you."

Giving him that burden to bear felt better than it should have, but I was too tired to analyze my lack of guilt and figured that at some point I needed to know when to relinquish control and allow people to help me.

I wrinkled my nose at the smell of burning flesh as they cauterized the wound. Chuck tucked his head under my neck, unable to watch what they did to my skin. I sensed a deep-seated frustration within him.

"Hey," I whispered. "This is not your fault. Your magic has done a lot to save me, but this wound is beyond anything we've dealt with before."

His little shoulders hunched in defeat as he looked up at me with sad eyes. I gave him kisses on his head and smoothed down his ruffled wings, noting the angry red coloring on his chest. After a few strokes on his back he calmed down and his underbelly took on a buttercup yellow.

"Why have you and Chuck never communicated telepathically?" Jareth asked out of nowhere. "You seem to be able to do so with a variety of faerie animals."

I gazed at Chuck in surprise, having never thought of that before. He stared at Jareth, looking a bit miffed.

"I don't think he appreciates being called an animal," Cedric said.

"Try telepathy with him," Jareth urged.

I sent out a few thoughts toward Chuck, but he just stared at me with a playful smile on his face.

"Did you get any of that, buddy?" I asked.

Nothing but the stare. Communicating with Chuck through telepathy seemed more like a one-way radio. I shrugged, feeling like it didn't really matter.

"Chuck and I don't need telepathy to communicate, do we baby?"

He let out a sweet chirp and licked my cheek.

Adris and the rest of our group chuckled at his antics while Kheelan and our healer continued to work their complicated spell on my side. Heat built up along my skin and my core pulsing heavily for quite a long time before the feel of magic slowly dissipated.

As they lifted their hands, I stared at the skin on my side, noticing a blue ring around the dark, damaged skin. "What did you do?"

"We looped some of your core magic to the outer areas of the bloodletting spell. A few threads of your winter magic will take a detour here to stop the progress of the spell, but it is not a permanent solution," said the healer. "Your core must fight *griesha* as well. For you and Terise to thrive, your bonds with your fated mates must be rectified as quickly as possible."

I tested out my fingers as the numbness wore off. Jareth helped me to a seated position and let me twist from side to side.

Still numb in that area.

Good. I could handle numb.

"Thanks, you two. I'm feeling much better now."

The healer gave me a loving look, but Kheelan could barely meet my gaze.

I grabbed his hand to get his attention. "I know you're beating yourself up for this, and you should to some extent, but Terise and I will pull through this."

Kheelan swallowed hard and finally looked at me. "You both had better, or I'll never forgive myself."

And he wouldn't. I knew that for certain. Kheelan was made for brooding, the tortured, bad boy at his most repentant it would seem. I could handle this Kheelan so long as the arrogance took a hike for a while.

It was unfortunate that it took the impending death of the two women he cared for the most for his arrogance and pride to go on hiatus.

Then I thought about what Zelres had taught me. Experiences, motivations, everything that fueled our decisions. Kheelan wanted contentment, love, and acceptance. Something he hadn't received from his father. Something he thought he could gain by making the choices he had made. I didn't want to understand that, but I did.

Understanding begets compassion.

I felt lots of compassion for Kheelan.

Damn him.

I pivoted in my seat to assess Terise's condition, placing a hand at her core, closing my eyes, and visualizing the complicated threads of magic that linked us both to Kheelan. The frayed threads that tethered her to him leaked so much magic, magic that could have been fortifying her body and healing the disease.

I thought back to what Kheelan had said. The only way to free Terise from this was by relinquishing my incomplete bond with Jareth and fully bonding with Kheelan.

I just couldn't accept it. Not yet. Once we had the diadem and stone, we'd find a way. We'd have our answers. Something strong enough to combat Kheelan's half-finished bonding spell.

I opened my eyes, taking in her pockmarked face and feeling a desperation hit me. I couldn't lose her. I couldn't lose any of them. At the end of the day, I had to accept the fact that I might have to make choices I wouldn't want to, but if I fully bonded to Kheelan, what would happen to the rest of the realm?

Would I need Kheelan to help me power the diadem or would the anchor of our fake fated mate bond be enough to control the crown's power? I needed the fated mate bond with Jareth, but if we didn't undo Kheelan's spell, there was a good chance Terise and I wouldn't live long enough to utilize the diadem's power. There was also a good chance I would be too sick to wield it either way.

Fully bonding with Kheelan or keeping things as is did not solve our problem. Neither solution guaranteed the eradication of *griesha* or the ability to overcome Moridan and Titania, and weren't they just about the worst duo to have ever joined together?

Crazy meet crazy and throw enormous power in there for good measure.

"Terise doesn't have much time, and based on how fast this disease is now spreading, I'm not sure how much time I have either." I stared at my wonderful family who surrounded the bed, giving me varied looks of worry and concern. "We head to the Lake of Beatha now. Time to find the diadem."

$$\infty \ \infty \ \infty$$

"Now that we're here, any plans on next steps for those of us who absolutely cannot live without oxygen?" I asked.

Our group stood on the sandy beach, staring across the choppy waves of the lake. Inky storm clouds had already moved overhead, sprinkling us with a misty rain. The smell of ozone and the sudden change in weather surprised me. I'd never seen the Lake of Beatha bathed in anything other than sunlight. A swift wind kicked up as we stood there, contemplating our situation.

"To be clear, the diadem is in the lake, yes?" Paio asked.

"Yes." Chantara took a step forward, allowing the water to pool around her feet. "Unfortunately, Oberon left very little instruction other than that. This body of water may not appear too daunting on the surface, but the world underneath is quite vast, holding several different kingdoms and thousands of species of creatures and faerie, some friendly, some not so friendly."

"In other words, let's not become anyone's next meal." Kheelan didn't look worried. Neither did my father, Jareth, Cedric, or Nuallan for that matter. In fact, there was an eager, boyish excitement leaching from their auras.

I rolled my eyes in disbelief. Leave it to thrill-seeking warriors to find the idea of being eaten by an underwater monster invigorating.

"Which kingdoms are we talking about here?" I asked.

"The Drac kingdom for one," Chantara said. "Normally, they refuse outsiders passage into their underwater sanctum, but you've managed to win those royals over, so I don't believe this will be a problem should we need them. The mer kingdom is a different story."

"But aren't you the mer-queen? You are the first of your kind."

A look passed between Chantara and Paio that spoke volumes. Too bad I didn't understand the language. After an awkward pause, Jareth cleared his throat.

"Chantara's mate passed away several centuries ago. Although the crown should have remained with her, she handed responsibility over to her mate's second wife."

"Second wife?" I stared at Chantara in shock. "Second *wife?*"

"The male to female ratio for the Merfolk is sadly imbalanced and has become worse over time. Not to mention the lack of fertility. It is common for males to take on more than one wife."

"Sounds complicated," I said, studying Chantara as her eyes flashed ebony for a moment.

"Believe me, it has been."

"Father's second wife also made the outrageous claim that I was her son," Paio said.

My jaw about dropped at that absurd notion. "It's one thing to doubt who the father is, but there's no mixing up a mom as the baby is being born."

"Rena and I gave birth around the same time. Her baby boy didn't live through the night, but she failed to let anyone know he had passed. Instead, she came to my birthing quarters and attempted to switch out her dead son with mine."

"She sounds nuts. You gave this woman the power to reign in your stead?"

Chantara let out a bone-weary sigh. "The death of a child is traumatic, more so when it is a male due to how badly we need them. She lost her mind for a while, but through the years, she overcame her grief and we mended our differences."

"I'm sensing a big, fat b-u-t..."

"My responsibilities as the first of our kind gave me powers that no other Mermaid has ever had. I oversee the magical distribution within the whole of these waters while dealing with domestic affairs for all kingdoms within the lake. Ruling my own kingdom while attending to my other duties became too big a burden once my mate died. Rena became my regent, overseeing the daily rule of the Mer kingdom."

"And with that power came certain power struggles," Jareth said. "In my opinion, Chantara has been very patient with Rena."

"Yes," Chantara said, "but a confrontation has been brewing for some time now. I hope she won't interfere with our current plans."

"What are those plans?" I asked. "I'm hoping they involve breathing under water."

"We'll get to spell casting in a minute. We need to discuss how we plan to find the diadem in this large body of water," Jareth said.

"I've thought long and hard about it," Paio said. "I think our best bet is to go over our own histories within the Mer world. If the Goblins had writings discussing the task Oberon gave to their first Goblin King then there must be something similar within our own writings."

"I'm surprised you have writings," I said. "I guess I just picture your world of water and wonder how you could write anything down that wouldn't get destroyed."

Chantara touched Paio's shoulder. "Are you referring to the ancient libraries within the Dry Lands?"

"The Dry Lands?" I asked.

"With magic, we have created various pockets of dry areas under the water. It's where we do our schooling, record our histories, and hold gatherings that require dry land."

"I think we should journey there first," Paio said.

Chantara shook her long dark hair. "We'll have to notify Rena of our arrival and our intent."

"You're the queen, Mother."

"I am. I'm also aware of Rena's pride and inherent jealousy. Let's not poke a sleeping Vorsha if we don't have to."

"Vorsha?" I looked between Chantara and Paio. "Do I even want to know?"

"Vorsha are fascinating creatures in that their skeletal structure is humanoid in nature, but the rest of them, their outer appearance is far different. Think of an octopus and its tentacles. A Vorsha has four-foot-long tentacles that fan out around their humanoid head, constantly swirling as it spins them in a forward motion."

"That's crazy. I'd love to see one up close," I say. "What language do they speak?"

"No, Crysta, you don't understand," Jareth said. "They are sentient beings, but intelligent in the way a large predator such as a shark or baracuda might be. There is a large difference between Faeires who live under the water and actual water creatures. Though they appear humanoid, they are most certainly not, and they are definitely carnivorous."

"I'm guessing the tentacles aren't for handshaking?"

"The tentacles aren't what one needs to worry about, although they are capable of restraining you," Paio said. "It's the jelly-like threads that cover their bodies. The threads are connected by tiny bulbs. It looks similar to a DNA strand if it were cut in half and then attached to the body...everywhere."

"What do those do?"

"No one knows."

"Excuse me?" I stared at Paio in disbelief.

"No one has lived to share that secret. All we know is if one comes into contact with a Vorsha and its jelly-like threads...they immediately die."

I turned to Chantara. "And you just compared Rena to a sleeping Vorsha? I really don't think we should have anything to do with this particular Mermaid."

Chuck let out a snort of agreement and burrowed himself into my arms.

"If we offer her the proper respect, all will be well. Then we can head over to the Dry Lands and research our next move." Chantara's reassuring smile did nothing for me. Her obsidian eyes said it all. She did not want to have a run-in with this Rena chick.

"Okay, so now that we have an idea of what we do once we arrive, how do we get there without asphyxiating?" Hated to keep harping on the lack of oxygen issue, but...hello!!!!

"There are many spells that will enable us to accomplish this. We simply need to figure out which spell you can maintain considering your current health issues," Adris said. "We also need to discuss who is going. As much as I wish to go with you and look after Crysta, I'm afraid my presence will only be welcome within the Drac kingdom. Rena has an aversion to our kind." She noticed my confusion and added, "We're not quite beautiful enough to enter the Mer kingdom."

I clenched my fists. "Rena doesn't like you because she thinks you're ugly?"

"To be fair to her, we are quite ugly." Adris gave me a wide smile meant to exaggerate her crooked, yellowed teeth. I reached up and touched her face, brushing away the stringy strands of her gray hair.

"Adris, you are exceptionally beautiful to me."

Her smile turned genuine as she patted my cheek. "That's why you're my princess. It takes wisdom to see past the vessels carrying our spirits. I think it best if a few of our group stay behind to keep an eye and ear out for movement from Titania and Moridan. They're not remaining idle as we continue our search."

She was right. We needed to get a few steps ahead of our enemies before they struck again.

I turned to the rest of our group, assessing how they felt about the situation. My main concern rested with Lily. She stared at the water with severe trepidation. I wanted all of them with me, but my trip to Zelres' volcano had been done alone. I didn't want to enter the Lake of Beatha on my own, but keeping track of our large group didn't seem feasible in this situation. There were too many unknowns within the depths of this lake.

"I think it best if Lily, Graul, and Cedric remain with you," I said. "I think between your collective gifts, you'll be able to scout out our enemies' plans."

"Excellent. Lily stay out of water. We keep you safe from here," Graul said.

He appeared relieved. Poor Graul. There were most likely moments where he was torn between his loyalty to me and his loyalty to his fated mate. I grabbed his arm and leveled him with an intense look.

"If it's a choice between Lily's safety and gathering intel, you will protect Lily no matter what. Graul, I'm not kidding. Go into hiding if you have to, but your first priority is her. Understand?"

His shoulders slumped with gratitude. "I protect Lily. Understand."

I gave him a quick hug, grateful to have lifted some of that burden from him. Chuck squawked at being crushed between us.

I patted him on the head and handed him to Lily who snuggled him close to her chest.

"Chuck, I need you to help Graul protect Lily and gather intel in the process. The water won't suit you, and I'm counting on you to protect my friends."

That little sweetie puffed up his chest, his underbelly turning blue, showing me he took his charge very seriously. I knew he wouldn't let me down.

Then I turned to Adris and Chantara.

"Which spell should we try first?"

"You are going to try a simple breathing and pressurization spell. The rest of the group will do a transformation spell."

"Hold up," I said. "Are you referring to the transformation spell that involves glamoring blood and cells, effectively changing the biological make-up of your body? That dangerous spell?"

"Correct," Chantara said. "They are familiar with this process and are not impaired by any injuries."

"I performed this spell to get on the royals' floor back at the Seelie palace. I can do this."

"Crysta," Jareth said, "My species is nearly identical to yours. You only had to change blood and cells to mimic his, which you never should have attempted in the first place." He pinched the bridge of his nose as if the very thought gave him a tension headache. "In this instance you will have to transform into a completely different species, creating new organs and body parts. We're talking fins, tails, gills, two hearts and an extra lung."

That fascinated me. "You have two hearts and three lungs?" I asked Chantara.

"One lung pulls in water, the other two lungs separate the oxygen from the water, sending it throughout our bodies while two hearts pump the oxygen at a more rapid rate."

"That sounds complicated."

"It is." Her soft smile reached her worried eyes. "You understand why a simpler spell is necessary for you? We'll need to get you to our palace as quickly as possible. I'm not certain how long you'll be able to hold the spell, and the underwater pressure will crush you without it."

"Have I mentioned how much I dislike Oberon?" I muttered. "He just had to hide the diadem in the damn lake. Does that mean your kingdom is below the water like the Drac kingdom?"

"To some extent, yes. There are certain parts of the kingdom completely engulfed in water. Merfolk can also decide if they want their abode to be engulfed in water or not. Our way of life is varied and magical, but I think you'll find it interesting."

"Okay. Let's do this spell and get this show on the road."

"Shows and roads," Graul muttered, patting Chuck on the head. "I never understand."

"You're going to encase your body in a pressurized air suit of sorts. You'll have full mobility with the added benefit of not getting wet. This will cover your head as well, allowing you to breathe." Chantara placed her hands on her hips as if prepping herself for some tough coaching.

"I'll use up all the air in this pressurized suit," I said.

"The magic continually reproduces oxygen. It will be a constant drain on you, but it takes less magical power than a transformation spell. You must say the words *inspiramus atque respiramus.* Repeat it three times. As you do so, draw on your core and visualize a thin casing of air surrounding you. Visualization is key. It drives intent and purpose, giving your magic the direction it needs."

"Got it," I said. Jareth had already taught me all about visualization.

Your thoughts are your reality.

Seemed like all those self-help books I had read as a lonely, desperate foster kid had hit on something pretty important, whether you were directing magic or the power of your own will, your thoughts were your reality. Visualization became self-actualization.

I closed my eyes and repeated the words three times as I visualized a thin casing of air covering me from head to foot, encasing me in a pressurized air suit that would protect me from the heavy depths of the water while offering me life-giving oxygen. My core responded immediately as threads from all three magics worked their way through my cells and over my skin. I half expected a major drain on my magic, some sense of weakening due to my condition, but I felt surprisingly energized. As I focused on my core, I noticed a small pulsing of gold near my heart, a faint imprint of the glyph for crown glowed near my core, giving me a bit more power than I'd have normally had.

I silently thanked my lucky stars for the added power of those glyphs I had absorbed, not fully understanding what it could all mean, but knowing their power had become my birthright and would be the thing that sustained me.

I opened my eyes, taking in the approving nods of the group.

"This spell seemed pretty easy," I said. "Why not have everyone do it?"

"This spell is a minor one, but it leaves a person a bit vulnerable to attack," Jareth said. "Transforming into a water creature allows us the advantage of speed and physical traits that we can use to defend ourselves, and defending you will be our top priority."

"I do not like this one bit." I'd become the weak link in this scenario. "I need to be able to swim just as fast as the rest of you."

"You will be. I'll never let go of your hand."

He took my hand in his and gave it a squeeze. Jareth needed the control this time around, the knowledge that he could protect me, and any attempt I made with this particular transformation spell would not be well received. My separation from him as I'd found Zelres had taken a toll on him. He'd reached his limit as far as any risks to me were concerned. I opted to hold off on my insistence that I try the transformation spell, even though I felt that the spell I had just cast left me vulnerable in a different way.

"Let's get this over with," Nuallan said. "Nothing worse than growing extra body parts."

"Not something I ever thought I'd hear someone say." My cheerful smile made Nuallan's lips twitch in amusement. He had a handsome face and a fun personality.

"Nuallan, have you ever been married?"

I should have waited to ask that after he had finished his transformation. He was so startled by the random question, he became stuck with a fin half formed on his back.

The rest of the group chuckled as he muttered under his breath, having to start the process of glamouring his body all over again, which looked painful. Remembering how badly it hurt to change my blood and cells to match Moridan's I couldn't even begin to fathom how badly it hurt to grow body parts. Things were definitely shifting around as Jareth, Nuallan, Kheelan, and my father's skin bubbled, bulged, and stuck out in strange places.

"I might be sick," Lily said in a breathless voice as she squeezed Chuck and watched Jareth's hands grow skin between his fingers. Webbed hands. I looked down, noticing he'd already removed his shoes to easier create webbing between his toes.

"Really? I was hoping for a tail," I said.

His smile was filled with sharp, pointed teeth similar to Chantara's.

"Just wait until we get in the water. Our legs will naturally fuse together."

I took him in, seeing scales scattered here and there along his arms, torso, and lower legs. He didn't have a fin on his back like Nuallan did. It seemed that everyone had created their own version of an underwater creature. One thing was similar in that their chests had expanded, giving them more room for that extra lung and heart.

"Did it hurt?" I asked.

"You have no idea," Kheelan said, looking a bit winded after that. He had three slits on each side of his neck, with spikes shooting out of his elbows and the back of his neck. He looked pretty intimidating. "This is why I never volunteered as a liaison for our kingdoms. Transformation spells are the worst."

I took note of the bright colors covering their bodies, my father's chest in particular was covered in splashes of red and orange.

He noticed my scrutiny and said, "It makes other underwater creatures think I'm poisonous. They eat me, they die."

"Clever." Flaming pixie wands, I wanted to create some crazy body armor of my own. I laughed at my own petulance. Feeling sorry for myself just because I wasn't allowed to shoot spikes from my elbows.

With my own injuries and *griesha* taking hold, I had to own my limitations at the moment.

With one last longing look at all of my shapeshifting companions, I grabbed Jareth's hand and pulled him toward the water.

"I'll teach you how to grow a tail later," he promised.

I glanced at him with a wry grin. "You always know just what to say." He had to know this chaffed a bit, relying on everyone else to swim me to the Mer kingdom. "My fated mate is the best."

"Your fated mate needs to watch his elbows. Did you have to create such long spikes?" Kheelan asked as he drew up beside Jareth.

"I did it in the hopes you would keep your distance."

"You've succeeded. I'll simply stick close to Crysta." Kheelan moved to my other side and held fast to my elbow. With Jareth and Kheelan on either side of me, we dove into the lake.

Crysta

*I*t felt strange to swim through the water at the rate we were going and feel hardly any resistance. Since I couldn't actually feel the water, the experience could have been compared to flying, flying above a watery bed dotted with vibrant patches of indigo. Indigo colored grass? Tiny, yellow schools of fish darted in and out of the foliage, coming up for a moment to chew.

As we continued forward, the patches of indigo lessened. The floor sloped downward and Chantara and Paio swam ahead, guiding us into open water. Other than the jagged cliff on either side that grew further apart as we continued forward, there wasn't much to look at, not even many underwater creatures.

"Why is it so barren all of a sudden?" I asked. I looked at Jareth. "Wait, can you hear me?"

He chuckled, but his words came to me a few seconds after his mouth moved. The sounds were muted, but still discernible. "We can speak underwater. As far as this area goes, we're simply working toward our first kingdom. The Mer kingdom. It will take several minutes of swimming before we reach the outer limits of the kingdom and go through the first set of sentries."

"Sentries? That sounds not so great."

"Rena does like her security measures. I'm actually not looking forward to this initial confrontation with her."

"Why not?"

"She has a thing for Jareth," Kheelan said, "and she's never been subtle about it."

A flash of irritation hit me. "Is there a female within this realm who hasn't made a pass at you?" Jareth's amusement added to my annoyance.

"I cannot take credit for my manly physique, dashing good looks, or soft silky hair."

"Oh, for cripes sake—"

"You don't have to worry about Rena." He gave my hand a reassuring squeeze. "The only one who has my heart is you."

"I know. I'm not worried."

"I am." Kheelan grimaced. "Rena is a hard woman. She also wants what she wants. I'm not at all certain she'll cooperate with us. I think it would be better to enter the Dry Lands without her being the wiser."

"Unfortunately, Rena knows everything that goes on within her kingdom. She has sentries everywhere," Paio said. "Mother is correct. We must have Rena on our side if we're to make this work."

We fell into an uneasy silence after that, swimming through darker areas of the water as we descended deeper within its depths.

After about fifteen more minutes of this, we navigated toward a steep incline. I was totally unprepared for the incredible landscape that opened up as we crested the ridge. My eyes were bathed in lighting that glowed from a series of stone posts standing on either side of a long bridge leading toward a palace made of coral the color of ivory. The palace consisted of seven enormous columns or sections in an open triangular shape with the largest structure placed at the tip of the triangle and the smaller constructs tapering off at an angle behind. On either side of the bridge, hundreds of lights dotted the interior below, hinting at a large epicenter of activity where the city's inhabitants went about their daily routines.

As we drew closer to the bridged area, the enormity of the place became clearer and clearer. The homes were carved from the sides of the cliffs below the bridge, with varying paths weaving back and forth between homes, businesses, and the actual bridge to the palace. I didn't see the necessity for roads, paths, and bridges when you could just swim your way to your next location, but then I picked out details I hadn't noticed before.

Hundreds of faeries with appendages ranging from claws, to tentacles, to actual legs, were meandering slowly along the bridge, heading toward the epicenter of the palace. I'd never in my life seen such colorful faeries. Not to mention the Mermaids. Bright shades of cerulean, indigo, tangerine, marigold, and amber, and that only covered a tiny fraction of what I saw. The shades of hair ranged from silver like Jareth's to Jet black like Chantara's and every variation of color in between. Their tails sparkled as if sequins had been sprinkled over the whole of them. Some tails matched the hair color, while some didn't.

I could have floated there, hungrily absorbing every colorful detail for hours if I'd had the time.

We slowly descended, reaching the start of the bridge and moving closer to a gated entrance with gold bars tipped with nasty looking barbs. Two Mermen flanked the entrance on either side. Their tails matched each other in aqua-green tones with silver slashes breaking up the solid color. Their chests were covered in a gold breastplate and they each held a golden spear. Their hair was a jet black, much like Chantara's, and the pupils of their eyes were slitted like hers as well. Upon seeing her, they immediately stretched their tails out behind them and bowed their heads. It looked like the equivalent of Mermen kneeling. A bit awkward, but probably normal for them.

"Your Highness," the one on the right said. "We were unaware you planned to return this day. I'm afraid your Regent is currently entertaining important guests from the Drac kingdom."

"Excellent," Chantara said. "We'll need to speak to a representative from the Drac kingdom as well. Less travel for us."

The guards appeared uneasy. "Highness, Rena is discussing the abhorrent marriage between their prince and an unworthy Hag. She is most displeased with the alliance."

"Excuse me?" I said, barely restraining myself from swimming over to the guard and popping him on his ebony-haired head.

The guards gave me a curious look as Chantara placed a staying hand on my shoulder. She gave a subtle shake of her head.

"If you'll send the guard a message that we are on our way, I would appreciate it. We'll be happy to fill Rena in on the alliance and why it was necessary."

I don't think I'd ever seen two dudes appear more disgusted.

"You approve of this alliance? A Drac and a...a Hag?"

"Can I spell them?" I muttered under my breath. "It'd be a real treat to castrate these two."

Kheelan let out a half laugh, half cough behind me. Jareth put some pressure on my other shoulder to keep me from saying anything else, but I saw the mirth in his eyes.

"Announce our arrival." Chantara's expression brooked no further arguments. The sentries gave her another weird bow and then placed their hands on a large column that glowed a bright blue around their fingers. They bowed their heads for a moment and closed their eyes before acknowledging Chantara and motioning us forward.

As we swam past them, I couldn't help but give those sentries the evil eye. Abhorrent Hag? Idiots!

"What was it they did on the column of coral?" I asked.

"It's like a telephone. They can communicate with different sentries stationed all throughout the kingdom by directing their thoughts to a particular spire. Saves on swim time," Paio said.

No kidding.

As we swam across the bridge, Jareth pointed upward, urging me to look at the interesting overhang. What looked like enormous, transparent mushrooms towered over us, supported by their version of a stem, but the stems were as thick as tree trunks. Aqua green veins spread under the soft tissue, letting off an eerie glow that also added to the illumination.

"What are those?" I asked.

"Ankat," Jareth said. "I think the closest thing I can compare it to from your world is Jelly Fish. The tentacles are topside, however. The Ankat catch prey and sting creatures that swim too close to the city structure."

"Nice. Nice and lethal. Is there nothing fuzzy and cuddly down here?" My thoughts turned to Chuck, suddenly missing my sweet companion.

"I'd avoid any cuddling with anything sentient in these parts," Kheelan advised.

Yeah. Good idea.

I feasted my eyes on as much of the view provided, taking in creatures that looked similar to crabs, dolphins, fish, and even eels. The Mer folk bustled about the city below. The women were attired in bone plating that covered their chests, looking like an exposed ribcage. Armor, maybe?

The males all wore gold plating, but the plating looked a bit thinner than the ones the sentries wore. It seemed as if this community expected to be attacked at any moment.

"Chantara, do your people always wear chest armor?"

She flipped her tail, pulling closer to me. "These waters can be dangerous, Crysta, but so can we." She flashed me a mouth filled with sharp teeth.

"You know you're crazy scary when you do stuff like that."

Her musical peel of laughter buoyed my spirits.

"That's good, Crysta. I have a feeling we're going to need to appear extra intimidating."

As we reached the end of the bridge, a large oval screen emitting more aqua-green blocked the entrance. It looked like someone had stuck an oversized bubble in front of the entrance, daring us to pop it.

Another sentry gave deference to Chantara before withdrawing and motioning us to proceed.

"We're going through the bubble?" I asked. Then I watched in awe as Chantara swam forward, allowing the thing to completely engulf her. Once inside, her beautiful tail quickly split into legs as her scales formed themselves into an elegant, sequined dress of the most dazzling ocean blue I had ever seen. She walked out the other side and disappeared from view.

Awesome. I really needed to take a break for a bit. The constant use of the spell had drained my reserves.

"It's not a bubble," Jareth said, giving me a teasing grin. "This is a muma. It helps the body adjust from the varying pressure of the sea to a dry room. Rena prefers the entire palace be dry, and I don't blame her. Water tends to ruin most everything over time."

He placed a hand at my back and guided me forward. I stepped through the thin coating of the muma, shivering at the gelatin-like feel as I passed through its outer layer. Once inside, my spell dropped without my having to do anything. Seemed as if the muma did that for me. I nearly stumbled forward as influx of power returned to my core. I managed to keep myself upright and took another step forward, heading out the other side, but dang if I didn't feel a bit woozy as my body adjusted. Chantara quickly enveloped me in her arms, giving me a good once over.

"You look okay, but I don't like those weird streaks in your eyes. I wonder if holding that spell for so long was too much for you."

"Streaks?"

Before Chantara could explain, Paio followed next. His Aqua tail split into legs and his scales rearranged themselves into a shiny coating of gold and green armor. Scaled strips of seaweed green ran down the length of his arms and legs, surrounded by layers of copper and gold colors.

Kheelan, Nuallan, and my father soon followed behind, letting down their transformation spells and magically dawning formal attire. I felt a slight rustling cover my body and looked down, surprised to discover myself ensconced in a gorgeous dress, icy blue in color. The tight sleeving covered my arms all the way to my wrists and the bodice cinched my waist.

I stared at Jareth in astonishment.

"What the hell is this?" I asked.

Kheelan and Jareth broke out into boisterous laughter, although Jareth's glittering eyes did not leave my figure. It gave me the shivers when he looked at me like that.

"This is a dress," my father said.

"Did you just dress me like I'm a two-year-old?"

He took my hand in his and smiled. "I never had a chance to dress you when you were two. It's my privilege to drape you in gowns of the finest fabrics and the latest fashions."

"Latest fashions? This is so sixteenth century England."

"Rena is a bit particular concerning court dress."

I took in the rest of the group, all dressed as if they were attending a costume party. Then I looked at Chantara whose dress was definitely more modern in appearance.

"I want that one," I said.

Chantara simply chuckled, grabbed my hand, and pulled me through an archway of bright purple coral. The sentries led us into a grand room with a vaulted ceiling made of the same material as the muma.

"That's nifty," I said, staring up at the various fish and Merfolk swimming above the palace.

I studied the walls of the structure, completely taken in by the ivory colored corral where tiny water urchins darted in and out of pock-marked holes along the walls. It looked as if they were swimming, which didn't seem possible since there was no water within this room, but their movements indicated they swam through something. Several little creatures that looked like sea horses shot from a tiny hole in the wall and immediately flew toward us. I marveled at the paper-thin fins running along their spines and curled tails. The seahorses swam straight for me, circling around my waist, creating a cool little breeze that misted my skin before circling upward and then disappearing through the ceiling.

"Interesting," Chantara said with a knowing look. "The Nola rarely welcome guests to the palace."

"Is that what they were doing?"

"They showered you with their protection."

Hmm. That reminded me of the pixies I'd encountered when I first arrived in the Fae realm.

"It certainly felt like a shower."

Nuallan bit a fist, trying not to laugh, but Kheelan couldn't restrain himself. "In other words, they shot magical spit on you. Welcome to the Mer kingdom."

I glared at him but stuck close to Chantara as she guided me past corridors of Ivory coral with various creatures popping in and out of the walls.

I nearly embarrassed myself by screaming in terror when a crab the size of a human being entered the corridor on six spindly hind legs. Its three eyeballs widened in surprise and then its mouth pincers flexed open in what I could only describe as a crab grin.

"Your Highness," it said, its voice coming out reed thin, but not unpleasant. Its arms appeared to be segmented appendages, but there were no pincers at the end. Just five long claws on each hand.

"Criva, it is so nice to see you again." Chantara released me and quickly moved forward, allowing herself to be enfolded in the giant crab's embrace before leaning back and giving him a smile. "Please come meet my guests." She brought Criva over, motioning me to come forward. I blinked away my shock and tried to compose myself instead of standing there slack-jawed like some moron who'd never seen anything other than humans.

"Criva, I would like you to meet Crystiana Tuadhe d'Anu, Princess of the Unseelie Court."

"Oh, such a pleasure," he said, managing a graceful bow on his back legs. "I've heard nothing but wonderful things about our queen in training."

I reached forward and took his clawed hand, enfolding it in mine, which made all three of his eyeballs blink over and over again.

"I'm very honored to meet you, Criva."

I released his claws and did my best to focus on his middle eye since I had no idea which one I was supposed to look at. Middle is best. Then it seemed as if I looked at all three.

I thought I heard Nuallan chuckle behind me. That faerie was gonna get it. I'd set him up with the female equivalent of Criva and dub it a blind date.

"The Princess honors me with her favor," he said. "I must admit, I'm relieved to see you all here, especially you, Highness." He turned toward Chantara again. "Rena is accusing the Drac king and his wife of conspiracy and treason due to this alliance with the Hags. She thinks they are planning a coup."

"Oh, of all the paranoid, idiotic, nonsensical..." Chantara took in a deep breath before saying, "Not everything is about Rena. No one wants to take her position as Regent."

"No one would dare, if I may be so bold." Criva's eyes did this weird thing where they popped forward a bit as if to punctuate his words with emotion. Then they moved back into their sockets.

So great. I loved this place already.

"Take us to the throne room, Criva. I assume that's where Rena has deigned to receive the Drac."

"Oh, most certainly. Anything to intimidate and belittle," Criva said, turning around on his...well, he turned around anyway. We quickly followed Criva down a few other corridors, making a left then a right, then a few more rights. No way I'd ever remember how we got there...or how to get out.

Criva finally led us through a receiving room and into a hallway that poured into the throne room with several sentries flanking either side. The throne itself appeared to be made out of sea-green coral, the high back of the throne spanned out in a clam shell design with three spiked points shooting up from the middle.

And perched on that ostentatious throne was a real stunner of a Mermaid. Her rich copper hair matched the copper tones of her tail, and her fair, creamy skin complemented the colors. Her fin in question seemed to fan out as if silken folds had been attached to the end of each fin. Her hair was adorned with a golden crown of five points, with dangling earrings to match. Her breastplate covered her ribs, mimicking the bone structure, making it appear that she had an exoskeleton just as the other sentries.

A few feet in front of her stood two people I recognized. The Drac king and queen appeared tense around the eyes, calm laced with a hint of anger.

How they managed that with spears pointed at their heads remained a mystery.

"Why is she in mermaid form?" Kheelan muttered.

Chantara let out a weary sigh and whispered, "She feels she looks more regal in her true form, rather than seated on spindly legs."

I didn't like her, and judging by her displeased glared as she stared at us from the haughty position on her throne, she didn't seem all that thrilled to see us.

"Chantara," she said in a sickeningly sweet tone. "How interesting you should show up at this very moment, especially when these two claim you were already aware of the alliance between their son and a Hag." Then she did a double take as her eyes landed on Paio. "My son, you, you're home. How is this possible?"

"Hello, auntie. It is good to see you again." Paio gave her a dutiful bow, but I noted the expression of disdain he wore, wiping it off his face as he stood straight.

Rena's expression did not gel with what I had expected. For someone who seemed intent on claiming Paio as her own son, she didn't necessarily seem all that relieved to see him.

Or maybe I was imagining things? Just as quickly as that stunned look surfaced it was gone, replaced by an expression of relief followed by a few tears. It felt a tad insincere. She stood and opened her arms to Paio. Chantara didn't give her the chance to do anything else.

"Lower your spears immediately," Chantara commanded.

Without hesitation, the sentries lowered their spears and stepped back. Rena made a sound of protest. Chantara approached the Drac royals.

"I apologize for this misunderstanding."

"Not at all, Highness. We are happy to forget the incident, considering all you and your friends have done for our people. Our race has never seen so many fated mates."

"Lies," Rena spat out, taking her seat. "Fated mates are a thing of legend."

"They speak the truth, Rena." Chantara placed a hand on the Drac queen's arm. I saw the tension in the queen's shoulders relax at her touch. "You're aware that *griesha* has become more prevalent, targeting those with less magical ability. Their immunity to the disease is nonexistent."

Rena shrugged a creamy shoulder, not bothering to hide her complete lack of concern. "Faeries die, Chantara. Survival of the fittest is a principle we should all appreciate. Consider it a cleansing of the realm."

My eyes narrowed at her words. They hit far too close to Titania's views on the unfortunate label known as lesser Fae. This racism ran deep within the Fae realm. I'd done my best to make changes, but every ruler of every race needed to come to terms with the new order of things and lay down their ignorant prejudices.

Or they would be answering to me.

"The disease has recently gained enormous power and potency, Rena." Chantara took a few steps forward and even though Rena was poised above her, there was no denying the true ruler of the Mer realm. Compared to Chantara, Rena looked like a petulant wannabe, constantly competing for something forever out of her reach. "We're learning that no faerie is completely immune to the disease. The Hags and the Land Dwellers were originally hit the hardest, but the Unseelie princess discovered a fated mate bond is the cure. Due to this rather remarkable revelation, Prince Jareth and Princess Crystiana have succeeded in recreating the fated mate bond between Land Dwellers and Dark Elves and Drac and Hags."

Rena's mouth remained pinched for a moment. "I had heard rumors of fated mates being discovered between species. I thought it ridiculous. Are you saying Adris' daughter and the Drac prince are fated mates?"

"That is correct. There is no conspiracy here, Rena. Our mission, simply put, is to stop *griesha* and save lives. Now that all has been explained," she turned to the Drac king and queen, "you're free to go with my deepest apologies for this unfortunate misunderstanding, but I hope you'll dine with us before you take your leave."

Rena made a sound of protest in the back of her throat, but no one paid her any attention, which gave me some petty satisfaction. Chantara had effectively taken over the meeting while seamlessly showing exactly who ran the show, and she did it with all the diplomacy of a first-rate politician.

Bravo.

"It would be our pleasure, Chantara." The Drac King didn't have to feign his appreciation. He and his wife had been terrified at the prospect of going toe-to-toe with Rena.

"Wonderful. Criva will show you to your room where you can freshen up a bit. We'll have a meal prepared within the hour."

As the Drac royals turned to take their leave, they both spotted me and immediately approached, embracing me at once. I hadn't expected it, but I didn't hate it either.

I hugged them back, chuckling at the unexpected affection and the sweet warmth filling my center.

"Thank you again for the happiness you've given our son and many others within our kingdom. The changes have been enormous, improving relations and understanding between our races," the queen said.

"That's been my goal from the very beginning. Promote understanding and good relations between races. I'm thrilled everyone is so happy with this unexpected development."

The king took my hand and covered it with his own. "You're meant to save us all, Princess. Once again, we pledge to you and the Unseelie court our unfailing loyalty."

I blinked away a few tears and gave him a grateful smile. "Likewise. Whenever you need me, all you have to do is ask."

"Thank you, Princess."

My eyes followed them as they left the throne room. As I directed my gaze back to our group it was to see them staring at me with varying looks of approval on their faces. I wiped at my damp cheeks.

Geez, these faeries.

Jareth enfolded me in his embrace, kissing the top of my head. "This is merely one of the things that makes you great, Crysta."

"What?"

"The genuine love and care you hold for all faeries. It's something that simply cannot be fabricated. Your capacity for love is infinite. Ruling with love is not something we see too often among the courts." He pulled back and brushed a strand of hair from my face, rubbing a thumb against my cheek. "You're the cure on so many levels."

I cleared my throat to regain my composure, but I never seemed to have much of that around this particular faerie.

"Well, now that we have everything cleared up, I'd like to meet the faerie that the fates have chosen to pair with my sweet Jareth," Rena said, effectively ruining the moment.

She stood this time on legs instead of tail, her gown a deep copper of sequined scales.I noticed her hand clenched around her scepter. Her expression held sweetness, but her eyes could have melted the face off a Mountain Troll.

Queen Rena was jealous.

I'd just inherited another enemy.

Crysta

ena sized me up. I refused to squirm under her intense perusal, but I also thought about the age difference between myself and everyone else in the room. Faeries were timeless in a sense. As long as illness and accident didn't occur, they were pretty much immortal. I'd lived a whopping eighteen years while my fated mate and Rena had lived for a couple centuries give or take. I couldn't imagine what it was like for Rena, a woman with power, position, beauty, smarts, and ego, facing off with an inexperienced eighteen-year-old girl, a rival taking away her not-so-secret crush.

It had to be a bit humiliating for her.

Over the years, I'd become an expert at reading the room. You had to get a feel for the players you dealt with, especially in an environment full of threats. A woman like Rena had the same personality type as Rhoswen. Jareth and I being a coupled grated, her narcissism wouldn't stand for it. And just like Rhoswen, I didn't doubt for a moment that Rena would get rid of any obstacles in her way, including me.

"It's an honor to meet you, Regent," I said. I wasn't about to refer to her as queen. Chantara deserved that title.

By the narrowing of her eyes, I saw she registered the slight even though I'd technically done nothing wrong in calling her that. Maybe it wasn't wise to poke the bear, so to speak, but I had to hold my ground here. I couldn't let a woman like Rena intimidate me if I was going to eventually rule the Unseelie Court.

Game on.

She didn't step down from the platform, no doubt preferring to stand above us to deliver her own subtle slight. Too bad nobody cared.

"Chantara," she said, never taking her piercing cerulean eyes from me, "I wish you would have given me some warning of your arrival. I would have prepared a massive feast for you."

"Kind, but unnecessary." Chantara kept her voice level and serene. Interesting when comparing these two. Chantara seemed comfortable in her own skin, her own power. She knew her place. Rena, for all her stunning beauty and misplaced pride, looked a bit insecure in Chantara's presence.

She cleared her throat. "What exactly are you doing here?" The question came out strained. I think she wanted to demand answers and rant and rail against Chantara's interference, yet she had to remain civil.

"As you've just learned, Crysta and Jareth are traveling the realm, assisting those faeries hit hardest with *griesha*. I thought it time we take our travels here and assess the situation amongst our subjects."

Not a bad cover for why we were actually here. In fact, I didn't think it a bad idea. If species of underwater Fae suffered from *griesha*, I wanted to know if any were on the brink of death.

"Merfolk are not susceptible to the disease, Chantara. We are a powerful race of Fae."

"True, yet Crysta has treated several powerful races of Fae for the illness, including the Formage. The disease escalates by the hour."

For once Rena appeared at a loss for words, until she finally sputtered, "The Formage? There are cases of Formage suffering from *griesha*?"

Chantara approached Rena, holding out her hand to help her descend the platform steps. I thought it a classy gesture, all things considered.

Rena hesitated, but finally accepted her hand and joined the group at the foot of the stairs. Chantara's news had unsettled her. Relief coursed through me. I had to believe her reaction meant she wasn't completely heartless.

"What do you need?" she asked.

Chantara gave her a kind smile and squeezed her hand. "Please send your messengers throughout the waters. Tell them we need a tally of any races hit with the disease and an estimate of those ill within each race. Those closest to death should be sent to the palace. We need to know what we're dealing with."

Again, a great cover for why we were really here, but I also felt a bit anxious to check on this underwater realm now that Chantara had brought it up. I could sincerely go about helping these races while we all simultaneously gathered information from the Dry Lands on anything that might shed some light on the diadem's location. Chantara's race might not have any knowledge of who Oberon gave the diadem to, but there were plenty of "fish in the sea". There had to be an underwater race who knew something about the diadem.

Healings would be off the table, considering my health, but dealing out hope could be just as beneficial.

Rena gave Chantara a respectful nod and headed toward an exit near the back of the room. Before she left, she said, "I think it best we consult each other before binding any other interracial couples. We wouldn't want to cause alarm or confusion among some of the more aggressive races."

Chantara remained serene as she said, "An excellent idea, Rena. Our underwater realm must be advised of the current situation. Once we have our numbers, we can converse with the leaders of each race as to next steps."

Yeah, that hadn't been exactly what Rena meant. She wasn't on board with the Hag and Drac marriages. Not a fan of interracial mingling, apparently.

Her attitude disturbed me. She might appear compliant, but I guessed she ruled her kingdom and interfered with others according to her own prejudiced beliefs. Chantara's presence changed the order of things. Any mismanagement on Rena's part would not go unnoticed with Chantara in attendance. Rena would have to play nice for now, but I had a feeling she would eventually bare her claws and make her move. Chantara seemed prepped for it. As she'd stated before, a confrontation loomed on the horizon.

"Next steps?" I asked Chantara after Rena had departed.

Air hissed between her teeth as she flung her hands in the air. A purple coating of dust shot from them, coloring the room around us and casting us in shadow for a moment.

"What is this?" I asked, holding out my hand.

"Coral dust. It's a soundproof spell. We need to discuss our plan without prying ears."

We gathered in a circle, Chantara wearing a grave look.

My father spoke for the first time since arriving in the throne room. "Rena is plotting something, and our presence here compromises her position."

I gave my father a curious look while Chantara grimly agreed.

"I fear you are right, Highness," she said. "Rena is not happy to see us."

I raised my hand like a schoolgirl. "Can someone clear up something for me. Is the Lake of Beatha ruled by the Unseelie Court or the Seelie Court?"

"We remain neutral and govern ourselves. We must remain partial since the lake is responsible for dispersing the magic created within."

"So Rena doesn't answer to the courts."

"No," Jareth said, "but she does answer to Chantara, and even now she chafes at it."

"I've been absent for too long," Chantara said. "It isn't good to leave Rena alone. I suspect I shall have to rein her in a bit. However, that has nothing to do with our next steps. The Drac may have their own legends concerning the diadem. I will make preparations for dinner within the hour. We can question the Drac then. It's a starting place, anyway. Tomorrow, while Rena is gathering the information I asked for, I will have Paio take you all to the Dry Lands to do a bit of research within the libraries there."

At least we had a plan. Much better than swimming around this underwater world with no ideas as to where we should be looking.

"Criva," Chantara said.

I turned in surprise. I'd completely forgotten he was still in the room.

"Yes, Highness," he said, scuttling his way over to us.

I stared at the way his many legs skittered along the ivory corral, finding it amazing that his tiny legs had the power to carry his heavy body, shell and all.

"Please show our guests to their accommodations. I'm sure they could use a bit of rest before dinner."

"Of course." His mouth pincers slid to the side. I think he smiled at us? I didn't know and I didn't care. I simply liked him. Quite a bit.

"Right this way," he said.

Jareth placed an arm around my shoulder as we followed Criva, leaving the same way we came in.

∞ ∞ ∞

"This is like *The Little Mermaid* on steroids," I said as I scrutinized the room Jareth and I shared.

I stared at the coral walls, still fascinated by the tiny creatures bobbing in and out of their little hidey-holes as if there was any water to swim in. I thought about Chuck right then and couldn't decide if he would have enjoyed playing with these tiny things or possibly eating them.

A large bubble in the corner surrounded what looked like a seaweed cocoon. I eyed the water within, trying to figure out why the room remained dry while everything within the muma remained wet.

"Mer folk enjoy sleeping within the water in an upright position. This contraption gives them that option, and since Rena insists the rest of the palace remain dry, the muma encases the cocoon in the same pressurized environment you would find while traveling through the lake."

"Very cool." I fixed my eyes on the large bed covered in glimmering turquoise bedding. It looked so pretty, I didn't want to mess up the covers.

I reached my hand out to smooth down the blanket and stared in shock at my wrist. Tiny red dots extended past my wrist line.

"Jareth," I said.

I lifted my arm to show him. He pushed the sleeve of my tunic up, revealing more dots peppering my skin all the way up to my elbow. The look in his eye as he studied it scared me a little. There were a crap ton of things Jareth could handle. As far as I was concerned, he was damn near invincible,

196

but I was his Kryptonite. He always lost focus and became emotionally erratic and overprotective whenever threats to my safety presented themselves.

He turned on his heels and headed for the door.

"Jareth, where are you going?"

"To get Kheelan. We're going to figure out how to break his bond to you now. I'm going to beat his thick head in until he releases you from this spell he created. Once he does sever his bond, I'll beat him a little more."

I grabbed his arm, forcing him to look at me. The anguish, the frantic look in his eye, and the stern set of his jaw told me Jareth had taken about all he could when it came to threats to my safety.

"I truly believe that Kheelan would have done so already if he had the power to."

"No, he wants you for himself. I think he's bluffing, waiting for us to fold first, waiting for us to swerve first. He is playing Turkey."

"He..." I furrowed my eyebrows in confusion before I finally caught his butchered reference. "You mean he's playing Chicken."

"Whatever. They are both birds humans eat."

I stifled a chuckle since he looked so grim. Not necessarily a time for joking around.

"You didn't see him while he watched over Terise. I think Kheelan can only go so far when it comes to risking those he loves. When he first cast this spell, he had no idea he'd be bound to Terise. He had no way of knowing Titania would return, further strengthening *griesha*. He didn't know he'd be risking the life of his fated mate...or me for that matter. He has developed strong feelings for Terise. I think if he could undo this he would."

Jareth ran a hand through his silver hair, his eyes looking wild and panicked.

"You're in the early stages of this, Crysta, and you're powerful enough that I think it will take quite a bit of time for you to succumb to the disease, but we have no way of knowing what Titania's presence within our realm will do to you or Terise. We have to find a solution here. The sooner the better."

"Why do you think I'm suffering from this when you and Kheelan aren't?"

"I think much of it has to do with the bloodletting injury. Kheelan and I do not have Dark Magic and a severed bond draining us. My bond to you is partial while you and Terise are stretched thin, and Kheelan's bond feeds from both of you."

"Yeah. Not ideal."

I bit my bottom lip, hesitating to suggest this since I knew it was our last resort, and I didn't think we were quite there yet, but I figured it needed to be discussed.

"Our semi-bond is not constrained by Kheelan's magic, Jareth. I wonder if it would be possible to sever it completely." I grabbed Jareth's shoulders when he made a choked sound. "Listen to me. I'm not trying to get out of being your fated mate. I think Kheelan's diabolical bonding spell gone wrong will right itself, releasing Terise in the process, if you and I sever ours. Once that's done, we can immediately bond Terise to Cedric, and I will be out of danger. It will buy us more time to figure out how to get rid of Kheelan's spell completely, without risking Terise's life or mine in the process."

Jareth had his jaw clenched so hard I was afraid his teeth would crack.

"No," he whispered.

"Jareth—"

"No!" He wrapped his hand around the nape of my neck, pulling me flush against him. "I only have half a bond with you, but I won't allow anyone to sever it. I worked too hard just to get that far with you. It's the only thing that keeps me from losing my mind whenever I think of part of you being linked to Kheelan, part of your core being joined with his when you belong to me. Losing that is not an option. There is no guarantee you'll be able to sever a full bonding with Kheelan, and the repercussion could be lethal, much like The Rending."

"Kheelan and I aren't true fated mates like Titania and Oberon. I think once we find the diadem, we could make things right...somehow."

"But you don't know for certain. You don't even know if it's possible to sever our bond without causing you serious injury. Kheelan's spell is not functioning properly. It was never meant to deal with another added core, and we have no way of knowing what it would do to Terise."

"Jareth, we have to make a decision soon. Terise is not going to last much longer."

"But you will," he said.

I stared at him in astonishment. "What did you just say?" I tried to shrug him off, but he wrapped his other arm around me and forced me to stay, forced me to look him in the eye.

"Terise may not survive this, but you are stronger than she is. Your disease will not progress as fast as hers. You have more time." His expression shone hard as granite. "I love Terise. She is my friend and someone I also consider to be a sister, but you are more important, not just because you are my fated mate, but because you are the future of this realm. Without you, none of us will survive. What you propose is a calculated risk I will never be willing to take. Too many lives are at stake. We find another way. We can work together to break down Kheelan's bond, but you will never suggest breaking ours again. Never again."

I chaffed at his authoritative tone. I'd do as I damn well pleased, especially if I thought it was the best course of action. "That's not how this relationship works. You don't throw your weight around just because you can't handle the hard decisions," I said. "We decide this together, or at the very least we compromise."

His jaw held firm, his eyes hard and unyielding. "Not on this matter. There will be no meeting in the middle on this. I've had about as much as any male can take when it comes to losing their fated mate. I don't care if I have to tie you up for the rest of this quest, you are not, under any circumstances, allowed to sever our bond."

I opened my mouth to protest, but Jareth had other ideas. His lips descended on mine in a harsh kiss fueled with all his pent up frustration, anger, worry, and stress. I'd like to say that I held on to some sense of female power here, maybe kicked him in the shin and declared my unquestionable independence.

Nope. I was irked for about two seconds, and then I returned the intimate exchange just as fiercely. He braced the nape of my neck and pulled me flush against him, kissing me in a way that marked me as his, that dared anyone or anything to take me from him.

When he finally let me up for air, I was both furious and...annoyingly turned on. We stared at each other, our own mental game of Chicken. My defiant glare against his possessive, authoritative one.

"You're an overbearing tyrant," I finally said.

The corner of his mouth quirked up in amusement.

"I'll show you an overbearing tyrant." With that, he picked me up, causing me to instinctively wrap my legs around his waist. He was already kissing me senseless by the time he eased us onto the bed. He bore the brunt of his weight on his arms as we continued to kiss with all the pent up passion and frustration our situation warranted. I think I needed that emotional release as much as he did, and I found myself okay with Jareth asserting some measure of control over the situation. I held him close and gave him all

I had, never wanting him to think that my suggestion meant I actually wanted to be separated from him for any reason.

As our intimacy became more heated, a warning bell sounded in my brain. I wasn't necessarily opposed to the idea of going all the way with him at this point. This was the faerie I intended to spend the rest of my life with, but our first time shouldn't have been under massive duress with the fate of the Fae realm in such a precarious state.

Unfortunately, my hormones really didn't agree with the logic my brain offered up. Just as I was about to throw caution to the wind and push for more, a loud knock at the door brought us out of our passionate exchange, clearing my head for a moment.

"It's Criva, your majesties," the crab said, his voice muffled behind the door. "I'm to tell you you'll be dining in ten minutes. If you're ready, I can escort you to the dining room."

Jareth placed a delicious kiss against my neck and rested his forehead on mine, groaning in annoyance at the disruption.

"Give us a moment, Criva," I said, hoping the crab didn't note my breathy tone.

"Worst timing ever," Jareth said in a husky voice. "Can't a male seduce his wife without interruption?"

"Is that what you were doing?" I asked. I drew back a few strands of his silver hair and lifted my head to give him a soft, lingering kiss.

"Flaming pixie dust," he said. "Do you have any idea how difficult it is to be with you, to love you more and more every day, to worry about losing you every minute, and to want you in my arms every second without being able to consummate this marriage?"

I slapped his shoulder playfully. "We're not married yet."

His expression gentled. "Yes we are, Crysta. I don't need the rest of the bonding spell or any other formalities to dictate what I feel in my heart. You are mine, and I am yours. Not even Kheelan's bond can change that."

A single tear trickled down my cheek, the tenderness in his gaze stealing my breath away.

"I've never once thought I deserved you," I said.

"I know I don't deserve you." He dipped his head, kissing my upper lip and then the bottom. "Promise me, you will not try to find ways to sever our bond. Promise me, you'll wait until we've exhausted all our resources. I'm not so bullheaded as to deny that your suggestion might be our only option in the long run. At the end of the day, I will do whatever it takes to save you, even if it means severing my bond with you." He tried to speak, but emotion overwhelmed him. Moisture formed within his eyes, causing their blue depths to sparkle in the light. "Just not yet," he said in a hoarse whisper. "Please, Crysta. Not yet."

I caressed his cheek, running my fingers along the sturdy line of his jaw. "Not yet," I agreed. "We try everything else first."

He swallowed hard, relief flooding his gaze. Then he rested his head against my shoulder, keeping himself propped up on his elbows.

I gave him another kiss, trying to unpack the full weight of my love and adoration in that simple show of affection.

A throat cleared loudly from behind the door. "Five minutes, your Majesties."

I thought I heard a few sniffles, but quickly dismissed it.

Jareth moaned in displeasure and then rolled to the side, getting to his feet and scooping me up into his arms.

"I can walk to dinner," I said.

"I know, but I'm feeling particularly possessive at the moment. I need to hold you."

"Fine, fine."

Jareth opened the door, and Criva stood there, wiping at his teary eyes with a clawed appendage.

"Criva?" I asked, feeling concerned. "Are you okay?"

"You two are simply the sweetest," he said. He wiped all three of his eyes even though his shoulders shook for a moment. Then he patted us on the arm. "It will work out for the both of you. I'm a big believer in happy endings." I stared at him in amusement as he continued to dab at his eyes. "If you'll...just...follow me," he said, letting out a soft little sob.

He scuttled down the corridor. I stared at Jareth in bemusement, but he didn't seem to be at all surprised by Criva's emotional display.

"Krees...Criva's species...uh...they tend to be sweet, sympathetic creatures."

Sweet, sympathetic crab attendants, huh?

Who knew?

15

Jareth

ish was not necessarily my favorite, and by the dubious look on Crysta's face as she watched Paio load his plate with something both fishy and filleted, she definitely agreed.

My thoughts turned to the little experiment I'd tried when first getting to know her, suspecting her physiology to be similar to mine. The way her captivating eyes widened when she saw the various plates of food spread out within her pitiful looking living room.

I'd needed to know her. I'd needed to understand the light we shared and the instant connection I'd felt. Even then, I knew she was mine. On some level, I understood that my life had irrevocably changed.

All for the better.

I gently nudged her, guiding her down the buffet line toward foods that were far more palatable for most of us. Crysta skirted around Paio, giving him a loving pat on the back as he continued to fill his plate full of various types of fish.

"I'm guessing you're making up for lost time," Crysta said, nodding toward his plate.

He gave her a wide smile. "Moridan wasn't one for buffets."

Her smile managed to convey both amusement and compassion, her eyes letting him know she understood. Her ability to connect with people, sympathize, put them at ease, and show how much she cared never ceased to amaze me.

"Save you some fish?" Paio asked, offering her his plate with a teasing grin.

She scooted down the line, following her father as she waved Paio off. "I'll stick with the essentials."

Chantara had truly gone all out, offering a long buffet line that was both elegant and casual, something for which I felt truly grateful. Formal meals with ambassadors and royals were tense ordeals, and we were all past that at this point.

I stifled a chuckle as I considered how Crysta would have managed a gathering like this. Instead of bone china or high-priced coral cutlery, she would have lined up paper plates and plastic utensils for the unsuspecting masses, never thinking twice about it.

Thank the goddess I'd found her.

We took our seats at an oblong table made of a shiny substance that appeared crystalline in nature. Crysta stared at its surface in wonder, running her fingers along its smooth lines.

"This isn't coral," she said, almost in surprise.

Chantara, sitting at my left, looked eager to fill her in. "Many of our furnishings are made from minerals and gems found within the Earth's oceans."

Crysta leaned forward a bit, placing her head just under my chin. I knew it was her way of conversing with Chantara, but her intoxicating scent nearly overwhelmed me, and I already had my hands full attempting to contain my instincts when it came to her.

Fated mates were never meant to go so long without fully bonding and consummating their marriages. I'd only slipped up once and lost control when Kheelan took things a bit too far outside the waterways, but I was no saint, and Crysta smelled delicious.

"Do you mean to tell me you have faeries travel to Earth's oceans to bring back materials for your homes and furnishings?" Crysta asked. The idea clearly fascinated her. She leaned her head against my chest as she continued her conversation. I wrapped an arm around her shoulder and held her close.

Sweet torture.

"A great weakness of our race is a fascination for shiny, beautiful objects, much like the Goblins." Chantara's laugh lilted across the room. "This table, for example is made from a form of Beryl, aquamarine to be precise."

"It's certainly beautiful. As is everything else I've seen."

"If you have the opportunity while you are here, you must visit the Drac Kingdom," the Drac King said. "It is also a beautiful place."

"We may do just that," Crysta said. "It's partly why we are here."

Crysta looked to her father to continue, which I thought was a kind gesture, instinctively respecting his position and authority. Roderick gave her a grateful nod and got straight to business.

"As you know, we're doing all we can to reverse *griesha* and take down King Moridan, and we've discovered a way to do so, but we may need your assistance."

"We will help in any way we can," the queen said.

"It has come to our attention that a diadem, once owned by Titania, may have the power to reverse the illness and overcome Moridan's core magic. Unfortunately, Oberon removed a very powerful stone from the diadem, one we were able to recover, but the diadem itself is missing. We believe it is hidden within the Lake of Beatha, but we have no idea where to begin our search."

"How did you manage to locate the stone?" the queen asked.

Roderick quickly went over the information within Oberon's scrolls and the legend held within King Lothe's histories.

"Chantara is the oldest of the Merfolk, but her race has not passed down any knowledge of who Oberon assigned to hide the diadem," I said. "We thought you might have some legend or tale passed down within your own kingdom."

"Nothing comes to mind. Have you checked the archives within the Dry Lands? The histories of the races within the lake are documented there," King Omer said.

"Not yet." Chantara looked as disappointed as I felt. We'd all hoped for something concrete. "It will be our first stop, but you know how vast those archives and libraries are. If we knew which race to be looking into, it would narrow things down for us and save us valuable time."

"The Drac have no legends of hidden diadems let alone treasures. You may find something documented within our histories, but I cannot think of anything that bears any resemblance to hidden treasure. I'm so sorry." The Drac King appeared distressed at the thought of not being able to help.

"It isn't your fault," I rushed to assure him. "This happened centuries upon centuries ago. We knew this wouldn't be easy."

"Wait a moment," Queen Olean said. "Chantara have you considered looking into the Missing Ruins?"

"Missing Ruins?" I asked. "I've never heard of anything like that." The whites of Chantara's eyes disappeared beneath obsidian. Never a good sign. "What is it?"

"The Drac Queen has brought up a fair point, one I had not considered since all underwater Fae are taught to avoid the Missing Ruins."

"What are they?" Kheelan asked.

"There are different spots along Earth's oceans where magnetic fields align with one specific point within our lake. Many of Earth's ships have disappeared in those areas only to reappear here within the lake. I'm unclear as to when it started or if it had always been. Many of the ships carried supplies and passengers who either survived by swimming to shore or drowned in the lake. That's one vein of ancestry that Land Dwellers can track. Many of those survivors were handsome men who eventually mated with Mermaids. Other ships carried treasures beyond your wildest imaginings."

Crysta's hand tightened around my thigh. I glanced at her questioningly, but she didn't seem to realize what she was doing. The notion of lost sailors mating with Mermaids had intrigued her. Curiosity painted her expression. A small smile twitched at the corner of my mouth. She was ever fascinated with the workings of the Fae realm. I adored her inquisitiveness. Unfortunately, Nuallan spoke before she could press for more ancestral details on the Land Dwellers.

"So it's essentially a ship graveyard." He folded his arms and leaned back against his chair. "Well, that doesn't sound too horrible. Why would any of you avoid it when many of the underwater races are known for their love of gold and shiny gems."

"That's exactly why we avoid it," Paio said, looking a bit green around the gills.

No pun intended, although I was tempted to say it out loud and show off my ever broadening slang and colloquialisms to Crysta. Even an eye roll from her would have been worth it, but now was not the time for such things.

"There is a race of creature that long ago made one of their nests within these ruins. Far easier to make your home where the treasure magically appears rather than leave anything to chance."

Unease brewed within my gut. I prayed he wouldn't say—

"Vorsha. A pod of Vorsha dwell amidst the ruins."

Kheelan, Nuallan, and I couldn't contain our groans. Roderick even paled a little at the notion of an entire pod. One Vorsha was dangerous enough. A pod held anywhere from ten to twenty Vorsha, depending on how many breeding females could be found within the pod, and how many alpha males vied for dominance. Those fights tended to end in death.

"May I remind everyone that we have no solid evidence suggesting the diadem is hidden within the Missing Ruins," Chantara said.

"True, but it would have been the perfect place to hide the diadem. That pod of Vorsha have lived and procreated there as far back as our Mer histories go," Paio said. "Surely the Ruins existed while Oberon was alive."

"Then that is one of the many things we need to ascertain. When were the Missing Ruins first discovered, and when did the first few Vorsha arrive and settle there? If these things occurred after Oberon had the diadem and stone hidden, then we can likely rule the Missing Ruins out."

"It's a good lead," I said. "Much better than what we arrived with, which happened to be nothing." I gave the queen a grateful smile. "Thank you for your help. If you can think of anything else, we will forever be in your debt."

"You mentioned that the very first Goblin King referred to the stone as the Stone of Destiny," King Omer said.

"That's right. I found it odd since a specific title had never been assigned to the stone in Oberon's scrolls."

He thought for a moment and glanced at his wife. "Olean, do you remember several of our forefathers making their home in Ireland for some time?"

Her eyes lit up in surprise, clearly making some connection. "The Stone of Destiny and the Sword of Light. Do you think...?"

"What?" I asked.

The King nodded for his wife to explain. "Some of our early ancestors decided to break from our group and live in the many waters surrounding Ireland. Ours weren't the only races of Fae to do so. Your ancestors decided to make their place among the humans, Prince Jareth."

I knew this just as most Fae did. A human's spirit held energies that most other races within other realms did not, and those energies gave our cores an immense boost in power. Now that I knew humans held magic throughout their entire bodies, thanks to Lily and Graul's bonding, it made sense. Unfortunately, humans were once kidnapped and sucked dry of such energies by predatory races of Fae.

Some faeries were ruthless about it, other faeries, such as my race, absorbed human energy through more intimate and pleasurable means, enthralling those victims and either bringing them back to the Fae realm or merely using them for as long as time would permit, though I suspected many of my kind at some point must have fallen in love, stayed, and developed families among the humans, sharing energy and magic with their chosen spouse to prolong the human life. Even before the ban, however, I had never been interested in participating in such activities. Draining any individual of energy never appealed to me.

Kheelan...well, he'd had a few trysts he still enjoyed reminiscing about.

"I know of several members of the Tuatha d'Dannan race who opted to stay and settle down with humans," I said.

"Well, there was a story many of our Drac ancestors shared regarding your race. It was said that the Tuatha d' Dannan line desired to grant their human families knowledge that would enable them to prolong their lives. Various spells and shared energy gave birth to the races known as witches and mediums. They brought gifts to their human families of Ireland, gifts that would enable them to enact these spells and prolong their lives. The two gifts or relics most made mention of were the Stone of Destiny and the Sword of Light."

There was a moment of silence as we contemplated what that could mean.

"Moridan peppered Chantara, Grizelda, and I with questions about what the diadem could do, even touching on eternal life," Crysta said. Her eyes looked a bit haunted as she thought back to her imprisonment. My grip on her tightened, not liking where those thoughts might lead. She shook herself and straightened in her seat. "It definitely sounds similar, but the timeline doesn't necessarily track. Didn't Oberon live for thousands of years?" Crysta asked.

"Yes, but The Rending took place around 300 BC, according to the human calendar," I said.

"And the Tuathas settled in Ireland by 600 BC," said Roderick.

"Tuathas?" Crysta asked.

"They were basic units or petty kingdoms of what is now referred to as the Gaelics."

"Gaelics? Man, you guys really did make your home in Ireland." Crysta wore a self-deprecating expression. "You know more about human history than I do, even though I spent all my life in the human realm."

"Under duress," I said. I gripped her hand, thinking about all she'd had to endure at the hands of her foster fathers and other males caught under her spell, something she'd had zero control over. She'd been surviving for so long. At some point I wanted to see her thriving and nothing else. I wanted her happy and safe, and I would never give up in my attempts to give her that life she so richly deserved. "Not much time for delving into the history of Gaelic Ireland."

"Fae history has always been intricately tied with humans, Princess," King Omer continued. "Fae are well-versed in our many excursions to the human realm. I would not be too hard on yourself. You are young yet. Plenty of time to learn."

I gave the king a grateful smile. Crysta was far too critical of herself.

"It's entirely possible that King Oberon entrusted the diadem to a member of my line during that time," I said.

"But the stone was entrusted to the Goblin King and he immediately hid it," Paio said. "And the diadem was given to a member of the Drac race. So that doesn't match up, either. Why would Oberon entrust the diadem to one of Jareth's line if he wanted the diadem hidden within the lake? Why give it to a Drac later on? And why this detour to the human realm?"

Fair questions, every single one. The legend seemed to make reference to the stone, but nothing else made much sense. And the diadem was not a sword.

"Wait a second," Crysta said. "According to this legend, the stone and sword were used to lengthen life, correct?"

"Yes."

"Okay, bear with me here because this is a stretch...but, we know the histories state that Oberon used children when attempting to rectify The Rending before the diadem and stone were dubbed too dangerous to be wielded. Your histories say that gifted children with more than one elemental magic were used, but those children failed."

"Crysta, what are you getting at?"

"What if Oberon decided not to risk any more faeries when it came to fixing The Rending? What if he had some of his subjects take the stone and diadem to Ireland and experiment on humans under the guise of bringing great knowledge and everlasting life?"

My eyes bounced from Roderick's, to Nuallan's, and then Kheelan's. We were all beginning to connect the dots.

"If that pans out—and we'll need to read more of Oberon's scrolls to discover the truth—then it is completely possible the stone and diadem were separated and hidden only after they were taken to the human realm."

"Which means?" Paio asked, looking a bit confused.

"Which means, we're not looking for a diadem," Crysta said. "We're looking for a sword."

∞ ∞ ∞

Crysta

"Whether sword or diadem, how does that help us locate it? How does knowing whether or not it was used in the human realm before it was hidden help us at this point?" Paio asked.

I held up a hand to prevent the questions I knew everyone had. My epiphany was just that. "We don't know if what I've theorized is even accurate," I said. "We need to read Oberon's accounting of that part of history as soon as possible, but if it is true, then that means we can look for any mention of the diadem or the Sword of Light within the archives, not to mention any of those terms tied to the Missing Ruins."

"It really is a good spot for hiding the diadem, but I have a hard time believing anyone would risk themselves to hide it within the Missing Ruins. That assignment would have been a suicide mission," Nuallan said.

I agreed. If the Vorsha were as dangerous as everyone said they were, then I didn't see the poor sap assigned to hide it escaping with his life. Then again, maybe that was why the Merfolk and the Drac didn't have any myths or legends discussing the diadem the way the Goblins did the stone. The one entrusted with its care never lived to document his failure or his success.

I said as much, which encouraged a new debate concerning other dangerous areas the bearer of the diadem could have hidden the precious artifact while perishing in the process. The back and forth of it all made me feel a bit weary.

It was time to act.

"I think we need to start digging. We came here with zero idea as to how to proceed once we reached the Dry Lands. We were quite literally going to start opening up books and begin reading. We've narrowed things down a bit. I say we take these leads and get started first thing tomorrow."

Jareth's eyes held a hint of pride mixed with some heady desire. Heady for me, anyway. Darn the man, the things those eyes, not to mention those lips, did to me.

"I agree with Crysta. Tomorrow we familiarize ourselves a little more with Oberon's accounting of history. Then we proceed to the Dry Lands and search from there." He motioned to the Dracs. "You are more than welcome to accompany us, but I fear it might be dangerous. Moridan and Titania have not yet attacked us again, but that doesn't mean they won't."

"We appreciate the invitation, Prince, but we must return. We have pressing matters to attend to. More bouts of *griesha* have broken out."

"Oh, no," I said. "How many?"

"We believe a few hundred have been struck with the disease. Princess. We know you will feel responsible to help in some way, but I think Titania's Diadem takes precedence. The sooner you find it, the sooner you can heal us all. But we must return to create order from the fear and chaos."

My eyes watered, thinking about all the faeries who were dying and would die as we tried to locate this relic. I couldn't save everyone. Not in time. It was a hopeless feeling, and I despised it.

"I'll fix this," I said. "I won't let you down."

The king gave me a smile that made my heart hurt a little. "We have absolute faith in your abilities, Princess."

"Thank you."

Kheelan shattered the touching moment by lazily getting to his feet and sauntering back toward the buffet.

"Well, I don't know about you lovely folks, but thinking of the next day's tasks leaves me feeling famished." He picked up a sparkling red bowl from the buffet and offered it to the masses. "Leafy greens, anyone?"

Crysta

"**W**hy didn't we continue reading this blasted book earlier?" Chantara asked as we all sat within the Merfolk's version of a study. The tiny creatures crawling in and out of what qualified as bookshelves distracted me to no end.

They were just so colorful. So diverse.

"We thought the information concerning locations was more important than anything else," Nuallan said. "I agree that it was an unfortunate oversight."

I gazed at our group, noting the tired lines etched in everyone's faces, not to mention a few smudge marks under the eyes.

Looked like no one had gotten much sleep last night, and the information Chantara had just discovered made for future nightmares.

"They were children," she said, hand shaking as she closed the scrolls. "Whether human or faerie, after that first child began wielding magic and lost his mind, my father should have seen reason and stopped."

"Not just children," I said.

Oberon had sent out several of Jareth's line to experiment on the unsuspecting, uneducated masses of Gaelic Ireland. According to his writings, his male subordinates spent several years finding humans of all ages who possessed strong energetic properties that could be used or channeled into various elemental magics. He wanted to test the energies of humans used to fuel faeries' cores, suspecting there might be more to these energies than met the eye. He aimed to bring forth multiple elemental magics within humans, magic strong enough to reverse The Rending.

He'd already destroyed several Fae children, why not try the experiment again with a different species?

Definition of insanity, anyone?

And boy did these humans deliver. Unfortunately, not in the way Oberon had hoped.

"When the stone and sword were used on these humans it resulted in magnified powers that the humans couldn't control, driving them madder than a hatter on steroids," I said.

"Please remember not all of us possess a slang dictionary, Princess," Nuallan said.

"They went nuts. Their physiology went nuts. We're seeing the birth of werewolves, vampires, witches, and who knows how many other paranormal creatures, all created from this experiment gone wrong. Not once were any of these humans' energies tethered to something that could keep them sane or keep the magic from bleeding out and changing them forever."

"The fated mate bond. It's always been the key, the anchor," Jareth said.

"Yet there were no more fated mate bonds," Kheelan said, shifting in his seat. "It never would have occurred to Oberon that this was the anchor or tether needed, the conduit through which the magic must run, because fated mate bonds had been destroyed. In order for his plan to work, he needed the very thing he was trying to restore, yet had already destroyed. It was a total Catch 22."

I raised my eyebrows at Kheelan's literary reference.

"What?" he said. "I had plenty of time to read while visiting the human realm."

"It still states that Oberon gave the diadem...or sword...to a Drac, yet King Omer and Queen Olean have no knowledge of this, no legends or histories that support this," Roderick said.

"It doesn't mean nothing has been recorded in their histories. The Dry Lands must be our next move."

"Is anyone trying to wrap their head around how the diadem became a sword? Why is it referenced as both things? It can't be both? And how is the sword used in conjunction with the stone?" I asked.

"At one point in our histories, ruling monarchs used various means to channel their powers, one being a stone centered at the apex of their crowns. They also used these crowns to aid them in battle by adhering them to their sword where the crown then became the hilt. The stone remaining the center point of their power. Imagine wielding a sword that channels and amplifies your power."

"It's something meant for kings," Chantara said.

"Yes, rarely did a female use such devices," said my father. "Yet from the sound of it, I think Titania must have been quite bloodthirsty after the deaths of her sons. It doesn't surprise me that she had her own sword fashioned in that manner."

"So there is a sword out there that amplifies power and was once wielded by a crazy, bloodthirsty queen who dabbled in the Dark Arts? Well, that's terrifying."

Jareth chuckled. "I think we've gathered as much information as we can. We need to move on to the Dry Lands and pinpoint an exact location."

"Agreed, but we must keep our destination a secret from Rena," Chantara said. "The last thing she needs to learn about is a powerful relic or where she can find it."

"What do you suggest?" my father asked.

"We'll need to leave the palace without tipping off the sentries. No one can know we've left, and no one can follow us."

"Mother, are you suggesting—"

"Yes. I'm giving you permission to sabotage the wards."

Paio rubbed his hands together like a happy child granted a full day of mischief.

"Won't that alert...everyone?" I asked. The rest of the group laughed, shaking their heads at Paio's antics. I gazed about in confusion. "What am I missing, here?"

"Paio has a rather unorthodox gift for imitating spells in a way that allows him to blend in as if he *is* the spell."

"Excuse me?"

"He can breach the ward by making it think he is an actual part of the ward. I learned that early on after he kept disappearing as a young child, giving me one heart attack after another."

Paio gave me a cheeky grin. "In other words, dearest Crysta, we'll take a hidden route out of the castle, and as I slowly breach the ward and become one with it, the rest of you will pass through safely."

"Pass through what?" I said, still not understanding how him becoming one with the wards was going to allow us to do the same.

"My legs."

I turned to Jareth. "Let me know when he's making sense."

"However undignified it may be," Chantara said, giving me a little smirk, "we will all be crawling in between Paio's legs to get past the wards unnoticed."

Really? I expected Mission Impossible antics here, and instead, we were going to crawl in between Paio's legs? "That's like the faerie equivalent of doing it the ghetto way."

"Ghetto?" Nuallan asked, giving Jareth an expectant look.

Jareth shrugged. "I can't translate everything she says."

∞ ∞ ∞

We had to play it cool for the rest of the day since sneaking out of the palace in the evening after we had all retired to our room was far more advantageous. Chantara stated that her room was linked to various hidden caverns and passageways running within the palace that only she knew about. One of the many things she had never bothered to share with Rena.

Wise.

Fortunately for us, she'd made sure Criva gave us rooms connected to hers through all those awesome little passageways. We'd be meeting up in her room tonight with Rena none the wiser.

Jareth suggested we rest in our room for a while. He'd suggested it for my sake. Between *griesha,* my wound, and the constant drain on my magic, epic waves of fatigue hit me at the worst moments.

As soon as we returned to our room, he scooped me up in his arms and nestled his warm nose against my cheek.

"How are you, Crysta?"

I decided to lie since showing him the red spots that had climbed past my elbow to my shoulder would only worry him, and I needed less alpha male in my corner.

"Just a little sleepy. Not a thing to worry about."

"Says the woman suffering from *griesha.* You'll tell me when you need to rest? We don't have to leave with the others. There are plenty of us to look at the histories if you need to stay and conserve your energy."

I narrowed my eyes, pulling back from his nuzzling—it was super distracting—and giving him a suspicious glare.

"Are you trying to get rid of me? You don't want me coming along?"

"You'll have to use another spell to swim to the Dry Lands, and it's a good fifteen-minute swim from here. It will drain you, causing *griesha* to spread. Crysta, the more magic you use, the faster the disease eats away at you. I think it would be best if you remained here."

"Not a chance. I'm going. There will be a ton of records to go over. They'll need my eyes just as much as they'll need yours. We can't be down two people when it is so vital that we find out exactly where the sword or diadem is."

Jareth looked frustrated, but not a bit surprised. More like resigned to it all. He gently set me down and put his arm around me, and I couldn't have been more grateful. My legs had almost given out on me. Showing him just how bad off I was would not do much in the way of convincing him I could handle the journey to the Dry Lands. I needed some food and some rest if I wanted to make it out there without showing the wear and tear on my body and energy.

I rested my head against his chest and asked, "Just how much do you love me?"

"I think you already know the answer to that."

"Excellent. I'll need several bowls of fruit, a large salad, heavy on the dressing, and an assortment of nuts." I tapped him lightly on the nose. "Don't forget something to drink."

"I require payment first." Jareth's eyes lowered to my lips, becoming hooded with desire.

"How much is this gonna cost me?"

"At least a full minute of sweet kisses."

I lifted up on my tip-toes and gently kissed his yummy lips. "I think I can handle that."

And the minute was absolutely delicious.

Jareth gently released me, and it took everything I had to stay on my feet. My illness combined with Jareth's kisses were enough to make any woman's knees nonfunctional.

"I'll be back in a few."

The moment the door shut behind him, I sank to my knees, feeling too lightheaded to make it to the bed. After a few moments of rest, I finally managed to make it to my feet, just in time for a sharp knock at the door. I answered it, thinking it was Criva, but the happy smile I'd prepared for him froze on my face at the sight of Rena standing in the hallway, looking serene in a way that had the hairs on the back of my neck raising in alarm.

"Regent? Can I help you?"

Her smile didn't reach her eyes, and I noted those eyes didn't miss anything. Sharp and calculating, I wagered she saw through most anyone. Good thing I'd already slipped my game face on.

"I wanted to come by and give you a report of the races afflicted by *griesha*." She handed me a stack of papers.

I tried not to look startled, but I couldn't account for this visit to me. "That was fast. I'm amazed you were able to gather this information so quickly."

"We haven't a moment to lose when lives are at stake. Wouldn't you agree, Princess?" She blinked wide, innocent eyes. I had the strangest urge overcome me. One that ended with her flat on her back after my fist met her face. I pushed away the feeling of aggression.

"I do agree. Thank you so much for getting this report to me as quickly as you did. Were you able to give a copy of the report to the queen?"

Rena visibly tried to rein in her temper at the mention of Chantara's title. "Of course." She pasted on a smile. "I thought it best that you both have one. I took the liberty of calling an assembly together to discuss the current state of affairs and your plans with the ruling monarchs in our lake. They will be most anxious to discover how you wish to cure the plague. I've informed them you'll be able to do so immediately. We must have confidence in our future heir to the Unseelie Court, after all."

She'd already called an underwater assembly to order and made promises we were nowhere near ready to meet. She'd overstepped her bounds for sure, and she knew it.

She must have caught my troubled expression.

"Oh, were you not planning on doing for them what you did for the Drac and the Annis?"

I was surprised she'd referred to them by Annis instead of Hag. It was just so politically correct of her.

"We are. We simply need to see which races will be most compatible with the others. We will also need Lord Raith present to discern fated mate bonds between races and couples."

"Oh, I apologize. I didn't realize things would be so involved. Fortunately, the assembly will not happen until tomorrow morning. I'm sure that will give you plenty of time to contact Lord Raith."

Rena had backed us into a corner and taken up precious time that should have been spent searching the histories of the Dry Lands. Not to mention over-promising. I couldn't do any more bondings. The toll it took on my body and my magic was too much for me. All that we would be able to accomplish with that assembly would be informing the races we had a cure and discussing pairings. And it wasn't something we were prepared to do just yet.

Rena had called our bluff by organizing an assembly without Chantara's consent.

I couldn't allow Rena to know that she'd rattle me.

"I'll have Jareth contact Lord Raith right away. I know the Dark Elf is just as anxious to save others from *griesha* as you are."

Her smile faltered for a second at the mention of Jareth.

"Yes. Jareth. He does have many friends in high places, doesn't he? Not to mention lady friends." She leaned in as if getting ready to pass on a dirty secret. "I vividly recall a dinner I held here...oh...must have been a few years ago...when he and Rhoswen announced their engagement. I couldn't have been happier for him. Yet it surprised me when he began making overtures to me. It isn't uncommon for royalty to engage in affairs, but I had thought he was wholly devoted to Rhoswen, though I can't deny my own ability to charm males."

"Oh, yes. There's no denying you're something else," I said.

Her eyes narrowed for a moment but that predatory smile never left her face. "You're such a young, innocent thing. It won't be your fault when he strays here and there. Just know this is part of keeping your prince happy. A few little trysts here and there are nothing. At least, they were simply fun and games when he and I had our little fling."

The very thought of Jareth ever partaking of this heinous wench's wares nearly had me laughing out loud. I knew what she was doing, and I knew Jareth's character. She wanted to create a wedge between me and Jareth.

Pathetic, really.

"I'm grateful for the advice, coming from someone so well versed in sharing husbands, I'm sure you understand how necessary it is for men to meet their needs. Though I truly believe that you and Chantara deserved a husband a bit more faithful."

Ah, it was spiteful. Never was much for the high road.

Plus, I didn't agree with a word I'd just spouted.

Rena maintained her smile, but if that tick in her jaw was any indication, it cost her big time.

"Yes, well, it's been so wonderful to chat with you. Can't wait to do it again."

"Yes, I'm sure you know I feel the same. Thank you again for your help."

She inclined her head in response. "I'm always so happy to give it."

"I'll bet you are."

She stared me down for a few more seconds, brightened her smile, and then turned on her heel and headed down the corridor with a few sentries in her wake.

I shut the door and rested my forehead against it, feeling a pounding headache crossing the back of my skull.

Her comments about Jareth hadn't hurt me at all. I was more worried about the assembly and the time it would waste. I blinked heavy eyelids and turned toward the bed, barely making it to the mattress before I lost my balance.

So tired.

I set the report to the side and bowed my head for a moment, taking in deep breaths to steady my nerves as I pulled the sleeve of my tunic over my shoulder. The dots hadn't gone past the fabric. Good sign. I lifted the sleeve of my other arm and noticed spots covering the length of it.

Hmmmm.

Well, that was new. I lifted my tunic up, exposing my belly and gasped in horror. Not only was my stomach covered in red dots, some of them were larger than they had been before, looking red and angry.

I pulled my tunic down, staring at my hands without really seeing them.

If I showed Jareth the progress my illness had made, he wouldn't let me go to the Dry Lands. Jareth could only be pushed so far, and I knew I wouldn't win if he had any idea how bad this had become.

I may have been the cure, but I was carrying the illness, and I didn't have more than a few weeks left to go before the disease took me. If I was getting this bad, then Terise was probably much worse.

We were running out of time.

∞ ∞ ∞

"I'm glad you were able to make it," Chantara said as the rest of us gathered in a semi-circle to face her.

"The passageways were a tight fit," Nuallan said under his breath.

I stared at him in surprise, taking note of his pale features and the sheen of sweat covering his forehead. How nice to find another claustrophobic in our midst. Misery loves company.

"I'm afraid our timeline has been upped. We'll need to be back by early morning," Jareth said, sharing what I had told him about Rena's visit.

"Yes, Rena was kind enough to let me know she had already called the assembly together," Chantara said. Her obsidian eyes gave away her irritation. "You'll have all night to look for clues in the Dry Lands. I'm going to remain here and keep up appearances. I'll gather the assembly together and start explaining our findings. Lord Raith should be arriving tonight, so at the very least, he can begin explaining his part in the pairing process." Chantara's concerned look switched to me, and she hesitated for a moment before saying, "Crysta, I'm afraid you and Jareth will have to do at least one bonding, just to show our fellow underwater Fae that this is possible. I worry it will be hard for them to believe let alone accept. We have varying degrees of openmindedness amongst the different races of Fae."

"We can manage one," I said, speaking up before Jareth could refuse the request. The grim set to his jaw spoke volumes, but we had little choice. Rena had forced our hand.

"If you're going to have to expend that kind of energy, perhaps it is best you stay put and rest," my father said.

"Ah, Dad, not you too."

He wrapped an arm around my shoulder. "You don't look well, Crysta."

"I'll be fine." I gave Chantara a firm look. "Where do we exit from here?"

Chantara stared at me for a moment, measuring my stubborn expression. She wanted to argue, but she also appeared proud of my persistence.

"Follow me," she said.

Chantara led us through her master bedroom and straight into a gigantic bathroom that rivaled any spa I'd ever seen...in magazines, that is. I hadn't had much money or time to spend pampering myself.

She immediately walked over to a full-length mirror wide enough for two people to stand side-by-side and still be seen.

"When this palace was first created, I had a very talented Goblin create this mirror for me. While it does the job it's supposed to do, it also acts as a hidden muma."

"A muma?" I asked. "Do mean there's a muma inside?"

"I mean, it *is* the muma. The substance that makes up the mirror will give with pressure. Simply walk through and you will step right into a muma that is hidden under an alcove near the wards, a good thirty yards from the outskirts of the palace and surrounding city. You'll need to spell yourselves before walking through so you will have time to adjust to the pressure. To return with no one the wiser, you must have Paio take you back through the wards and the hidden alcove. You can then return to your rooms via the passageways."

"How very cloak and dagger," Kheelan said. "I'm going first."

Within moments he had transformed back into the same underwater form he had taken on the shores of Lake Beatha. Jareth, Nuallan, and my father followed suit. I had to dig a little deeper to harness my core magic, recite the words, and recreate my own spell. I felt the drain immediately and could have sworn my legs were tingling as a result. I didn't know what that meant, but I also didn't look forward to finding out.

"Remember, get back here before the assembly," she said.

Kheelan went through first, followed by Paio and Nuallan.

"After you, Crysta," my father said, concern coloring his tone.

I must have looked like hell. I walked straight toward the mirror before either he or Jareth could change their minds. There was a bit of resistance as my hands pressed on the mirror's surface, but then that pliability that reminded me so much of jello kicked in, and I stepped into the mirror, or rather, the muma. A heaviness descended over me as my body adjusted to the pressure of being under hundreds of pounds of water. I spotted Kheelan and Nuallan just outside the bubble, remaining in the alcove but keeping an eye out for passing sentries as Paio continued to sneak forward near a dome-like surface that glowed a bluish-green.

The wards. We really were close to them. I took another step forward, feeling the muma pop me out into the water like a bottle of soda shaken, not stirred. Kheelan immediately grabbed my hand as the momentum from the muma nearly launched me from the alcove. Jareth and my father followed closely behind.

Paio moved into position, turning to face us with arms spread wide. He slowly backed into the ward, moving his legs a far enough distance to create a crawl space for us. I watched in awe as the color of the wards slowly covered Paio's skin, as if he were actually absorbing them. Within seconds his entire body merged with the wards and blended in. The only outward sign of him were his glowing eyes and the outline of his body.

"You still have the stone?" I asked, suddenly feeling nervous about...everything.

"It's spelled and hidden on my person, Crysta. No one can take it from me unless it is given. Let's move."

I allowed their powerful fins to propel me forward. I didn't mind admitting to weakness when doing anything else jeopardized the game plane. I didn't swim fast enough, and honestly, I didn't have the energy to try. Kheelan and Nuallan had already swam their way between Paio's legs by the time Jareth and my father brought me over. I knelt down and used my feet to push me through the opening, kicking my legs only after I had cleared his so I could get out of the way while Jareth and my father swam through.

Then we floated a few feet away as we watched Paio back through the energy field until he had also cleared the ward. The color bled from his skin until he stood at the bottom of the lake's depths. Then he turned, and in a burst of bubbles, he transformed into his aquatic form.

I had to admit, Paio was every teen girl's fantasy when it came to mermaid romances. Jet black hair, eyes to die for, a physique that screamed protector. I had a lot of faerie friends who deserved a fated mate. I wondered where I'd find Paio's.

"We need to get moving," he said.

Kheelan and Jareth took me by the arms and swam me forward, following Paio's lead. The landscape before us was barely discernible this late at night. At these depths, it seemed that moonlight couldn't penetrate.

"How do you guys know where we're going?" I asked.

"Sorry, love," Jareth said. "Our forms allow for special night vision. The suit you're encased in probably doesn't offer up special perks like enhanced eyesight."

"No kidding." I kicked my legs to aid in the swimming, but after a few minutes I stopped. Better to allow them to do all the work while I enjoyed the sensation of flying through a dark and endless abyss. I think I could have fallen asleep for a few minutes if I hadn't been so amped up with adrenaline from our sneaky escape.

"Are you doing okay?" Kheelan asked.

I remained silent for a moment, needing to tell Kheelan my concerns for Terise, but not knowing how to do that without spilling the beans to him and Jareth about how far my own disease had progressed.

"Do you remember what we talked about, concerning Terise?" I asked.

I didn't like the whole zero visibility issue. I'd only ever been able to read Kheelan's true emotions, the man behind the facade, so long as I could see the facade and read his eyes.

"What of it?" he finally said.

"She has the right to choose, and you'll need to give that to her. Soon."

"She can't choose. She's been cursed...because of me."

"Kheelan—"

"There are heroes and there are villains in every fairytale, Crysta. Please remember who always gets the girl in the end."

"I believe our more modern fairytales have become pretty progressive. Women and men pave their own way and make their own choices, and those choices aren't always black and white. They're not always clean and precise. Love is messy, Kheelan, and people are complex. Terise is no Disney Princess."

He chuckled low and squeezed my hand. "Well, I think it's safe to say that I am no Prince Charming."

"You're right. You happen to be so much more."

Jareth let out a low laugh on my other side. "What my wise fated mate is trying to get you to understand is Terise doesn't want or need clean and precise. She's not interested in Prince Charming. She's looking for Flynn Rider."

"Flynn...who?"

"You're the one who referenced a male Disney hero," Jareth grumbled. "Did you never watch *Tangled?*

"Why in the world would I have ever watched...wait, did *you* willingly subject yourself to an animated Disney movie?"

"The things you boys will do for your fated mates," I said. "Heaven help you if Terise ever discovers the six-hour, BBC version of *Pride and Prejudice.*"

Crysta

*A*fter several more minutes of swimming through complete and total darkness, I sensed us taking a sharp right as our speed gradually decreased. We dove lower, slowly moving into a single-file line with Kheelan pulling me behind him and Jareth taking my waist and pushing me forward. Up ahead I saw slight illumination that grew brighter the further we went. After a few more minutes, we entered a circular cavern where the illumination came from above.

Jareth caught me in a cradle hold and then shot us toward the light, breaking the surface of the water in the process.

I gazed about the circular pool and then watched as Paio swam toward a set of steps leading up to a door made of onyx. His tail swiftly morphed into legs as he ascended the stairs. He pressed his hand to the area where a knob should have been and faintly whispered some unintelligible words. The door swung inward, and Paio looked behind him, beckoning us forward.

"You'll be able to drop your spell the moment we get inside," Jareth said.

Good. Exhaustion lapped at my energy like a parched dog in a desert oasis. We followed Paio through the door and into a small entryway that then opened up into a larger area, I'm talking ballroom sized, with ceilings a good thirty feet above us. And within this enormous location were housed hundreds of bookcases so tall they nearly reached the ceiling. It was grander and more ostentatious than any library I'd ever visited, not to mention a few legendary libraries in Europe that I'd merely dreamed of visiting.

A beautiful woman wearing a sequined gown of light blues and pinks slowly approached us, her smile serene. Her blue and pink stripes of hair were weaved into a side braid that reached her waist. Obviously a mermaid, but I wondered what her tail looked like based on her colorful dress and hair.

I loved the diversity.

When she caught sight of Paio, her eyes widened and her face paled. She stood for a moment looking about ready to wilt.

"Paio?" she said.

Paio smiled wide and caught her up in an exuberant hug, totally overwhelming her.

"I've missed you, Shay. How have you been?"

"How have I...you..." she pulled away, staring at him in disbelief. "You have been missing for over two years. We all thought you were dead."

"Held against my will by King Moridan is more like it, but my friends helped me escape," he said, gesturing toward us.

Shay barely acknowledged us as she continued to stare at Paio like she'd seen a ghost. I truly hated my gift for reading people. It was damn obvious that she had feelings for Paio, had been mourning his loss, and now he suddenly showed up out of the blue while she scrambled to deal with the knowledge that this male she cared for was indeed alive.

She swallowed hard and blinked a few times before pasting on a smile.

Paio appeared oblivious to her tumultuous emotions. It appeared that the males in this realm were just as clueless as the ones in the human realm.

"My Prince, we had no idea you intended to visit the Dry Lands. I will alert the other scribes as to your presence and bring you refreshment."

Paio gently placed a hand on her shoulder, causing the woman to blush a charming pink.

"No need, Shay. In fact, we would prefer that only a very few are aware of our visit. Don't alert anyone, especially Rena."

Shay's face hardened. "As if I'd ever give that harpy information concerning you or our queen. I'm convinced she is the reason you..." She took a deep breath, catching herself before sharing something important, I suspected. I figured she didn't want to say too much in front of the rest of us. She had no idea who we were or if we could be trusted.

I liked her already.

"How can I be of service then?" she asked.

I stepped forward. "We're looking for books on the Missing Ruins, histories of Fae in Ireland around 300 BC, Drac histories, and anything concerning the Sword of Light."

"Oh, ah, and you are?" Shay appeared extremely uncomfortable.

"It's fine, Shay. My mother is aware of our presence here, and she would want you to help us. May I present Crystiana Tuadhe d'Anu and King Roderick of the Unseelie Court. You know the rest of these men."

Shay's lips paled in the face of so many royals.

"So nice to meet you, Princess. We have heard rumor after rumor of your return to our realm. I never imagined I would have the opportunity to meet you." She came forward and grabbed my hand, placing her forehead on my knuckles and whispering a few words in a language I didn't understand.

"She's giving you an old Mer greeting to welcome you here," Paio said.

"Oh, well, here's a greeting from the human realm," I said.

I stepped forward and embraced Shay, giving her a hearty hug much like Paio had. She stiffened only for a moment before she laughed and engaged in the hug.

"Thank you, Crysta," she said as she stepped back. "And yes, I know exactly where our volumes on those subjects are. If you'll just have a seat, I can bring them to you."

She indicated an area in the center of the mass of bookshelves where several pieces of furniture sat cozy and inviting. I eyed the cream-colored sofa. Just the thought of curling up on those soft cushions made my eyes involuntarily shut.

Our group moved toward the lounge area, all except for Nuallan, that is. I watched him as his eyes followed Shay until she disappeared down the hall behind a bookcase.

"Nuallan," I said in a hushed tone.

He continued to stare after Shay, his brows narrowed, and his mouth pursed in a thin line.

"Nuallan," I said, more forcefully this time.

His gaze snapped to me, startled as if he had forgotten where he was and who he was with.

"Are you okay?"

He let out a slow hiss of air before stepping forward. "I'm fine."

I stared after Shay and then watched Nuallan find a spot on one of the couches next to Paio. He seemed fine, but that look on his face as he'd watched Shay walk away indicated he felt anything but fine.

I recognized that look.

I saw it every time Jareth looked at me.

A heady mixture of longing and desire.

∞ ∞ ∞

"I can't find anything in the Drac histories about a sword or a diadem," Nuallan said as he slammed another book shut.

"I'm not exactly faring any better as far as Irish histories go." Jareth kicked his leg up on an ornate table and flipped another page. "As far as I can tell, our ancestors mixed and mingled with humans, passed down specific powers, but there is nothing here about a sword or stone mutating humans or driving them insane. Certainly nothing to report as far as Oberon handing off a magical relic to a member of the Drac race. Whatever we're looking for, it wasn't documented here."

I closed the book I read and massaged my temples. "All I've discovered about the Missing Ruins is the answer to several human mysteries in regards to some missing ships such as the San Miguel and The Merchant Royal. Apparently, places like the Bermuda Triangle are not just an old wives' tale. I can't imagine all the ships, boats, not to mention humans, who've gone missing in that area alone. The good news is, the first discovery of the Missing Ruins happened round 300 BC. So we know it existed as far back as Oberon's reign, but it doesn't say when Vorsha settled in the area."

"Maybe it isn't relevant as to whether or not the Vorsha were there during that time. A graveyard full of ships isn't a bad place to hide treasure." Nuallan said.

"It is if there is nothing there to guard it. The stone was guarded by a dragon and several dangerous tests. I highly doubt Oberon tasked a Drac to simply dump one of the most dangerous relics of our time in an area that would have been teaming with other treasures. Without Vorsha to ward off intruders, the place would have been picked clean by faeries and underwater creatures alike."

"So we need to know if Vorsha were present during that time. If not, then the Missing Ruins is not where we should be focusing our energies. All I've found here are documentaries of those who lost loved ones to Vorsha while exploring the Missing Ruins, and even then there isn't much to report, and not a hint as to when Vorsha settled there." I rubbed my eyes this time, hoping Kheelan or my father had found something in the pile of books they'd been going through.

"We're running out of time," my father said. "We have theories and speculation. No concrete direction. We can't go searching dangerous areas unless we have probable cause for doing so."

"How about we take a break. I'll grab us some snacks, and then we'll get back to work," Paio said.

I excused myself to use the restroom, but as I walked down one of the book aisles, a sudden thought occurred to me. I turned around and went in search of Shay. I found her a few aisles over, peeking through a space on the shelf. I slowly approached and looked over her shoulder. A small smile tugged at the corner of my mouth as I spotted Paio returning with food.

"He is quite handsome, don't you think?" I asked.

Shay jumped, spinning around quickly with one hand over her heart.

"Oh, Princess, I am so sorry. I wasn't trying to spy on you."

I waved my hand. "I don't think you're spying, Shay. I think Paio intrigues you and you're getting a better look at him without him being the wiser."

She bit her bottom lip, but not before I caught the embarrassed smile.

"It's nothing. To be honest, I was watching all of you. I suppose I've been stuck cataloguing these books for far too long. I probably need to start socializing more instead of behaving as if I haven't seen people in years."

I wanted to press her further, but she looked so embarrassed I decided to give her a break.

"Shay, I know this will sound bizarre, but do you have any books on the Vorsha?"

She pursed her lips for a moment. "In the many years I've worked here I have never once catalogued or cleaned any manuscripts pertaining to the Vorsha, but that does not mean they do not exist. As you can see, the libraries are vast, and this is but one area of our archives."

"This is one area? Just how many areas...no, never mind. Let's just focus on Vorsha."

"Come with me," she said, appearing eager to help.

We went in the opposite direction of the lounge, past the many aisle of books and through a separate door that opened up into an ivory room with a simple well of water in the middle. Shay approached the well and ran her fingers through the aqua colored water.

"Since you are the one seeking the book, I think it best you make the request." She ushered me to the well.

"I don't think I understand."

"The Well of Knowledge has been spelled with all the books' locations. Think of it as your own personal computer."

"You've been to the human realm, I take it?"

Her smile faltered for a moment. "Not for long. My mother took me on a brief trip, but we never returned."

It seemed like a touchy subject, so I decided to push away the nosiness I felt and not pry.

But ignoring the impulse wasn't easy.

"So this well can tell me where the histories of the Vorsha might be located?"

"Vorsha. Dangerous aquatic species." I jumped at the female voice emanating from the well. "Ancestral origins unknown. References accounted for within area two, aisle seventeen, shelf 1346."

Shay beamed up at me and clapped her hands. "I know exactly where that is. I'll take you there at once."

She grabbed my hand and pulled me away from the well.

"Thank you," I shouted back.

"You are welcome," the well said in an eerie monotone.

Shay laughed as we passed through the door. "I don't think I've ever thanked the Well of Knowledge before. The fact that she answered back is hilarious."

"Seems like a very ancient piece of architecture. Just how long have these libraries and archives been around?"

"A long time," Shay said.

We took a left and headed down another corridor where a long hallway opened up into another huge section of bookshelves.

"This is area two. We just need to find aisle seventeen...let's see, ten, eleven..."

I allowed her to lead me along, enjoying her enthusiasm and the chance to be around another female who appeared as young at heart as I wanted to be. I didn't think anything got Shay down for too long.

"Seventeen," she declared, taking another right and pulling me in between the bookshelves. She absently brushed away a pixie as she searched the shelves looking for 1346. Once she found it, she began studying the titles of the books on that particular shelf and finally pulled out a thin, blue book that looked to be in mint condition.

Seriously, it didn't seem like anyone had turned its pages in years.

I grabbed it and flipped it open, only to discover yet another foreign language I couldn't read.

"That was the only one on the shelf. Honestly, I'm surprised we even have one. Not many would dare study the creatures, and I can't imagine anyone living through that kind of research. We only know what we do about them due to the few who ever survived at the expense of others being taken."

I put my arm around her and gave her shoulders a squeeze, feeling happier by the minute as my eyes landed on a drawing of an underwater shipwreck, a Vorsha, and a Drac bearing a sword in defense of his life.

Telling information right there. I'd hit the jackpot.

"Shay, you are my new best friend."

"Oh. Well, thank you, Princess."

She appeared truly touched by my flippant words which made me decide right then and there that my flippant words were actually something I meant. I wanted her to be my friend.

"Once all of this settles down, how about a slumber party at the Unseelie palace."

Her eyes glowed with happiness as she said, "Can we do mani-pedis? I've always wanted to do them, but other Mermaids here don't get the appeal."

I couldn't hold back my laughter as I steered her toward the lounge.

"Mani-pedis and pillow fights."

She let out a happy sigh. "Perfect."

"This book was actually written by the Drac who was charged by Oberon to hide the diadem," Jareth said.

"He even drew his own battle with a Vorsha," Nuallan said.

Jareth read the thin book after skimming through some of the events that matched up with Oberon's scrolls.

"Neither faerie nor human can wield the diadem and net the results we so desperately desire, even when attaching it to Titania's sword. All our attempts at righting The Rending have failed, bringing greater calamities to humans who cannot handle the influx in power nor the disease that once afflicted our own people. Plagues have broken out among the humans. Magical creatures, once human, now roam the human realm. I fear we have tampered with something we do not understand, and Titania's power is dangerous, reaching through realms and dimensions to continue wreaking havoc. Puck fights us at every turn, attacking human and faerie alike, waging a war he cannot hope to win, and blaming our king for his loss of power and the woman he loved."

"Interesting," I said. "Oberon never mentioned anything about Puck losing his power, but I can see how they might be at war with one another over the banishment of Titania."

"The war lasted for so long," my father said. "Our histories state that Puck was more the hero and Oberon the villain, but it is helpful to know the truth. Puck and Titania wanted mass genocide. Titania was sent to hell, so to speak, Puck was stripped of his powers, though I'm not sure how that happened, and blamed Oberon for the loss of everything. So while Oberon was trying to right The Rending, Puck continually brought war to his front door."

"How did he wage war if he lost his power?" I asked. "Wouldn't core magic be crucial when going up against Oberon and his soldiers?"

"I doubt Puck fought at all," Jareth said. "Most likely he had his followers battle for him." He skimmed over the page, stopping in the middle and taking more time to read.

"Puck circles ever closer to Titania's power, and the sword is unstable. It cannot be destroyed, but it can be dismantled. It is our only option at this point. I have been tasked by Oberon to take the sword and diadem to a

242

place Puck will never be able to locate. A place he will have no magical power to survive."

We waited as Jareth fell silent, his eyes widening in disbelief. He cleared his throat and continued. *"I have barely survived with my life. Upon traveling toward the Drac kingdom, I happened upon a graveyard of two enormous ships."*

"Just two? There are hundreds of ships in the Missing Ruins now," Paio said.

"The presence of these ships was alarming," Jareth continued. *"Even more so due to the human craftsmanship. I could not understand how human ships had arrived at the lowest depths of our lake. I decided to investigate, swimming into the broken hull of one and finding chests filled with treasure beyond anything I had ever seen. The bodies of drowned humans were also present. They hadn't been there long, but every single one had drowned. There was no saving them. Such a waste of good men."*

"Jareth," I said. "Do you think the use of the stone and the sword in the human realm might have caused various imbalances in Earth's electromagnetic fields, causing Earth and the Fae realm to be connected through the lake?"

"Now that is a good theory," he said. "No one has ever had an explanation as to how the Missing Ruins could be tied to Earth, and with only two ships present at the time this Drac discovered it, well, the timeline certainly seems to match up."

"The enormity of what Titania's diadem can do," my father said looking shaken. "To hold enough power to cause so much destruction, even tampering with the lines between realms on a global level. How do we know Crysta will survive wielding such power once she has it? It could kill her."

"It won't," I said, faking confidence. I couldn't afford for that thought to get planted in anyone's head. The diadem was our last hope here.

"I agree, Crysta. Once we attain the diadem, there's no telling what it might do to you," Jareth said,

"Hold on. Listen. This is the only choice we have. Without it, I die anyway. With it, I have a fighting chance, and so does everyone else." I grabbed Jareth's hand. "Never forget we have something Oberon could never have: a fated mated bond. We can do this, Jareth." I reached up and caressed his cheek. "I can do this. Now keep reading."

Jareth's jaw clenched tight for a moment, but he got himself together and flipped to the next page. *"The treasures were valuable to be sure. I felt it imperative that I alert my brother, The King, to the valuables found within our waters."*

"Our waters?" I interrupted. "Did Drac rule the lake back then?"

"If you'll remember, Crysta, my mother was the first of her kind and a mere child during this time," Paio said. "She didn't ascend as queen of the Merfolk until there were actually enough Merfolk to consider them a tribe, then a village, and then an actual race. Once she gained enough power, the rule of the lake and its magic was granted to her by Oberon. There was some uneasiness and discord for a while among the races of the sea, but everyone grew to love my mother."

"I can easily believe that," I said.

Jareth cleared his throat, reminding me we'd gone off on a tangent.

"As I swam from the hull of the ship, hurrying to report my findings and deliver the sword to my brother, I encountered one of the Vorsha, a deadly creature my kind has failed time and time again to kill. I had not expected its presence, their hunting grounds were several leagues from this area, and yet one floated before me, its tentacles spinning from its head. Its humanoid form all the more eerie due to the fact that it is a creature, a predator with nothing but animal instinct for intelligence. I wielded Titania's sword high, forgetting momentarily that the stone had been removed. I could have

defeated it with the stone. Without it, the magic was gone, the sword heavy and cumbersome underneath the water. One tentacle lashed out, grabbing the end of the sword and pulling it from my hands. The moment the Vorsha wrapped its hands around the hilt, a bright light flashed, the signal that always preceded certain death for anyone unfortunate enough to run into a Vorsha."

"I closed my eyes, prepared to meet the goddess, but after a moment nothing happened. I opened my eyes to find the Vorsha gone. A noise behind me alerted me to another's presence. I spun around and found that same Vorsha clutching the sword to its chest, staring at me with those soulless eyes as two other Vorsha flanked him. I did not hesitate. I did not fight. I simply fled. Oberon believes the sword to be hidden somewhere safe within the Drac kingdom. He shall never know the truth, and I fear I have destroyed the fate of the Fae realm. There is one who will wield it again. One who will save us all. The Fates have decreed it. Yet I alone know the sword and diadem shall never be found again. Goddess save us all."

Kheelan exploded with some colorful language. I felt like throwing out a few four-letter words myself.

"It's not just in the Missing Ruins. It wasn't deposited in some chest within one of the wrecked ships. Oh, no. Handed over to a Vorsha. Do you know what this means?" Kheelan asked. "It could be anywhere. We have no way of knowing if that sword stayed with the pod of Vorsha living in the Missing Ruins or if it was fought over by others, taken to other hunting grounds, other pods, or if the creatures got sick of the shiny object and simply abandoned it at the bottom of the lake. We are never going to find the damn thing."

"At least we have a place to start," Nuallan said. "We go to the Missing Ruins. We do reconnaissance. We figure out where their nest is, and we find a way to lure them out."

My father appeared shaken by this. "Do you have any idea what a pod of Vorsha could do to us? We would have to make certain that we lured everyone out and combined our magic to spell them all at once. We'll need Chantara's aid in this. I'm wondering if we need to call on Adris and Cedric as well just to increase our power."

"You're thinking we perform an *Iuncturam Imperium*," Jareth asked.

"Can you think of any other way to paralyze them as we send someone in to raid the nest and look for the sword and diadem?"

"What's a...whatever you just said?" I asked.

"An *Iuncturam Imperium* is literally translated to mean joint power. We combine core powers to fuel a spell, making it much stronger and further reaching than it would normally be. To paralyze the Vorsha, we would need extensive aid. If we are dealing with nearly twenty Vorsha, then several powerful magic wielders must be at work."

"Well, everyone in our group is a royal or from a powerful race. Add my powers into the mix, and I think we have more than enough of a chance to subdue the Vorsha long enough for one of us to go looking for the relic," I said.

All the color drained from Jareth's face as the room became uncomfortably quiet. He looked at me as if I'd lost my mind.

"Absolutely not," he said in a faint voice.

"Huh?"

"You're not going anywhere near the Missing Ruins."

"Excuse me?"

"I'll not allow it."

"*Allow it?* You don't exactly have a choice. You guys need me, and I am not being benched for this."

I noticed Nuallan slowly inching away from the room, the rest of the group doing the same.

Jareth's eyes grew hard as stone, his expression as unyielding as granite. "I've put up with about as much as I can handle when it comes to risks to your safety, and I will do absolutely everything I must to keep you from leaving the palace. You are not going with us. You will not be put at risk. You're not even remotely ready for something like this."

Anger flared within me. I knew I was weak and fragile. I knew that I had massive power, but still lacked the appropriate training, but I'd been doing pretty damn good so far, even improvising off the cuff and saving all their arses in the process. I could do this, and I needed Jareth to believe in me. The fact that he didn't sent a sharp pang through my chest.

"You can't keep me out of this. I'm going to be queen someday, and I can't hide behind my fated mate every time something is dangerous."

"Hide?" He let out a derisive snort. "You've never hidden from danger a day in your life, and I've put you right in danger's path time and time again."

"You need to start believing in me," I said. "I'm not some fragile waif."

His eyes burned with fury. He grabbed me roughly by the arms and shook me a bit as if trying to get me to wake up. "Believe in you? I've never stopped. I know exactly what your destiny is and what you must accomplish, but you can't have any of that if you go barreling in without considering your situation. When do I get to protect you, Crysta? When will you trust me enough to follow my lead and take my counsel? There is a time to fight and there is a time to withdraw. You are compromised by *griesha*. Every single spell you cast accelerates your illness. This is not about you proving some point. This is about the thousands of Fae you put at risk every time you put yourself at risk."

I swallowed hard as I realized he was right. I'd been trying so hard to prove myself, trying too hard to avoid being that weak link, that my own pride had gotten in the way, fueled by my insecurities.

And it was killing me. Literally.

"You're right," I said.

Jareth opened his mouth as if to argue but stopped short at my words. "What?"

"You're right. I am compromised, and I am being reckless by pushing my own limits. This isn't about proving myself right now. This is about achieving our goal, even if I have to sit this one out." I lifted my hand and pushed his hair away from his stormy eyes. "I know I'm headstrong and stubborn, but I hear you, and I know you are right. I need you to carry my share of the load for now. Then, once I'm healed from *griesha*, we can go back to carrying this burden on an equal playing field."

Jareth blinked back some moisture. "Goddess, you're amazing, and I don't deserve you."

He took his lips with mine, enfolding me in his arms and pouring his love and affection into each tender movement. A girl could get used to attention like that.

"We'll need to return to the palace soon. I don't like that we'll have to attend this assembly without you getting any sleep." He tucked my head under his chin and rubbed his hands up and down my back.

"It won't be a waste. The assembly would have been necessary in the long run. I'm sure most everyone is going to want the opportunity to find their fated mate."

"With the diadem we won't have to bond people one-by-one. At least, that's the theory."

"Or wishful thinking." I closed my eyes, relaxing in Jareth's embrace and tuning out our troubles for one moment. If I never had a moment's peace afterward, I would look back on this and remember that Jareth and I once held each other in a beautiful library underneath a magical lake.

"Once the assembly is over, we'll meet with Chantara in her rooms, and go over our findings with her. We can plan from there."

I pulled back and planted another kiss on his lips. "We're going to figure this out, and the moment we do, I'll get better, and so will Terise."

Jareth's smile didn't reach his eyes. He looked weary, the stress of my well being weighed heavily upon him.

"Just be very careful when you go to the Missing Ruins," I said. "I can't lose you."

"I'll never allow that to happen."

I knew Jareth would do everything in his power to find the diadem, but I also knew, no matter how powerful Jareth might be, he couldn't control all the variables.

Let alone fate.

Crysta

The assembly reminded me quite a bit of the Faerie Council. A large infrastructure comparable to that of an underwater Greek amphitheater, except the large amphitheater was in the palace and completely dry. Insert hundreds of representatives from various underwater races.

Same format, different faeries.

And I'm talking different.

Due to the diversified nature of the assembly, many ambassadors and royals of their race were ensconced in large bubbles filled with lake water since breathing air was not really their thing.

One particular species I had a hard time *not* gawking at were the Kelpie royals. Holy crap.

I'd never known much about Kelpies, other than they were rumored to be shapeshifting horses who could turn into humans if they wanted to. Well, apparently the queen of the Kelpies enjoyed her humanoid form, with a mane of flowing black hair, smooth black skin, and flames for pupils.

That's right. Flames. Downright freaky.

However, the king enjoyed remaining in his more natural state. The biggest, blackest, most frightening horse I'd ever laid eyes on, but there were massive differences in his appearance. His mane was made up of jagged fins surrounded by wriggling black snakes, or maybe worms? I had a hard time figuring it out since the wriggling things were thin looking, yet had bulbous heads on the end. The king's hooves were flipped backward. Like if you told him to run forward he'd go in reverse.

I thought he'd sink like a stone in water, but apparently the guy was pretty buoyant, not only capable of swimming, but also running across the surface of the lake.

His flaming eyes caught me staring at him, but I couldn't stop, especially when the flames grew brighter and he bowed his head. When he lifted his head, his upper lips pulled back to reveal a mouth full of knives.

Okay, they may as well have been knives.

"He seems to like you," Jareth whispered as we stood before the assembly next to Chantara. "I've rarely seen King Hepheron reveal his teeth in deference."

"That was deference? I thought he was letting me know how badly he wanted to eat me," I whispered.

I gave Jareth an elbow nudge when he laughed at me, but I found myself immediately distracted by other faeries. Jareth had helped me identify Nixies, an amphibious looking race with webbed feet and reptilian skin. Their noses were flat like a snake's, but their eyes were round, black orbs. The leather green of their skin was spotted with white, and their long tail was thin and a bit see-through. Thin membranous fins replaced what would have been ears, and six-foot antennae sprang from their forehead like thick cords draping down to their feet, along with a full head of gorgeous chestnut hair.

I loved the look of them as they quietly floated within their large bubbles. The female was slightly smaller than the male with tiny curves and a softness to her body in direct contrast to the musculature of her mate. He continued to sweep his eyes around the room and immediately checked on her. I zeroed in on the worry in his eyes and studied the female more carefully. A few red dots here and there. I hoped it was just a colorful skin pattern rather than *griesha*.

I really hated this illness.

There were Selkies who preferred to remain in seal form. From what I understood, they never left their seal skins unless they were unmated and wished to find a mate outside their species. I remembered some folklore I had read on Selkies. Males and females alike would shed their seal skin, hide it along the shore, and go in search of temporary mates. The females didn't return until they were pregnant, and the males didn't return until their human mate gave birth and the child was old enough to return to the waters with him.

Sounded horrible, and I had no idea if any of it held much truth.

Then there was a race that had dolphin tails, a subspecies of sirens and mermaids known as Encantado in Brazilian folklore. A species made up solely of males. They looked a bit like Mermen, but their massive tails were a shiny gray, and they had managed to keep their lineage going by making pilgrimages to different parts of the Amazon River where they seduced women by hypnotizing them and then impregnating them.

Male children were born with an instinct to seek out their kind at the River. Apparently, it was a whole ritual where males traveled to the river two to three times a year to retrieve the young males waiting for them.

Again, horrible.

I tried to remind myself that my cultural views on family and parenting didn't necessarily gel with other races and species. Tried not to judge, but it seemed like a better option to start retrieving the female children they created so they could start reproducing amongst themselves rather than humans.

Then again, what in the world did I know? Maybe any female offspring they produced were infertile...and maybe The Rending had something to do with that. Or *griesha*. Or a hundred different other things.

And here I was suddenly trying to solve everyone's infertility problems.

I did a double take when my eyes landed on Lord Elsly in the top right corner. His glower made my spine tingle.

"What in the word is he doing here?" I asked Jareth as I moved my eyes toward the annoying Lord.

Jareth's brows narrowed. "It wouldn't surprise me if Rena invited him to cause some trouble."

Awesome.

I spotted King Omer and Queen Olean a few seats above. They both gave us encouraging smiles as Chantara cleared her throat and called the assembly to order.

"I'm so pleased so many of you could be here. As you know we recently sent out inquiries as to the races effected by *griesha* and their numbers. I went over the reports just last night and I'm alarmed at how high the numbers have become within the last few days."

"Are you going to give us the same song and dance that the Princess gave the Faerie council. All about finding the key to Moridan's destruction and ending the illness once and for all?" Lord Elsly shouted.

Chantara's glare could have petrified water.

"Lord Elsly, I'm quite surprised to see you here."

"I'm following up on the promises made by our Unseelie Princess. I do believe the Faerie Council is reassembling in less than two days to see if she has made good on her promise."

"We have already solved that issue, Lord Elsly," my father said, coming to stand beside me. "I assure you, we will be ready to report our findings to the council. At the moment, we are concerned with this rampant illness and assessing how far it has spread."

"Pairings and fated mates," Lord Elsly scoffed. "I'll admit that forming a bond between a Land Dweller and the king of the Dark Elves was impressive, but not everyone can be saved in time."

The murmurs among the assembled grew in volume. I wanted to smack Lord Elsly's smug face. The underwater faeries didn't know much about the cure or our findings. Better to hear good information from us than a stripped down account from this buffoon.

Chantara quieted everyone and then shared the measures we had taken to save the Land Dwellers and the Annis. The stunned silence that followed didn't last long.

"We cannot have fated mates, though we would wish it," said one of the Encantado. I wasn't sure if he was the king or a representative. "We have no females to mate with, and our species has only ever survived by joining with humans."

"I don't deny that there will be some necessary changes. I can't travel to the human realm and find human fated mates for you. They would never survive living within the depths of the lake," I said. "But we can attempt to find species similar to yours. The Mermaids, Sirens, or even the Drac might do."

"We do not breed with lessers," a Merman sentry called out.

Chantara sent a blast of water into the sentry with so much force I was surprised he survived it. The action immediately quieted the group, a tense hush filling the room. He slowly got to his feet, unable to meet her gaze as Chantara glared at him and then moved her flinty gaze to the rest of the assembly.

"Times are changing, and so must we," she said. "Interracial marriages and offspring are not anything new to us since many of you mate with humans, but we have never before been faced with an illness so devastating it could wipe out our entire realm. Nor have we been offered a cure so wonderful it could save us all and allow us to find what we never dared dream. Fated mates." She took a few steps closer to those assembled, making eye contact with as many as she could.

"If you wish to die of this illness, I will not stop you. I will force no one to take a fated mate if they do not wish to do so, but I will not allow anyone in this room to deny your people the same opportunity no matter how opposed you are to the idea of interracial marriages. There may be pairings between races you do not like, but they do exist, and they will help us survive. It's a gift. It's an opportunity. It's a chance to lay down selfish differences and unite our races rather than remaining suspicious and separate."

She looked at me and nodded. My cue to take up the cause and push through.

"I know there are prejudices here that run deep. Change is difficult and preconceived notions can be hard to alter, but I believe our differences, when shared and accepted, can work to make us all stronger. The Merfolk have much to offer the Encantado. The Selkies have much to offer the Kelpies and vice versa. There could be pairings among races that might never have occurred to you, but I promise a united realm made up of amazing differences will offer you all unique perspectives and massive growth in your communities. My fated mate, Jareth and I, can help you make that happen if you will accept it."

"Will you show us?" the same male Encantado said.

"What is your name?" I asked.

"I am Banvu, King of the Encantado."

"I'm honored to meet you, King Banvu." I must have said the right thing because his eyes widened in surprise and then gratitude at being acknowledged.

I turned to Lord Raith who stood a few paces behind us. "As you can see, we have a Dark Elf present. Lord Raith is able to sense potential fated mate bonds between couples." I turned to him and motioned him forward. "Any chance you see something in here that might help us solidify what we can do?"

Lord Raith gave me a warm smile.

"The Nixies are fated mates." A murmur flitted through the assembly, and the dawning excitement in the Nixies' expressions made all our struggles up until now so worth it. I think I loved creating marriage bonds more than the thought of ruling. "I always find it so interesting that fated mates find their way to one another, even when they don't know it."

I smiled at him and nodded for Chantara to continue.

She called the Nixies forward. Their bubbles of water slowly descended the steps until they stood right before us.

We encouraged them to place their hands at each other's chests, which involved them carefully joining their bubbles into one enormous orb of water, and then Jareth and I started the spell. He had to take over once again. All I managed to do was give him access to my core magic as he worked to bond them together. It took a few more minutes than I would have liked, but I felt a little comfort knowing the rest of those assembled had no idea how little time the process normally took.

The bright flash of light followed by an immense drain on my power signified the bond had worked. I watched the infinity rings appear for a moment before they winked out of sight. I also took satisfaction in seeing those tiny red dots on the female completely disappear.

As the Nixie king tenderly kissed his wife, I cast my eyes to King Banvu who stood stock still, staring at the Nixie couple with a longing that bordered on ferocious. I got the impression his race had suffered dearly with no females to really call their own. They wanted families but were stuck with older traditions that prevented them from thriving.

"What say you King Banvu?" Chantara asked.

He bowed his head and then looked directly at me.

"The Encantado will do whatever our Unseelie Princess sees fit."

My relief hit me so hard, I nearly listed to the side. Where one king accepted me, others would follow. Chantara gave me a smile as the rest of those assembled bowed their heads in deference and echoed Banvu's statement.

"Never a dull moment with you, Crysta," Kheelan said behind me.

If only Kheelan knew how badly I longed for dull. I gripped Jareth's hand as a wave of exhaustion nearly buckled my knees, but I remained on my feet for every last minute of the assembly as we answered more questions and discussed possible alliances and pairings between species. Lord Raith did spot a few more fated mates within the room that he quietly shared with me and Jareth.

We agreed that performing any more bondings was a risk my health couldn't take. Not to mention some of the fated mate pairings were a bit, inflammatory. As in, the Kelpie queen was not destined to be the Kelpie King's fated mate.

Yikes.

We were not touching that one with a ten-foot fishing rod.

Sometimes, you just didn't mess with the status quo. No sense in breaking up that royal pairing with information that could hurt them and their race.

By the time the assembly was dismissed, I could barely keep my eyes open. And yet Lord Elsly was still skulking around, waiting to be heard.

"What is it Elsly?" my father said.

"I demand you release Rhoswen. You have no grounds to hold her."

My father looked at him like the arrogant Lord couldn't possibly be serious. "No grounds. I have multiple witnesses, not to mention my own witness, of your daughter launching an attack on the Unseelie palace with not one, not two, but three Mountain Trolls in an attempt to kill *my* daughter. Her crimes have gone beyond treason and attempted murder. You're lucky she's still alive."

Lord Elsly actually appeared shocked for once.

"Mountain Trolls? There must be some mistake. She attacked the Unseelie palace? She would never do something like that."

"And yet she did," Jareth said. "I once cared for her, Lord Elsly, and out of respect for that relationship, and his concern for you, King Roderick did not have her executed as was his right, but she will answer for her crimes."

Lord Elsly looked as if he had aged ten years. "She is all I have left after everything—" His gaze hardened as he glared at me. "It's because of you. My daughter was driven to it by your claim on her fiancé."

"She has no claim. Crysta is my fated mate."

"You'll regret this." Malice poured off him in waves. "Every last one of you."

With that, he walked away, meeting up with Rena, who appeared to be offering him some kind of an apology. She actually looked worried. It seemed that there were a few faeries in this realm who intimidated her.

That's what she got for cluing him in on the assembly.

"I think I'm ready to crash," I said, grabbing Jareth's hand. He took one look at me and scooped me up in his arms. Yeah. I knew I looked as bad as I felt.

After making it back to our room—I had no idea how he found his way around the place—he gently set me down.

"Crysta, let's get you into—" Jareth stared at me in horror.

"What is it?" I asked.

He lifted his hand and gently rubbed the side of my neck. Then he abruptly lifted my tunic up and pulled it over my head. I'd never stood before him in my bra before, but the act wasn't sexual. He was genuinely worried.

"You're covered in spots, all the way up to your neck. Sweet Danu."

I didn't even bother looking at myself. I knew what I would find.

I simply wrapped my arms around him and held him close.

"It's going to be okay, husband."

He barked out a laugh and then held me tight.

"Nothing will be okay until we cure you. Let's get you into bed. Sleep will be the best thing for you. I'll make sure we contact Cedric and Adris. We'll need them for what we plan on doing tonight."

I didn't argue. I was barely standing, and the desire to join in had been replaced by a desire to simply do what was best for everyone all around. Me weakened, swimming around the Missing Ruins with a pod of Vorsha in play, was a liability nobody could afford. I didn't like it, but I could accept it. I slipped under the covers as Jareth tucked me in. Disembodied voices floated back and forth as I went in and out of consciousness. I thought I heard my father ask about the disease and its progress, but then I went under again and lost the thread of the discussion.

As I slipped deeper in to lah lah land, I dreamed of Terise covered in open sores, her life draining away as I tried desperately to get to her.

I woke up in a sheen a sweat, breathing heavily and crying.

"Shhhh, Crysta. It was just a bad dream," Jareth said, pulling me into his arms.

Not a bad dream. A premonition. A knowing that came from my own gut instincts.

Terise had less than a day to live.

∞ ∞ ∞

We assembled back in Chantara's room later that night and reported our findings to her. The more Jareth and I shared, the more alarmed she became. Cedric and Adris were already there waiting for us, having managed to sneak in past the wards and through Chantara's mirror-like muma with Paio's aid.

"This is a suicide mission," she said, her eyes black as a moonless night.

"We have a chance if we perform that spell," Jareth said.

"If we have all the Vorsha in one place," she said. "If we miss even one Vorsha who may be in hiding, none of us will live, and we're not even certain the diadem and sword are still there."

"You aren't raising concerns we haven't already discussed. We know it's a risk, but we have no choice. Crysta is getting worse."

All eyes switched to me. My stomach turned at the scrutiny.

Chantara stood silent, no doubt weighing our options and coming to the same realization the rest of us had. We had one shot at this. We had to make it count.

"Crysta, you're staying here, correct?"

"Yes." Why was that so hard to get out?

261

They talked strategy for the next few minutes as I stood by Jareth, feeling completely useless. I'd never been to the Missing Ruins so I had no context for the best way to enter and exit the area, where the Vorsha would need to be drawn to, and how to search the ships and even the nest, which apparently involved a series of underwater caverns.

The more they talked, the more insurmountable the situation became. My throat closed up at the thought of the spell going wrong, or the group getting ambushed. The desire to go, to remain in control, to ensure things went well and no calamities befell them warred with my knowledge that I had *griesha*. I could offer them nothing at this point.

"Crysta, you can remain here if you want to or you can head back to your quarters. Either way, we should be back before morning," Chantara said.

If they came back, and that was a big if. The reality of losing all of them struck me hard. What the hell would I do if this didn't pan out? In my condition, I couldn't go up against Moridan and Titania alone. I didn't want to continue on if any of them were lost to me. If Jareth was lost to me. Panic like I'd never known swept through me, causing a gust of air to sweep into the room.

"It's going to be okay." Jareth caught me in his arms, holding me close. He kissed my head, my cheeks, my lips. "It will take upwards to an hour to locate the Missing Ruins, but I swear we will return Crysta, and we'll bring back the sword. I'll not fail you."

"I know you won't."

He reached underneath his tunic and cast a quick spell, pulling out the stone and placing it in my palm.

"Hide it on your person. Fuse it to your core," he said. "It will be safest with you for now."

"How? That sounds complicated."

"I will cast the spell. You simply hold it to your chest against your skin."

I did as he suggested as he said, "*Foliagh*."

I watched the stone slowly merge with my skin and take on my skin tone. All I felt was a slight tingle at the joining. My core liked the relic pinned over it. Warmth spread through my achy limbs and joints, easing my pain. I wished we'd done this a bit sooner.

I took turns embracing my friends, my father, holding back tears since those couldn't help us at this point. Adris embraced me and stepped back, staring into my eyes again, not liking what she saw.

"You need to tell me what is wrong," I said as the other made their way through the mirror.

"It's a suspicion, nothing more, but we will discuss it when we return."

Jareth stood in front of the mirror, the last one to walk through.

His soulful eyes ensnared me, drinking in the sight of me with so much love it bordered on painful...for both of us.

"Don't you dare die," I said, my voice coming out husky. "You have to come back to me."

His eyes glistened as he said, "I am with you. Always." Then he stepped into the mirror and disappeared.

"So touching. A real tear-jerker as humans like to say."

I spun around, feeling my heart land squarely in my stomach as I stared at Lord Elsly and Rena standing side-by-side. It took me some serious concentration to keep my face a mask of calm.

"What are you doing here?" I asked. "It's extremely inappropriate for either one of you to be in Chantara's quarters without her permission."

Rena rolled her eyes. "Oh, please. As if we didn't see and hear everything. As if we didn't know your group is off to the Missing Ruins to find the very thing that will take down King Moridan. And I'm afraid I simply can't let you do that."

My eyes narrowed as Rena took a step forward. "Rena, you do realize we're fighting on the same side. If we don't take down Moridan, then we all suffer, *griesha* spreads, and everyone is destroyed. Why would you try to stop this?"

"Lies," she hissed. "Lord Elsly has told me everything. It is your fated mate bond with Jareth that has upended the balance of this realm. And the more false fated mates you create between races, the worse the disease becomes."

"Rena, *he* is the one who has lied to you." I looked at Elsly. "You know the truth. Why are you trying to convince her otherwise?"

He simply stared at me. His dead gaze gave me more cause for concern than the spiteful regent slowly coming toward me.

"I have a chance to get everything I want the moment I hand you over to Moridan. I thought handing over Paio would be enough, but Moridan still denies me total control over the Lake of Beatha."

"You are the reason Paio was held hostage at the palace?" I shouldn't have been surprised, but her reasoning was so faulty. "Moridan doesn't have the power to give you control over the lake. Chantara is the rightful ruler and the only one capable of passing that power to someone else."

"If she is dead, then the power goes to me, and Elsly has assured me he will take care of this. My sentries will take the precious stone and the sword and dispose of your friends at the Missing Ruins."

"You've sent your sentries to The Missing Ruins? You've betrayed your queen."

"I am queen," she hissed, spittle flying from her lips. Her eyes turned coral, her whole body hummed with magic as she slowly brought her hands forward. "Moridan wanted you delivered to him alive, to torture and kill you, no doubt, but I can't imagine he would be too displeased if I did his dirty work for him. I want that stone."

Her gaze flashed to my chest. The stone pulsed at the threat she represented.

Blood red light illuminated her core, slowly crawling up her shoulders and through her arms as a pervasive buzzing noise grew in volume. Whatever she geared up for would be excruciating. I pulled my shield forward, but it flickered and died. Rena scoffed, a maniacal laugh following as I pulled my shield forward again and held it in place.

"Do you really think that's going to stop me. My magic will tear through that like tissue paper."

"Your voice is as annoying as your empty threats, Rena. Less talking, more pain." I flipped my hand forward and sent a blast of frigid Winter magic straight for her core. She easily deflected and lifted her hands high, electricity crackling between her palms.

"I'm really going to enjoy this." Her eyes flared with malice just as she brought her hands down.

Lord Elsly moved faster than lightning, pulling out a dagger from his belt and thrusting it into Rena's back. Her mouth opened wide, caught in a silent scream before she coughed up blood and fell to the floor. Her startled eyes tracked Elsly just as mine did as he circled her and leaned over.

"Ah, Rena. Always so shortsighted. Always so disloyal. How am I to rule the Fae realm with someone like you in charge of the magical properties within the lake?"

She choked and gagged as blood filled her mouth, flailing around like a newly caught fish. Then her body went limp as her eyes glazed over.

He turned to me, that same dead look in his eye.

"I'm not going to thank you for saving my life since I'm pretty sure you still intend to kill me."

He let out a laugh. It sounded a bit off, like he'd never had much cause to do it.

"You know, fate can be a tricky thing, a Seer's visions to interpret even trickier. It took me a long time to realize that framing the Unseelie Court, specifically Rodri, for the murder of King Moridan's wife was a mistake."

"What?"

"Well, killing her wasn't a mistake," he amended. "Just blaming it on your family, convincing Moridan that your fated mate bond to Jareth would be the destruction of the realm when I'd actually needed you all alive all along."

"Wait. I'm reeling a bit here. I'm not following anything you just said."

Elsly settled himself on the side of the porcelain tub, looking for all the world like the dashing, debonair aristocrat he claimed to be.

"You know, I think I would actually enjoy explaining my diabolical plan to you." He carelessly swung the dagger around, talking with his hands as he continued. "I've kept this bottled up for quite some time. Really since the moment I fled Oberon's presence after he stripped me of my powers."

"You..."

Dawning realization hit me, a clarity that brought nothing but debilitating dread in its wake.

"Figured it out yet?" he asked, truly enjoying my reaction.

"You're Oberon's brother. You're Puck."

His wide smile set my nerves on edge. "Why, my dearest Crysta, for once in your life, you're one hundred percent right."

Crysta

"Since you managed to decipher Oberon's scrolls, you must know the true history concerning what happened between Oberon, Titania, and I."

"You wanted to rule the Fae realm alongside Titania, and you wanted to do it by killing off lesser faeries."

"That does sum it up nicely. After losing Titania, I spent decades fighting Oberon for power, fighting to avenge the love of my life, fighting for those goals she and I had so purposefully put together. Yet my plans never came to fruition since I had to rely so heavily on others for their magic."

"You have no magical abilities?"

"None whatsoever, but please don't assume I can't kill you before you attempt some weak spell on me. I've learned how to hone my skills in a land filled with magical beings." He waited for a moment to allow that message to sink in, and then he flipped his dagger, catching it by the hilt. "After that last massive battle with Oberon whereby my flying dagger pierced his heart and killed him—some wondrous luck in that moment—I had to fake my own death and go into hiding for a while, but I was never idle. I knew Titania and I still had much to achieve, and since she was banished rather than executed, I knew there had to be a way to bring her back. I also knew all about

Oberon's attempt at fixing The Rending with Titania's diadem. Her magical stone, her diadem, was the key to achieving everything we'd dreamed. I needed Titania and her crown, but more importantly I needed redemption."

"Redemption for what?"

"Leaving her. Abandoning her to her fate after Oberon struck that near lethal blow." For the first time since I'd met Lord Elsly, he looked truly grieved, guilt holding his expression hostage for a moment, his eyes haunted rather than dead.

"I wanted her back. Needed her to know I had not abandoned her. Bringing her back was something that had never been done before. The decades I spent creating the blueprints for the correct spell, not to mention what it would entail and the massive time it would take to go searching for Titania in the Netherworld...I didn't have the resources, didn't have the power needed to execute my plan."

"You slowly established yourself as Lord Elsly," I said. "Over the decades you moved up the ranks, aligning yourself with King Moridan, becoming his advisor and ambassador. You needed his power, didn't you?"

"Right again," he said, giving me a winning smile. "It would take Dark Magic to pull off something like that, and King Moridan was far too pure, his wife far too influential, a constant thorn at my side. The blasted woman never did trust me much. Which was fine with me since getting rid of her was all part of my plan. I murdered her myself and framed your family for it since Rodri and Insley would eventually be a roadblock I'd need to bulldoze into submission. The loss of Moridan's wife to murder was a hellish blow, but giving him a target, someone to hate, someone to destroy...that was the tipping point for him. It wasn't difficult to make a few off handed remarks here and there about bringing his wife back. Then he just so happens to discover specific pieces to the puzzle. Soon he turned to the Dark Arts, not only to bring his wife back, but to avenge her murder."

I eyed the dagger he kept flipping, catch release, catch release. Was it the same dagger he'd used to murder Oberon?

My thoughts turned to Jareth and the others. I had to warn them, but I wasn't going anywhere.

His eyes zeroed in on me as he squeezed the hilt.

"Then you were born, and Moridan's Seer came to me, petitioning to see his highness, bearing news that would change The Rending. I managed to persuade her to share this vision she'd had, only to discover that all my plans were to be ruined by a baby girl."

He leaned against the ivory wall, shaking his head with a self-deprecating smile. "According to her, a Princess was to be born, one who would unite the courts, bring harmony to the realm, and dispense with the social classes. One who would be fated mate to Jareth, though the princess was not of the same species. Unheard of. Dangerous. Not a chance interracial fated mates were possible after The Rending. Yet the Seer claimed the union would heal rather than tear apart the kingdom, and I had to believe her no matter how outrageous the concept. Titania and I were to rule the realm, get rid of the lesser Fae, and a princess upending my own future goals would never do. I wasn't quite ready to take action, but the timing actually felt perfect on many levels. So I...persuaded the Seer to change her vision, just a tad."

"You threatened her life and the lives of her loved ones," I said.

He shrugged, completely unrepentant. "Leopard, spots."

"You had the Seer tell Moridan that my fated mate bond to Jareth would be the destruction of our realm."

"Of course, I couldn't have you fulfilling your destiny. Highly inconvenient for me after being so close to putting my plan into action. So I planted it in his head that the fated mate bond would destroy the realm and all his attempts at bringing his wife back. He already blamed your father for his wife's death. It didn't take long for him to enact his vengeance. He could kill you and save the realm while killing Insley and taking away the very thing that Rodri had taken from him. Forcing a vampire to assassinate her was simply icing on the cake. He came up with the brilliant plan all on his own. Proud moment for me. That slow descent from morally clean to dastardly evil is not something anyone expects to have happen to them. They never see it coming, though evil versus good is merely a dogma used to put fear into the hearts of those afraid to live the lives they were born to live."

Man, this guy talked a lot. The evil monologue ground against my nerves. "You don't believe in evil and good? Wrong and right?"

"I believe in the strong and the weak. Anything else is just noise."

"Yet you made a mistake. You should have let me live?"

"Yes. Even when you returned from the grave, I still held on to the same belief Moridan did: you needed to die. Seems Kheelan and your fake father thought the same thing. I had nothing to do with that by the way."

He held up his hands as if they were actually clean. "I had no idea your blood was the key to bringing back my beloved, that your blood was the key to locating the stone and the diadem. We wanted you dead right up until Moridan made that astounding discovery after your binding spell became null and void. The last piece of the puzzle I had been working on for years finally emerged, and everything fell into place."

"Yet you sent Rhoswen to kill me."

The fond look on his face struck me as misplaced. "She did that on her own and was appropriately reprimanded, but her initiative impressed me. Such a bright future ahead of her once I get her out of that dungeon."

"She's really your daughter?"

"Do you think I remained celibate all these years? I needed a family to support the illusion."

"And you care for Rhoswen?"

He looked surprised. "Of course. She's my daughter."

Hard to believe he felt any true love for anyone. I decided to let that line of questioning slide even though the guy was a textbook psychopath.

"So what's the plan now? I assume Titania has no idea the part you've played in her return, who you are, or where you are. Last time I spoke with her she didn't have cordial things to say about you."

He swallowed hard, eyes flinty and unyielding. "The idea that you've seen her and spoken with her when I've yet to lay eyes on her makes me feel slightly murderous. I haven't dared set foot back in the Seelie palace since you and your friends breached it. I've been following you all carefully, knowing full well I'd need to return to Titania with stone and diadem in hand if I wanted her to give me a chance to speak before she struck me down."

So we had Elsly and Titania's minions shadowing us, attempting to get the relics from us. I felt foolish, blinded in a way, like I should have seen this coming. I should have known Elsly was involved.

But Puck?

Who could have seen that coming?

From the doorway of the bathroom, behind Elsly, I spotted something peeking through. It looked like an eyeball floating on a red string. I quickly moved my gaze back to Elsly who didn't notice my split focus. Then two eyes caught my attention, and it suddenly hit me who was standing just outside the bathroom door.

Criva.

"What now?" I asked, making sure Elsly's attention remained on me.

"I've been following your progress. I know you have the stone, which I shall happily take off your hands, and now I know the sword and diadem are in the Missing Ruins. Manipulating Rena was more than easy, and her soldiers are to adhere to my commands. The amount of manpower I've just sent to not only take care of the Vorsha, but your small group of heroes, should wipe everyone out within the hour. After that, it's simply a matter of scouring the Ruins looking for the sword, and since I've used it before, and am drawn to its magical properties, I shouldn't have any problems retrieving it. Once I present the magical relics to Titania and let her know I'd been guiding King Moridan into setting her free all along, she'll forgive me, and we'll finish what we started."

He let out a heavy sigh. "I do believe we've wasted enough time chatting. Time to die."

"Wait a second. I thought you needed me alive."

"To bring back Titania and retrieve the stone and diadem, but I highly doubt I'll need your blood as I pick over shipwrecks and sunken treasure. It's not as if there are any magical tests or booby traps I'll have to go endure. Fortunate that the Drac lost the sword in that mess." His eyes gleamed with malevolent light. "You always had to die, Crysta, just not as soon as I originally believed."

"You have no magical powers. How will you breathe under water?"

"Just because I can't cast any spells doesn't mean I can't get someone to cast them for me."

"We don't know it's even there for certain."

"No," he said, "but we do know there's a good possibility it's simply languishing at the bottom of the lake." He lifted his hand up, brandishing his dagger and taking a slow step toward me. "I finally get to finish you off. Can't say I'm sorry to see you go. Don't worry. I'll make sure Rhoswen takes very good care of Jareth."

"If he survives your attack."

"He'll be the only one to survive. A courtesy to my daughter. I'm not completely heartless."

I took a step back, wondering if I'd be able to make it through the mirror before he threw that dagger, when an enormous claw shot out of the doorway and smashed into Elsly's head. He sank to the floor, unconscious.

My eyes snapped to Criva who stood in the doorway, shifting back and forth while his eyes twitched something fierce.

"I have never raised a claw to a royal. Forgive me, Princess, but I saw no other alternative."

I ran right over to him and flung my arms around his thick shell.

"Criva, you pretty much saved the day. Anytime you want to bludgeon Lord Elsly with a claw, you go for it. I need you to help me get to Jareth and the others. We have to warn them, and I have no idea where the Missing Ruins are."

If a giant crab could lose its coloring, it would have looked like Criva. I swore the color bled right out of his shell.

"They've gone to the Missing Ruins? There is no surviving that."

"Criva, listen to me, your queen, Chantara, is about to get ambushed by some traitorous soldiers. We have to do something about it, and I'll have to cast a spell I'm not even sure I have the strength to sustain."

"What spell?"

"I have to be able to swim, and the stupid breathing spell I've been using doesn't allow for much speed. I've never been a great swimmer to begin with. I gotta go full-blown Mermaid."

"It will be a difficult transmutation spell, highness, and I understand you are not well."

"Not well. Not by a long shot, but I think I have enough juice to get there and warn the others."

Even if it kills me.

The only other option would be to stay, allow everyone else to get killed, and die anyway.

I wasn't going to wait around for my own funeral. I wasn't going to allow my loved ones to get ambushed.

"You with me, Criva?"

"Yes...yes, Princess. I will take you to the Missing Ruins."

∞ ∞ ∞

Criva caught me in a cradle hold so I wouldn't fall over once I created a mermaid tail for myself.

"Will you need assistance?" he asked.

"You're gonna need to talk me through it. I'm not exactly sure what the physiology looks like or the organs necessary for breathing. Placement. You know the drill."

We walked a dangerous line from Criva's descriptions, to visualization, to reality as I slowly and painfully shifted cells, created extra organs, and damn near tore myself from the inside out. The pain reduced me to silent weeping as my insides shifted and strained to accommodate an extra lung, an extra heart, scales, and a fusion of skin as my legs grew together. Sweat coated my entire body, and I tasted the coppery tang of blood as my legs grew fins.

Scorching pain licked along my spine, while tiny needles jabbed every inch of skin until my very cells ripped from the inside out and reassembled in a tidal wave of agony.

"Almost there, Princess. Hold your core steady."

I visualized one last section, one last advantage I could give myself in the form of an extra wide flipper at the end of my tail for speed, and then I let the spell go.

Criva spoke soft, unintelligible words to me while I shook, sweating and limp in his large arms.

I opened my eyes, taking note of my icy blue mermaid tail, though the color was a bit muted since droplets of blood covered my tail like early morning dew.

Black scales covered me from my waist to my chest, emitting a light sheen, yet also covered in droplets of blood. My fingers ended in sharp talons. Not necessarily a mermaid thing, but I needed an advantage. I ran my tongue along my teeth, wincing as their sharpened ends drew more blood.

My arms were pale as moonlight. My silver hair fell over my shoulder, containing streaks of admiral blue.

I'd managed the change, but I had zero strength left to swim a meter let alone a mile.

"You did it, Princess. I've never seen anyone manage a change like this for their first time."

"Criva, you might have to drag me along with you. I thought this would help me swim faster, but I've used up all my energy."

"Here," he said. A small antennae-like appendage moved from the side of his head. The tip of it sparkled with electric gold. He lowered the appendage to my chest, and the moment it made contact, my body jolted. Adrenaline surged through my system, an energy unlike anything I'd ever felt before, the equivalent of ten cups of espresso without the shakes.

"Flaming...what in the world did you do to me?" I croaked, trying to catch my breath.

"I shared some core magic with you. Just a little. Too much could kill you. Did I hurt you?"

I stared at Criva's eyes as they bobbed back and forth. I'd learned the twitchier his eyes the more emotion he struggled to contain.

"I'm fine, Criva. I had no idea you could do something like that."

"My kind don't do it often. It's...well...it's considered a bit intimate, something shared between family and loved ones."

"You are definitely family to me. So no worries."

All three of his eyes shot forward, rapid blinking ensued. "Thank you, Princess. I shall do my best to live up to such an honor."

I patted his crusty shoulder. "You already have."

His eyes started to water. I sensed his embarrassment at the emotional overwhelm.

"Let's get going, Criva."

"Yes. Yes, Princess."

He continued to carry me as he stepped through the mirror and into the muma. I didn't think I'd ever get over that jello-like consistency. We plowed right through to the other side, and the moment the water hit me I felt the most exhilarating sensation. The water embraced me like a long lost family member as I took my first breath. Oxygen and water filtered through my system. The sensation of new organs filtering the water from my lungs and carrying the oxygen to my blood made me wish I had time to simply hold still and process the experience.

We reached the ward and halted.

"I don't have a plan for breaching this thing," I said.

Criva took his clawed hands and punched two holes through the wards, spreading his arms wide enough to create a gaping hole that sparked and spit magic around the circumference of the breach.

"No time for finesse. We simply barrel through," he said, pushing me in and following closely behind.

Shouting rang out in the distance, but we'd be long gone before anyone spotted us.

I flipped my heavy tail and shot forward with Criva at my side. My eyes picked up everything before me, an underwater world of beautiful creatures going about their own business, colorful rock formations holding small civilizations of tiny water creatures. I saw everything with a clarity and richness I hadn't been able to see before.

Puck. Titania. Moridan's wife. My mother's death.

The diadem.

Clarity.

Things had finally come into focus.

∞ ∞ ∞

"We almost there, Criva?"

That jolt of magic he'd given me had kept me going for the last forty-five minutes, but my energy took an abrupt nosedive.

"I've never actually been to the Missing Ruins. I know their location due to maps I've studied, but when you've seen one rock formation you've seen them all. I'm wondering if we've circled around the ruins rather than made a straight path to them."

"As long as we find them, that's all that matters—"

"Wait. Up ahead."

My eyes tracked the direction of his claw, taking note of shadowy structures in the distance. Floating in the water while inching closer to the Ruins felt like hovering in a spaceship over an undiscovered planet.

Not that I'd ever done that.

It definitely appeared otherworldly compared to the rest of the lake. Like it was a section of the lake designated solely for the Twilight Zone. If I entered, would I ever make it out?

"Criva, I have no idea where the others might be. I don't even know if we're entering the ruins from the same direction they did, but actually going through them is going to be extremely dangerous. I think you should turn back."

"I may be afraid, but I'd never do anything so dishonorable."

"Criva—"

"We move forward."

A heavy ball of emotion punched its way through my chest. More lives at stake. I hated to risk Criva, but I knew he wouldn't leave me now. I felt both grateful and guilty. I bet my mermaid fin Criva had a wife and kids.

We slowed our speed, keeping our eyes open for sentries, Jareth and our group, or heaven help us any predatory Vorsha. As we neared the first sunken ship, we slowed even further. The ship had been gutted, leaning on its side like a beached whale. Its hull contained several splintered holes, as if it had been dashed upon a cliff side before sinking to its watery grave.

I didn't see much in the way of treasure, but I didn't intend to go looking for it. My first priority? Warn Jareth and everyone else of their impending doom. Unfortunately, we were probably too late for that. I'd wasted too much time listening to Elsly do the evil villain monologue. Then the transmutation spell took much longer than I'd have liked.

If anything, this was a rescue mission. One tiny princess ready to take on an army of seasoned Mermen. The odds were not exactly in my favor.

As we continued forward, another ship slowly came into focus on my left, and then my right. The murky water dimly lit by the soft illumination of the moon made the shadows appear menacing, holding untold horrors in their depths, any number of underwater creatures with jagged teeth and voracious appetites.

I tried to stay focused before I psyched myself right out of my rescue mission. A distant shout came from up ahead. I paused for a moment and held still to make sure I'd heard it correctly, but then it came again, along with the low din of magic at work.

"We've got them, Criva. Follow me."

I flipped my massive fin, reveling in the musculature at my disposal, but a powerful undertow pushed me back, bubbles traveling in its wake. It spun me a bit and then released me. I blinked my eyes, getting my bearings, trying to figure out what had caused the powerful current.

"Criva?"

He sputtered, pushing up from the sandy bed below where the current had pulled him down.

"I'm not sure what happened," he said, spitting sediment from his mouth. "There are no currents within the lake."

I shook it off and moved toward the din of what I now perceived to be a battle, but another rush of current, followed by a wave of bubbles, spun me in a spiral and then blinded me to anything else. Once I finally stopped spinning, I searched for Criva who had landed on the ground again.

"Princess," he yelled, pointing behind me.

I swiftly turned and sucked in a whole lot of water.

Several feet ahead of me, floating effortlessly above the floor, a creature both terrifying and awe inspiring stared at me with two orbs the color of sapphires. Its physiology was that of a human. The same arms and legs, yet covered in shiny black scales, with those jelly-like threads sticking out from its bumpy exterior. It looked to be male due to its musculature. Its long, gray tentacles spreading out like a fan around its head were not spinning as Chantara had described, but I wondered if that had anything to do with the fact that he simply floated rather than swam.

He hadn't attacked me yet. I studied his features, noting the high cheekbones and proud jaw. He looked like a warrior, not some animal.

Intelligence shone brightly from his eyes, a deep fascination as he stared at me.

"Princess, do not move," Criva said. I sensed him trying to make his way to me, but the Vorsha's eyes snapped to Criva, and he bared his teeth, hissing at him in warning.

"Criva, stop," I said, motioning him to freeze.

At the sound of my voice the Vorsha's eyes snapped to mine, widening in wonder. I slowly lifted my hand, and like a complete and totally idiot, I waved to him.

"Hi, my name is Crysta."

For a moment, he did nothing, just stared at me with zero comprehension. Then he lifted his hand and made the same movement. I smiled at him, and he obliged by lifting his lips, mimicking my smile even though it seemed awkward for him.

"I need your help." I waited for a moment, but he continued to stare, and then he waved at me again.

Crap.

"Do you speak?"

Silence on his end. We didn't have time for this delay, and not knowing whether he intended to kill me or simply stare at me ratcheted my anxiety. I decided to take action and gently moved my tail, gliding forward. His tentacles rose to attention, and he hissed at me just as he had at Criva. I held up my hands and halted my progress.

"Sorry," I said. "I'm not going to attack you or anything. I just need to get moving. I need your help."

I didn't lower my arms until his tentacles and the rest of his body relaxed.

Then I motioned him over. "Maybe you could come to me." I moved my arms as slow and deliberate as possible, urging him to get closer, to see that I didn't intend to attack or hurt him. I should have felt terrified, but the curiosity in his eyes made it impossible to feel anything but wonder. Despite some obvious physical anomalies, he looked so human.

After a few moments' hesitation, he glided a little closer, then stopped.

"Good. That's good. Yes." I smiled and received a grimace in response. For some reason it looked so funny to me I couldn't help but laugh. His eyes widened again, and a true expression of warmth crossed his features. I waved him forward, but he still remained hesitant. For a moment, I thought he'd either attack me or swim away, but then the tiny threads sticking out from his scales began to retract into his body until they were completely gone.

Did that mean he intended to shoot them forward and kill me? Before I could say anything to soothe him, a sharp stab to my chest caused me to double over as I cried out in pain. I felt myself sinking a little, and then I coughed, a coppery taste filling my mouth. In my pain-filled haze I didn't notice the Vorsha moving until he was right in my face.

I thought he had attacked me somehow and was getting ready to finish the job, but when I looked into his eyes, I saw nothing but concern. His hands went to my waist as he steadied me. Then he began checking my body, running a hand over my stomach, turning my head from side to side and placing a hand just under my neck.

"Why does she cough up blood?"

I blinked, trying to figure out if he'd spoken to me. His hand remained on my chest, sending weird waves of warmth through me.

"Not Mermaid. Transmutation spell gone wrong. Her male is foolish to allow this."

I took in a deep breath as the pain in my chest eased a bit. Then I reached up and placed my hand on his cheek and spoke to him telepathically just as I had with the Cù-Sith and the Bordesh.

"Thank you."

He jerked back in shock, his eyes meeting mine in complete and utter bewilderment. *"I heard you. In my thoughts. You spoke to me. No other race can speak to us. Do it again."*

"Thank you," I said. *"It's my first time ever performing a transmutation spell of this magnitude, and I had to do it under duress. Not my best work, I guess."*

He didn't make any exuberant noises that I could hear, but the telepathic equivalent came in loud and clear. He wrapped his arms around me and held me in a desperate embrace.

I returned the embrace, sensing his isolation and fear. A deep sense of loneliness and despair, followed by immense relief.

"Your people communicate telepathically?" I asked.

His grip on me tightened, as if each word I spoke was a special gift to him, and if he let me go, he would lose those words forever.

"As far as we know, we are the only race who does. We have no voice boxes. No ability to speak. We do so with our thoughts, but no race has ever taken the time to know this. They simply attack. I do not believe any other race is capable of this type of communication."

I pulled back a little to look at him. *"I guess that would make for some serious misunderstandings."*

"You have no idea."

"Princess," Criva said. "Are you all right? Is he hurting you?"

"That crustacean means you no harm? He was following you. I did not like the look of it." He peered down at Criva with a distasteful look.

"He is my friend. He helped me get here."

"This is a dangerous place to visit. I do not understand how your family could have allowed this. I am a more reasonable male of my species. Curious by nature, but we are always attacked by other races, and we have

learned to attack first rather than give our enemies any leverage to react. Any other warrior might have killed you on sight."

The mere idea of it caused him emotional pain. Weird to sense that through this telepathic link.

"It was necessary, I'm afraid." I cast my gaze down to where Criva sat tensed and ready to explode. "We are fine, Criva. I am communicating with him telepathically."

Criva's three eyes bounced around like bobble heads. "Extraordinary," he muttered, gazing up at us in disbelief.

I turned my attention back to the Vorsha. *"I'm trying to reassure him that you're not hurting me. What's your name?"*

"Venzoray. I am ruler of the Zolas."

"Zolas? We know you as Vorsha."

His eyes grew sad. *"Destroyer. That's what Vorsha means. I am not surprised this is what we are known as."*

"Zolas. A king then," I said. *"Your Highness, my name is Crystiana Tuadhe d'Anu, Princess of the Unseelie Court, and I am in some serious trouble."*

He blinked in disbelief.

"You call me king and show me respect, yet you are greater than us all."

He attempted to let me go, but I held on to the embrace, afraid the loss of contact would prevent us from communicating.

King Venzoray...

Ven, please. Call me Ven.

I gave him a grateful nod and said, *"I think we need to maintain contact to speak. We can always test that theory later, but I don't have enough time for that right now. My fated mate is in trouble, along with many of my loved* ones. *I need your help in subduing the traitorous soldiers sent by Rena to kill Chantara and my family."*

He jerked as if I'd hit him with a stun gun. *"Fated mate? That is no longer a possibility."*

"It is, and it can be for your race as well, but you must trust me. You must help me. If my people die, the fate of the Fae realm dies with them. I can explain everything to you later, but I need your help to save my friends now."

"This is the battle going on in the northern side of the ruins, yes? We were simply going to let them all kill each other. Not our business."

"And now?"

He lifted a hand to my face and placed his forehead against mine. *"You shall have it, Princess. I swear on my crown and my kingdom, I will protect you and your friends."*

I surprised him even further by locking him in a huge bear hug.

I was a hugger. Folks needed to get used to it around here.

"Thank you, King Ven."

Jareth

*I*t did not sit well with me, leaving Crysta behind, but the idea of her swimming about in the Missing Ruins and getting herself killed made every male instinct of mine go berserk. We chose the lesser of two evils, but this gnawing in my gut, the persistent unease prickling my skin had all my warrior instincts on high alert, and not just because we were coming up on our first sunken ship.

Without her in my field of vision, my body felt ready to combust at any moment.

"We could attempt a search within this first ship, but I'd rather be out in the open with more room to maneuver once the Vorsha figure out we're here," Chantara said. "There are only six of us, but I think that will be enough to pull out the pod of Vorsha. Their predatory instincts should demand it."

"Do we simply move forward within the Ruins or wait here on the outskirts?" Nuallan asked.

I opened my mouth to make a suggestion when my chest grew tight and my adrenaline surged through my system. An echo of Crysta's voice penetrated my thoughts, bouncing around in my brain. An image of Crysta writhing in agony enveloped my sight, superimposed against the backdrop of the sunken graveyard before me.

My skin burned for a moment as I blinked away the image, but the overwhelming sense of impending doom increased. I turned my head, looking back in the direction we'd come, straining to see any sign of my mate even though the very idea of her being here made the blood in my veins ice over.

"Jareth? Are you okay?" Kheelan asked.

I continued to stare into the aqua blue horizon, searching for some sign of her. I noticed a flash of light in the distance, a reflective illumination reminding me of light hitting armor.

"Down," I shouted, pushing Kheelan out of the way and then dodging to the right as a wave of magic hurdled past us and hit the hull of the sunken ship, exploding on impact.

We dove low and scattered, everyone finding cover behind what they could as another volley of magic shot straight for us.

The cluster of large rocks Kheelan and I hid behind would get pulverized with one hit, leaving us exposed if we didn't rally fast.

"Is this Vorsha?" he asked. The spikes along his arms and elbows were raised, his body armor engaged. A ball of electricity hovered above his hand, sparking and spitting, ready to be used, and Kheelan was lethal with defensive magic.

"Can't be. Vorsha don't possess magic. They're not faeries. They're simply creatures, remember?"

Another explosion made us think twice about leaving our cover.

"Then who is attacking us?"

After an onslaught of one explosion after another, the place grew quiet, eerily so. I slowly stole a look from the side of the rock formation, ready to pull back at the slightest sign of magical use, but the view before me was nothing I'd expected.

A vast army of soldiers spread out in battalion formation, at least sixty in number and armed to the gills. Each one held a golden spear, a way to amplify their magic and give it focus. One of Chantara's sentries was a formidable opponent, but this many against our six. The odds were ludicrous.

"Are they out of their minds?" Kheelan hissed. "They are attacking their queen."

Above them, Chantara spoke from what he thought was the bowels of the sunken ship.

"What is the meaning of this? Do you dare fire upon your queen and the rest of these royals? Are you imbeciles trying to cause a civil war?"

She slowly swam her way out of the hull and into open water. Magic encased her entire frame, a sparkling shield of protection. Her onyx eyes threatened to consume anything she looked upon as her skin lit with fury.

"She is a little scary," Kheelan muttered.

I carefully peeked my head around the rock again, noting the sentry front and center slowly swimming forward.

"We are under orders from the Regent to bring you into custody for crimes against the Merfolk."

"Rena does not have the authority to call my rule into question, nor does she have the power to arrest me. The proper procedure for any grievance she may have with me must be brought before an assembly of witnesses where she presents her findings against me and I have the opportunity to refute them."

"Those laws have changed."

"Impossible," Chantara spat. "I make the laws, and I have not changed them. If Rena has altered proper procedure without my consent then it is she who has committed crimes against the Merfolk."

"You will come with us or we will engage in combat. The choice is yours."

"No, Falhan." She lifted her hands before him, spreading her fingers wide as her sharp fingernails grew in length. "The choice is yours."

Without giving him a chance to respond, Chantara took action. Threads of lightning shot from her fingertips, nailing the sentry right in the chest before he had a chance to so much as flick his spear in her direction.

The sentry's blackened body sank to the floor as the shock of Chantara's attack left everyone immobile.

"Absolutely terrifying," Kheelan said.

"Looks like this is happening." I shot from the protection of the rocks, covering myself with several layers of shielding while I whispered a temperature control spell and sent it as a tidal wave in their direction just as the sentries finally seemed to snap out of it.

The spell hit the frontline head on, the boiling water disoriented them, blinding them, and melting several layers of their skin. Their cries of agony meant nothing to me. To turn against their queen was unforgivable. Their treasonous acts would not go unpunished.

A bolt of magic hit me square in the chest, flipping me head over fin. My shield remained stable, but the echo of that impact would no doubt leave me bruised and aching later.

Without needing to communicate, our group found cover behind outlying rocks and ruins as we battered them with every nasty spell we could think of, thinning their ranks as we were driven deeper into the Ruins. The sentries moved forward, systematically destroying our cover, laying waste to the already damaged ships and the many underwater rock towers.

No doubt they hoped the Vorsha would now take notice and force us forward. We'd be trapped between Vorsha and Rena's sentries if we didn't do something to halt their progress.

I spotted Nuallan up much higher, hiding behind a tattered sail atop one of the ship's decks. His fingertips glowed bright red. He placed his palms and finger together as if in prayer. Keeping his hands like that, he drew his arms straight out before him. The lava red glow shot from his fingertips like a laser, hitting the middle of the sentry formation and burning a hole in the ground. The laser never tapered off. Instead, it grew in height until a sheet of red ran from the bottom of the lake straight up, much higher than I could discern from my position.

Then he spread his hands wide...and the lake parted in two.

Sweet Danu, I couldn't believe he'd attempted something so dangerous. The enormity of the spell alone would drain his energy within minutes. Several of the sentries fled from the parting water, but several fell into the dry area, unable to swim fast enough. Their tails were completely useless at the bottom of the lake's floor, requiring them to take precious moments to find their legs, precious moments where they were no longer defending themselves or attacking us.

The rest of our group took full advantage, hurtling one magical spell after another, taking out at least ten sentries in the process.

Nuallan continued to widen the gap, trying to catch more sentries in its wake, but the element of surprise was gone, and I could see his strength failing him.

I sent a warning shot of magic just above his head where it hit one of the spars and exploded. He ducked down and lost the spell. The water slammed together in a rush, pulling the sentries on the outskirts into a tailspin and creating a rush of frothy water that shielded us enough to swim farther back and find better cover.

Unfortunately, one sentry had found his way past the chaos, swimming over my cover of rocks and pummeling my shield with the end of his spear. His magic cracked the shield, sending spidery veins along the surface. I let it drop and flipped backward, clocking the sentry in the face with the end of my tail, which just so happened to have poisonous spikes attached to it. As I righted myself, I took satisfaction in the sentry's immediate reaction to the poison. He convulsed for a moment before foaming at the mouth. His eyes glazed over as the slow pallor of death stole over his features.

I thought of Crysta and her sensitive disposition. I didn't know what she would make of this, of my ability to kill with zero remorse when defending my loved ones. It bothered me to think that she might find me less appealing. It was one thing for us to kill the Formage. Titania had already killed them in a sense. We had merely put them out of their misery, but there was no mind control here.

Simply treasonous sentries who deserved every horrible death they received. Yet it bothered me. Before I'd met Crysta, I'd spent decades assassinating threats to the Fae realm on my father's orders.

Yet how many of those people I had killed were truly innocent.

Just as Crysta had been.

I shoved the thoughts aside, not wanting to analyze them, knowing I couldn't or I would perish within seconds. I'd already paused too long, become too distracted imagining Crysta's reaction.

I didn't know how long we played this game of cat and mouse, finding cover, spelling the sentries, disclosing our own locations, only to have our cover disintegrated. Then bobbing and weaving toward another area of cover before getting hit with more offensive spells.

And as we fought, hid, cast spell after spell, and dove for more cover, I thought of nothing but Crysta. If Rena had sent sentries out for us, then she had already imprisoned Crysta or worse. I had to get to her before Rena killed her. I had to end this.

With a shot of resolve, or what Crysta would most likely refer to as a suicidal impulse, I swam out before the remaining sentries, figuring there were at least twenty left. Lifting my hands above my head, I suffused them with my core magic, ignoring the hits my shield took, and brought my fists down, sending a shock wave of electricity straight to the center of the group and knocking out three sentries in the front.

My shield took two more hits, and then a third one managed to get through, hitting me in the shoulder and spinning me around. I regrouped quickly as the rest of my companions gave me cover with their own attacks, distracting the soldiers as I geared up for another round of electrical roulette.

Just before I released my magic into the enemy, the sounds of battle ceased as if someone had pressed a mute button. The sentries stared at me in horror, frozen in fear.

My confusion turned to its own kind of horror as a chill danced along my spine. My scales rose as another shot of adrenaline hit me. They weren't staring at me.

They were staring *past* me.

I slowly turned myself, hoping against hope I wouldn't find—

Vorsha.

So many of them. More than a pod of twenty. More like ten pods worth of Vorsha spread out behind us.

And just as I'd feared, we were stuck between them and the sentries. There was literally no way out of this now. My hands still sparked, crackling with electricity. I could still use it on them if it came down to it, but even has I raised my hands high, I knew we were dead.

And so was Crysta.

Then the creatures parted in the middle, and a Vorsha larger than all the rest moved forward with...a Mermaid at his side. Deep blue tail, black scales from waist to chest. Her hair was silver and blue, and she looked to be linked arm in arm with the Vorsha as if she was one of them.

As if she was with them.

"Jareth, stand down," she said.

The sound of her voice shot my eyes to her face, recognizing both at the same time.

"Crysta?"

Seeing her in the midst of an army of Vorsha and floating like a sitting duck before the sentries made me age at least two centuries. My initial reaction was to fling all my power at the Vorsha at her side. With her arm through his, my mating instincts kicked in at a threat so near my fated mate, but she spoke again, causing me further distraction.

"Sentries, you have a very important choice to make. You can submit yourself to the will of Chantara, your queen, or you can continue to fight and be sentenced to death for treason. Personally, I'd prefer option A. There has been enough killing, but the choice is yours."

There was a moment of silence as the sentries contemplated their options while I stared at Crysta in amazement. She'd done a transmutation spell. How she wasn't absolutely covered in *griesha* and dying because of it, I didn't know. The Vorsha, for whatever reason, hadn't killed her. I glanced at Kheelan who floated tense and at the ready, hidden behind the large wheel of one of the ships. Nuallan was now in the hull of a different ship. I couldn't see the others, but I knew they were all still alive.

Crysta floated forward with the enormous Vorsha locked at her side. I noticed his hand giving hers a pat as if he wanted to reassure her. I locked eyes with him in surprise. His hard eyes gave me a once over, then he nodded his head in acknowledgment.

Flaming pixie dung! How was this possible?

"Do you surrender?" Crysta pressed.

I glanced over my shoulder and watched as the sentries chose neither option. Instead of giving themselves up, they fled.

I turned back to Crysta who stared at the large Vorsha for a moment as if they were communicating. He nodded his head then lifted his arm and swung it forward toward the retreating sentries. Several Vorsha swam ahead, chasing after our foes. Crysta tugged at her companion's arm, and they both swam toward me. I met them in the middle, ready to get her as far away from him as I could, but as I pulled up closer, a few of the Vorsha who flanked them hissed at me, revealing some very nasty teeth.

The one next to Crysta held up his hand and glared behind him, warning his entourage to back off. I stopped moving after that, afraid if I swam forward again it would be seen as threatening and put Crysta's life in danger.

"Jareth," she said as she let go of the Vorsha's arm and flew into mine.

She pulled back and gave me a desperate kiss, one filled with relief. I felt a primal need to mark her as my own, so I didn't hesitate to deepen the kiss, taking my sweet time to delve my tongue between her lips and dominate the exchange.

As we parted, I immediately glanced at the leader. His eyes were cold, but his lips tugged up at the corner in amusement. The mix of emotions I saw in his expression confused me. He looked like he approved of the exchange, but it was obvious to me how much he wanted Crysta based on the way his eyes flashed to her and then lingered there, softening with something so tender my instinctive reaction was to grab her and have my way with her right there in front of everyone, marking her as mine.

I held back my baser instincts and simply kept her close.

"Do you mind telling me what you are doing with an army of Vorsha, and how the hell you managed such a complicated transmutation spell?"

Her eyes sparkled with excitement, completely oblivious to the way her companion and I were sizing each other up.

"Jareth, may I present King Venzoray, ruler of the Zolas, or what we know as Vorsha."

The creature had a name?

She grabbed hold of his hand and said, "King Venzoray, I'd like you to meet Jareth, Prince of the Seelie Court and my fated mate."

There was a moment of silence as she and this King stared at each other. I didn't like it. Seemed a bit intimate. Then she smiled and turned her eyes on me.

"He said it is his honor to meet you and to assist you."

"Crysta, how do you know this?"

"I can hear him. In my mind. They have no voice boxes. They communicate telepathically, which is why no one has ever been able to see them as anything other than creatures with low sentient intelligence. He can't understand our language, but when we communicate telepathically, we can understand each other."

I stared at the king in amazement. All the attacks on his people over the centuries, all because we couldn't communicate and assumed them to be...well...lesser.

Yet Crysta saw people. She saw someone of worth. As she always did.

"I don't think it's possible for me to express to you how truly sorry I am for all the bloodshed, for the miscommunication," I said to him as I extended my hand. "I owe you a life debt for your aid today."

Crysta stared at the king for a moment as she told him what I said. His eyes widened in surprise and then he looked at my hand. His soft smile and grateful expression humbled me in a way nothing ever had.

He grasped my hand in his and pumped it twice.

"He says there is no need to offer such a huge debt to him. He was happy to assist and grateful that there is a way to finally communicate between the races." She paused for a moment, listening to whatever Venzoray said and then she blushed.

"What?" I asked.

"He said you are lucky to have such a resourceful fated mate."

I gave him a warm smile, hiding my need to pull Crysta behind my back. I figured she edited whatever it was he had said. She didn't blush easily, and I doubted he'd said exactly that.

But I couldn't blame the king for wanting Crysta. She was his first lifeline to the rest of the faeries, and as far as desirable went, Crysta was every single red-blooded male's fantasy come to life.

The rest of our group slowly made their way forward. I noticed several Vorsha tense at the movement, but Venzoray placated them...somehow...and they relaxed just a tad.

"It shouldn't surprise me that our Crysta has befriended an entire army of Vorsha," Kheelan said, giving her a sassy wink.

She laughed and gave the king's hand a squeeze as she paused to translate. I gritted my teeth, knowing it was necessary for her to maintain contact with him so she could communicate, but sweet Danu, the control it took to not lose my mind and swim her away from this scene nearly overloaded my brain. The only thing that kept me anchored to the here and now was my arm around her waist and the feel of her hand at my back, stroking my scales down as they rose off and on while we communicated with the king through her telepathy.

As long as she was alive and in my arms, I could handle another admirer of hers for a little while longer.

∞ ∞ ∞

Crysta

"This is Chantara, queen of the Merfolk," I said as she slowly approached and smiled at King Ven. I quickly told him the same thing in his head, but it almost seemed as if he hadn't heard me. His slight inhale followed by the widening of his eyes as he stared at her absolutely delighted me.

"Chantara, this is King Venzoray."

She bowed her head with deep respect, then she took her hand in his, brought his knuckles to her forehead and said, "We owe you our lives. Thank you, King Venzoray."

"She is thanking you and says we all owe you our lives," I said.

"An honor..." he said faintly. Then with more power he said, *"I am forever at the queen's disposal."*

Chantara's head snapped up in surprise. *"I think I just heard you,"* she said.

I'd never seen eyes blaze with excitement the way his did. He let go of my hand and grabbed both of hers. They were obviously communicating now, but I heard nothing once the contact was broken.

I smiled as they gazed at each other, having a conversation together that none of us could hear. I was tempted to touch his arm again so I could nose in on the convo, but from the way they looked at each other, I could have sworn they were flirting.

Brilliant.

"What's happening?" Jareth asked.

"It would seem that Chantara has the ability to communicate with him telepathically when she touches him."

"What are they saying?" Nuallan asked, wearing a knowing grin.

I chuckled. "I have to be touching him to hear it, but I think they are getting along."

Adris wiggled her eyebrows at me. "I do believe you're right." Then she grew serious, her expression gentling. "Such an astounding discovery, Crysta. It amazes me, the things you manage to do, the barriers between races you constantly break down. Well done, Princess. Well done."

"Yes. Thank you for introducing Chantara to Venzoray. The last thing I need is more competition from your many suitors," Jareth said.

"I have backed off for pity's sake," Kheelan said, sounding miffed.

Cedric's delighted chuckle at Kheelan's discomfort made me feel as if everything would be okay. A weird bit of normalcy amidst the chaos.

"Crysta," Chantara said, "please join the conversation. I do believe King Venzoray can help us."

"What are we discussing," I asked.

"Your beautiful queen has mentioned you seek out a very important sword, one that was left here by mistake by a Drac."

"Yes. We believe the sword carries the Diadem of Titania, a powerful relic we can use to get rid of the illness plaguing faeries."

"The red spotted illness?" he asked, his eyes focusing on me with earnest.

"Your people suffer from it as well?"

"Many have died already. We have no idea what it is or how to stop it."

"We do. We need the sword. Not only will it cure this illness, it will bond fated mates in higher numbers and end the threat Moridan and Titania pose to this land. Not to mention Puck."

"Puck?" Chantara said.

Yeah. Lots to share on that front. Chantara agreed to translate everything to the king while I spoke out loud, saving us some time. I shared with the group what had happened right after they left. Rena dead, Lord Elsly was Puck, and we had another enemy trying to get hold of the stone and diadem.

"Puck," my father said. "Hiding in plain sight this entire time. Unbelievable."

"We have to find the sword before he does," Nuallan said.

Chantara quickly translated.

"I can help you with that," Venzoray said.

"You know where it is?" she asked.

"Of course. I am the one who took it from the Drac."

Chantara let out a low, husky laugh, one filled with as much relief and joy as I felt. *"You'll take us to it?"*

He lifted a hand to her face and lightly stroked it, prodding a shy smile from Chantara.

Geez, I was such a magnificent matchmaker.

"For queen of the Merfolk and Princess of the Unseelie court, I will do most anything."

Good answer.

Crysta

*I*t fascinated me to watch the Vorsha swim. They did use their arms and legs, but what propelled them, and also assisted in steering, were the long octopus-like tentacles spanning out from the back of their heads.

A full head of tentacles, without the suckers on the undersides. I'd never get over the rich diversity in the races here. Besides their outward appearance, their customs offered some insight into who they were as a people.

Once it had been decided that Ven would lead us to the sword, he motioned for a large male from the ranks to come forward. He took the time to interpret the previous conversation, and once this male knew, everyone knew. Ven had the ability to speak to everyone's mind at the same time if he so wished.

Many of Ven's warriors gazed upon Adris, Chantara, and I with deep respect, while eyeing the males as if ready to throw down and brawl like any males who felt threatened within their own territory.

A universal response across races.

It would be difficult for thousands of years of programming to change just because we finally understood one another.

Chantara stayed linked at Ven's side with Jareth and I following closely behind. The rest of our group fanned out behind us and Ven's warriors flanked us all.

Swimming deeper within the ruins revealed an entire community of citizens living within dwellings made of...well...treasure.

"Ven says they have a weakness for shiny objects, and over the centuries they have smelted the gold, silver, and other gems to create their kingdom," Chantara said.

"I think he put all that treasure to good use."

There was a moment's pause before Chantara said, "Ven is happy you approve."

A rush of bubbles came barreling from the side, right into my chest, and before I knew it, I was staring at a Vorsha the size of a toddler, one who stared at me with violet, almond-shaped eyes. She sucked on the end of one of her tentacles and reached out for me. I ignored a few of the Vorsha who rushed forward in a panic and took her in my arms, cradling her like I would a baby.

"And what's your name?" I said.

"Veezee."

The child-like sound of her voice filled my head and heart, bringing a smile to my lips.

Ven had already turned around, looking at the child in consternation. I gave him a smile, trying to reassure him all was well.

She reached up and grabbed my hair. *"You are pretty. No one here has tentacles like yours. They are different."*

"Not tentacles, sweetheart. This is called hair."

"Hair. I like it, and I like you. I will keep you."

I could hear quiet chuckling in my head, coming from Ven and a few of the males around us. It seemed as long as I stayed connected to her, I was also connected to this large-scale mental telepathy.

"As long as your mommy doesn't mind," I said. *"Best not to bring unwanted pets home."* That got several more laughs from the warriors who seemed to be loosening up in our presence. I adjusted her at my hip, and we continued to swim forward.

"Veezee is not troubling you?" Ven asked.

"I'm not troubling," Vee said in outrage.

"I like little girls with big thoughts and curious minds," I said. *"How old are you Veezee?"*

"I have passed seven rotations."

Seven! She was so tiny, I hardly believed it, but I knew nothing about the growth rate of the race.

"We don't have many young who reach the age of maturity, and procreation has become more difficult as the years have passed." Ven looked back and stared at Veezee with fondness. *"She is one of our miracles."*

"You're struggling with infertility issues as well?"

He appeared startled. *"This is a common problem for other races?"*

"I think it has to do with the Dark Magic Moridan has been using, coupled with the lack of fated mates. I really think fertility will rise once we get rid of Moridan and his Dark Arts.

"And griesha," Chantara added.

Yes.

I stared at my arms, noticing the red spots looked more like welts now. I felt so tired, and my entire body ached. Now that my adrenaline had tanked, my body screamed at me to sleep for the next several weeks.

"You are sick," Veezee said. "You have the spots."

Ven stopped and spun, grabbing my arm as if the pronouncement was an affirmation of death.

And maybe, in a sense, it was.

The sadness in his gaze as he confirmed what Veezee said made me like him even more.

"I had not realized you are also ill."

"I'm going to be just fine." I focused my attention back to Veezee. *"Your king is going to help us find something that will get rid of these spots."*

Her lips pulled back in a wide grin. *"Then you can save mommy."*

I glanced up at Ven. His sad eyes took in Veezee, as if he knew her mother wouldn't make it, but he didn't have the heart to tell her otherwise.

I swallowed hard and closed my eyes.

I hoped her mother wasn't too far gone because I simply could not afford to cast another bonding spell with Jareth. It would kill me. I just knew it.

The sunken ships receded even further behind us, but what sprang up before us was a beautiful garden of colorful underwater flowers, bushes, and coral reefs, creating a pathway that led directly to a massive palace of amethyst.

Chantara sucked in a sharp breath. "Why have we never seen this before? You have an entire kingdom here."

"Our wards provide invisibility, and whenever anyone swims too close to our city or the palace, the wards act as a redirect, hypnotizing the mind in a sense, sending all unwanted visitors in a different direction. Most everyone who dares to come close enough to this area always ends up swimming around us. We are no longer in a constant state of war and unrest with other inhabitants of the lake."

Made sense to me.

I thought the king would take us right up to the palace gates. Instead, he had our group form a circle, grasping our hands together. I had to release Veezee, who gave me quick peck on the cheek and then swam her way out of the circle with a little giggle

"I shall apparate you and yours to the location." The rest of the group gasped in surprise, and I realized they could hear Ven due to us all being connected. *"I apologize for not showing you the way, but the location of our treasury is known by only a few."*

"We understand, King Venzoray. We simply appreciate your help in this matter," Jareth said.

Ven appeared pleasantly surprised at Jareth's voice in his head. This experience had been valuable for us all, figuring out how we could communicate with Ven and his people.

A swift tug at my center followed by some slight nausea sent me off balance as we apparated into a room filled with...weaponry.

I'd been expecting a room filled with gold doubloons and mother of pearl necklaces by the yard. Instead, there were several gold pillars rising up to hip height, each one supporting various weapons such as bows and arrows, cimeters, swords, katanas, battle axes, clubs, quarterstaffs...the list was endless.

"Where in the world did you get all these weapons?" I asked out loud.

Chantara quickly translated for him, listened, and then replied, "These come from all the many ships that have arrived here over the years. The weapons have fascinated the king for some time. He knows how to use a few of them, some he does not."

Ven pointed to a pillar holding...holy cow...was that a machine gun? Looked like ships were still finding their way to this place.

He led us to the very back of the room where a larger pillar stood on a dais. Atop the pillar floated a beautiful sword, its hilt made of the finest silver, coming to a point in the middle where a gemstone appeared to be missing. Then it flared out to the sides. I saw how the hilt was shaped like that of a diadem, one that might rest with the apex pointing down across the forehead so the gem would sit atop the middle of one's forehead like a third eye, but I didn't see how it would stay on anyone's head since it didn't seem to have the back band attached to it. Did it just magically fuse to a person's forehead?

Painful much?

Yet the more I stared at it the more fixated I became. The king reached forward and plucked the sword from the pillar. With reverence, he floated to me and placed it in my hands. A blinding light illuminated the room. I shut my eyes as everyone gasped. The light faded until only the hilt of the sword glowed as I held it in my hands.

Ven placed his hand upon my shoulder. *"The sword has never created light like this. I believe this means it has finally found its home."*

I swallowed hard, barely believing I finally held the sword and diadem in my hands. We had everything we needed. We could stop this now.

And then I coughed up blood.

Okay, more like blood exploded from my mouth while my chest felt as if it was being crushed by a monster truck.

"Crysta," Jareth cried as the rest of the group moved forward to assist me.

Jareth got his arms around me, but Ven already had his hand upon my chest.

He looked at Jareth in alarm and placed a hand on his shoulder. *"Her body cannot maintain the transmutation spell. There is Dark Magic festering an old wound, and her illness is much worse. She must leave at once and change back or she will die. Her chest cavity is already filling with blood."*

Crap.

Explained why I struggled to breathe.

Before anyone could do anything, an enormous explosion shook the treasury.

"Flaming pixie dung, what was that?" Kheelan asked.

Ven remained silent for a moment, then he touched Chantara all the while keeping his hand on me, warming my chest. It felt like healing magic, but I honestly didn't know. The pain was a bit distracting.

"My warriors tell me we have a battalion of creatures attacking our wards. They have eyes like lightning."

"Do they look like land Fae?" Chantara asked.

"The Formage," I said, spitting out a little more blood. *"If Titania is the one controlling them then they are basically dead, they can't drown either, their bodies would be under her protection."*

"I'll stay with the king to help him deal with this threat. Jareth and the rest of you, get Crysta back at once so she can change."

Chantara repeated her words out loud and folks got moving fast.

Another stab of pain hit me in the chest, but this time it felt like an echo of someone else's pain. I sensed Terise on the fringes of my subconscious and realized her connection was fading.

"Apparate to my room in the palace," I choked out.

Jareth didn't hesitate. One moment we were under water, the next we weren't. I held tight to the sword as we collapsed on the floor. Jareth managed to change back quickly, but I was stuck on the floor, soaking wet, trying to get my bearings and flopping my useless tail back and forth on the floor.

"Can you change back?" he asked.

I looked at the bed and noticed Terise's coloring was gruesome. She already looked dead, her lips blue, her skin pasty, covered in open red sores.

"I don't know. I—"

Another explosion shook the room, dust and plaster from the ceiling swept down, covering my dark blue fin. I stared at it feeling a bit disconnected from everything.

"What is going on?"

Kheelan and Cedric came rushing in, soaking wet and frantic as hell.

"We've got more Formage at the gates of the palace. They've been attacking for the last few minutes. Looks like a coordinated coup."

"Kheelan, I need you to do what you can for Crysta."

Kheelan knelt next to me and placed his palms on my shoulders, giving me a nice burst of energy as heat blossomed from my chest and unfurled like a flower around my heart. The pain eased, but my strength was completely gone. Blood drenched my arms, the red sores open and weeping.

"Crysta," Kheelan said, helping me to sit up, propping me against the bed. His face twisted in grief while Jareth held my hand, brushing the hair from my face. He came away with more blood. I figured I had sores all over my face now.

"They need you guys out there," I said. "No one is going to be able to...to take...on the Formage without your help. Get my father and Adris. You need to go."

"Not leaving you," Jareth said. His eyes welled with tears.

I felt so afraid. I'd run out of time, and I needed to help Terise, but I knew if they were all here, they wouldn't let me do anything.

Yet saving Terise would also save me. Somehow. I just knew it.

I touched Jareth's tear-streaked face. "I am not going to die, Jareth. I will still be here when you get back. You and Adris and Nuallan, you guys know how to work that spell, how to defeat the Formage and release them from their prison." Another explosion went off, shaking the very foundation of the palace. "You need to go now. If you're that worried about me, then leave Cedric with me."

I glanced to Kheelan. His eyes flickered for a moment, some sort of knowing coming over him. I prayed he would understand and move this along.

He cleared his throat and took my hand. "We'll have Cedric watch over you and Terise. Make sure you focus on your breathing, and under no circumstances do you shift until we return to guide you through the transformation."

I nodded.

Jareth leaned down and kissed my lips. "I'll come back for you. Don't you dare leave me before we can fix this."

"Not a chance," I said. "We still have to get married."

He pulled me against his chest, blood smearing his tunic. "We already are."

I swallowed back the lump of emotion, refusing to cry. I didn't have the energy, and Jareth would not leave if I started in.

Cedric took Jareth's place, holding my hand as he gave him a reassuring nod. "Get going. I'll take care of our women."

Jareth and Kheelan stood. Kheelan gave me one last look, letting me know he knew what I was about to do. I tried to communicate with him that I would respect his wishes on that front. I knew what he wanted, even if I didn't agree with it. Jareth and I locked eyes one last time before they hurried out of the room, the door closing shut behind them.

I didn't waste any time. Didn't have any to waste.

"Cedric, I need you to hand me that sword."

"You shouldn't be moving."

"We have to save Terise. She is literally at death's door."

He looked at Terise, swallowing hard, pain lancing through his expression. He handed me the sword. I studied the hilt, trying to figure out how the hell to separate the diadem from the handle. I ran my bloodied hands over the surface, looking for some tiny latch or crevice that might allow me to separate the pieces. As my blood filled the space where the stone should have been, the hilt began to glow, slowly breaking away and floating before me.

Of course. My blood.

Like that was a shocker.

The hilt transformed into a thin, delicate crown, spreading some seriously blinding light in the process. I lifted my hand to keep it levitating. Getting the stone to magically separate from my chest was a little more complicated. I sent a tiny burst of power to it and said, "*Separatum.*"

The stone fell from my chest to my free hand. With the stone floating below one palm and the diadem floating above the other, I slowly directed the two pieces closer together. Just as the stone hovered over its own resting place, I met with resistance. The more I forced the stone closer, willing it to lock in place, the more resistance I encountered, like pushing two magnets together that simply refused to fit.

My breathing grew more labored. Panic overtaking my motor skills.

We had no time left!

"I can't fuse them together. I don't understand why."

"What do we do?"

I knew the stone had power, and I knew the diadem channeled that power. The fated mate bond was the key, and I remained halfway bonded to two men, the threads of magic so knotted and confused, I wondered if my inability to fuse them together had anything to do with how difficult it had been to bond other couples together, progressively getting worse. There was no definitive fated mate bond for the stone and diadem to anchor themselves to. Not a complete one, especially with Kheelan's unfinished, mutated spell gumming up the works of all our cores.

The diadem and stone were confused.

I closed my eyes, trying to see exactly what I was dealing with again. I tugged at Kheelan's threads, wrapped around my core, then I gripped the stone in my hand and tried to channel its power to the threads, trying to find a way to sever them so I could free Terise and myself, but the magic of the stone ran up against a brick wall when it came to cutting through Kheelan's ties.

Jareth was only tied to me.

Kheelan was tied to me and Terise, not Jareth.

It's funny how truths will hit you with a suddenness that leaves you reeling, poignant moments where time is relative and nothing is more important than the inevitability of your next move and that next choice to be made, the ability to accept the only choice you have.

Kheelan's spell was incomplete and had to play out.

Dammit!

To unravel the knot, one tie had to be severed.

And it had to be Jareth's.

Once I did that, Kheelan's spell would reach fulfillment, fully bonding to me and releasing Terise in the process.

I swallowed hard and looked at Cedric. "I need you to do something for me," I said.

"Anything, Crysta. How do we save you and Terise."

My eyes stung, knowing how this would devastate Jareth. How it devastated me.

"I am going to sever my bond with Jareth, fully bonding with Kheelan."

His reaction killed me, the utter desolation on his face squeezing my chest. "You can't do that. She has to stay bonded to Kheelan or she really will die, and your fated mate is Jareth."

The room shook again as another explosion hit the palace. The muted sounds of battle carried through the windows. My throat ran dry and my cracked lips stung.

"It's the only way. This is the only way we undo what Kheelan did to our cores. This is the only thing the stone will respond to. It is dealing with too much interference from Kheelan's spell. It has no fated mate bond to anchor itself to. I am going to sever my bond with Jareth and immediately transfer Terise's bond to you. I won't need Kheelan's aid in that since I will have the stone and our completed fated mate bond anchoring me."

"Crysta," Cedric said, shaking his head in horror. "You can't do this. It will kill Jareth. You can't do this."

"I will find a way to fix this. I will, but this is our only option now. We don't have time for anything else. I am dying, and so is Terise."

Cedric glanced between me and Terise, clearly torn by his love for her, his concern for both of us, and his concern for what this would do to Jareth.

"What do you need from me?" he asked.

I let out a soft sob. "Just hold me while I do this. I don't want to feel alone right now."

He immediately put his arm around me and held me tight as I gripped the stone hard in my hand and closed my eyes. I channeled my power through the stone, relying on its strength to loop my power back to me as I located the thick cord bonding me to Jareth.

With one swift strike of the stone's powerful magic, I cut the bond in two.

The blow-back was nuclear, knocking the wind right out of me, casting the room in brilliant heat and bursting the windows as Kheelan's spell finally finished, his bond to me firmly linking to my core and releasing Terise in the process.

The gold threads running between us became a solid rod, pumping life back into me, filling me with energy and vitality. My wounds closed up, my body began to transform itself, aching to return to the form it knew best.

Once I opened my eyes, I felt it. My link to Kheelan was complete.

"Crysta! Sweet Danu, what have you done?" Kheelan said, his voice ringing in my head.

Telepathy. I nearly vomited as the reality of what I'd had to do, without running it by Jareth, overwhelmed me.

Yet it had to be done.

These difficult decisions had to be made.

Kheelan had been right on so many levels.

At the end of the day, I would make the right decision. I would make the necessary sacrifices to save the Fae realm.

And I had done just that.

I blocked Kheelan from my thoughts, shoved him out of my mind just as firmly as if I had slammed a door in his face.

"It worked, Crysta." Cedric helped me to my feet, but I didn't feel wobbly in the slightest.

I immediately levitated the diadem and brought the stone and diadem together, fusing them with a burst of light, not meeting any resistance now that it saw a clear path to my "synthetic" fated mate bond with Kheelan.

Placing the crown on my head, I felt power surge from my roots to the tips of my toes. I sat down next to Terise, placed my hand on her chest and ushered Cedric to my side with my other hand. He grabbed it and placed it on his chest.

Kheelan's Summer magic was now mine as well, swirling in my core and giving me all the elemental magics I needed to perform this bonding on my own.

"You ready?" I asked.

His eyes were already leaking tears. "Absolutely," he choked out.

I immediately performed the bonding, repeating the spell, creating a link between his core and hers. Kheelan's bond held strong within my core, taking the enormous power and funneling it through me, keeping me grounded as I passed the power through my hand to Cedric's chest. In a burst of white light, the bond between Terise and Cedric formed.

A synthetic fated mate bond, but one that would save her life.

And life, in that moment, had become very messy.

I shook a little from the magical overload, but nothing could put a damper on the sight that met me as Terise's illness completely disappeared replaced by healthy, glowing skin.

A strange impulse compelled me to lift my hand and place it at her temples. The contact made the room lurch a bit, then spin as if we were on a tilt-a-whirl, going faster and faster until my head hurt and dizziness slammed into me. Everything stopped spinning like a sudden punch to the gut.

I blinked heavy eyes, trying to get my bearings, but the room I stood in was not my room at the palace.

It was my room at my old apartment back in San Diego.

"What the hell?"

I raced into the hallway, calling out Jareth's name, trying to figure out how I'd managed to transport myself back to my apartment.

"Well, this is certainly a surprise."

I spun around in my living room, horrified to see Titania and Moridan staring at me. Pure evil permeated the room. It seemed like the natural light of the day could hardly stand to be near them, shying away as evil oozed darkness in its absence.

"What is going on?" I asked.

"You're stuck here, I'm afraid," Titania said. "Not necessarily the end I had in store for you, but there isn't much we can do to you here in this dream state."

"Dream state?"

"You switched places with that Land Dweller of yours. The one I cursed," Moridan said. "It's how I knew where to find you. I'm linked to the spell, and believe me, it was quite the shock to sense your energy here in her stead. A delightful shock."

"I can find my way out. I know how to beat this," I said, thinking back to Adris's coaching.

Titania smirked. "Yes, well, perhaps if you hadn't already been infected by my handiwork before Jareth rescued you from the Seelie palace, that might have worked. Fortunately, you're stuck in limbo land just as surely as my Formage, though I find it a dreadful shame I can't control you as I do them. That would require your heart first, which I have every intention of retrieving. Soon."

"I don't believe you," I said, feeling desperate. "I can get out of here any time I wish."

"Well, you are more than welcome to try, but I suggest you gaze upon yourself in your paltry mirror before you go assuming you are capable of what hundreds of Formage have yet to achieve."

I rushed to the mirror on the wall and stared at my face, sucking in a breath when I caught sight of my eyes. Streaks of silver flashed like lightning within them, a storm brewed within their depths, completely taking over my irises.

Just like the Formage.

"I've slowly been delving into your brain, taking over your cerebral functions without you being the wiser. The spell will complete itself once I have your heart, but as far as leaving this place, I'm afraid that little lightning display means you're good and stuck."

I spun around and faced them, wishing with all my heart I had some power in this dream state, but the diadem and stone remained in the Fae realm with my physical body. There was nothing here I could channel.

"Jareth and Kheelan will beat you. All of my friends will."

"Such unfounded optimism. Confidence with literally nothing to support it. I admire you, Crysta, truly I do, but once I have your heart, you're mine, and so is my diadem."

Her cruel smile said it all. She thought she had bested me. She fully believed she'd won.

"You have no idea who you're dealing with." I walked right up to her, not sure if she could hurt me in this dream state and not really caring at this point. With my nose inches from hers I snared her with my stare.

"My name is Crystiana Tuadhe d'Anu, Princess of the Unseelie Court, Ruler of the Fae realm, a serious force to be reckoned with, and *you* are absolutely nothing without that crown."

Whatever she saw in my eyes must have gotten under her skin. For one brief moment her confidence appeared shaken.

And then...she and Moridan disappeared, leaving me alone in my living room.

Epilogue

Jareth

*M*y knees buckled, and I fell upon the broken earth, nausea taking over. My chest felt as if it had been hollowed out with a searing hot blade. The cries of battle broke around me. Losing consciousness at this moment was hazardous to my health, but death seemed a welcome relief.

My connection with Crysta was gone, my fated mate bond with her severed.

And that could mean only one thing.

She hadn't made it.

My beloved had died.

Kheelan grabbed me by the shoulder and yanked me to my feet.

"Are you crazy?" he shouted. "You're going to get yourself killed."

A bolt of lightning landed a few yards away, shaking the ground and tearing up structures in its wake. Formage ran about casting illusions as material as the ground I stood upon. Citizens scattered while the rest of our group spread out to take on Titania's forces.

"Crysta is dead," I said, barely above a whisper.

Then Kheelan went down hard, grabbing his chest in surprise as he wrestled with an enemy I could neither see nor hear.

"Brother," I cried, kneeling down next to him. I could not lose him as well.

He concentrated for a moment, and then his jaw became slack. "What have you done, Crysta?"

What *had* she...?

And then I knew.

She wasn't dead. She hadn't perished. She had done what she promised me she *wouldn't* do.

She had fully bonded with my brother.

"No," I said, shaking my head in disbelief. "No. She wouldn't do this. NOT. THIS."

Kheelan grabbed my arm and shook me, forcing me to make eye contact.

"If Crysta severed your link, then there was a damn good reason for it, Jareth." He looked pale and shaken, no doubt dealing with the blow-back from completing the spell with Crysta while simultaneously losing his bond with Terise. "She'd never have done this if there had been another way. Let's get through this latest assault and get back to our women."

I couldn't process a thing he said. My only desire was to be at Crysta's side, begging her to reverse what she had done.

He squeezed my arm to get my attention. "Jareth, I swear on my life, I will make this right."

I shook my head, a fury building within me the likes of which I had never before known.

"There were other options." I sent a blast of magic straight into a Formage headed our way. The smell of burning skin was a sweet balm to my flayed emotions. "She could have done anything but this."

Adris reached us, planting herself at our flank and creating a protective shield as a line of Formage headed our way.

"As much as I appreciate everyone's need for some rest, this isn't exactly the place to be lounging about."

"We need to get to Crysta," I shouted.

"We destroy Titania's forces first. Crysta and Terise die if we don't, and so do the rest of us."

Adris's calm assertions broke through my crazed thoughts. Getting to Crysta as fast as I possibly could changed nothing in the end. She had made her choice.

And I would have to live with it.

I pulled Kheelan to his feet and lined up next to Adris as Roderick, Paio, and Nuallan joined us.

My heart was torn in two, but my family still remained at my side.

"We spell them now," Adris shouted.

The wind kicked up. Angry storm clouds covered the sky and darkened the land. The air smelled of fresh rain and spilled blood. The line of Formage grew in number, facing off before us.

They were many, but we were enough.

"On my mark," I said. "Three...two...one..."

Thank you for reading *My Fair Princess*. Please consider going online and leaving a review if you have enjoyed the series thus far. Be sure to look for the sixth and final installment in the *Paranormal Misfits Series* with *My Fair Queen*, coming out in 2020.

Until then, I hope you'll turn the page and discover more books to read. Happy reading, my friends.

The Healer Series

The Healer: Book 1
The Black Blossom: Book 2
The Grass Cutter Sword. Book 3
The Prophecy: Book 4

Supernatural Treasure Hunters Series

Double Booked

The Paranormal Misfits Series

My Fair Assassin: Book 1
My Fair Traitor: Book 2
My Fair Impostor: Book 3
My Fair Invader: Book 4
My Fair Princess: Book 5
My Fair Queen: Book 6
    (Coming 2020)

Other Books By C. J. Anaya
Written Under The Pen Name Cynthia Savage

Billionaire's Reluctant Wife Series

Marry Your Billionaire: Book 1
    Cynthia Savage

Crushing On The Billionaire: Book 2
    Jennifer Griffith

Trusting The Billionaire: Book 3
    Cynthia Savage

About the Author

C.J. Anaya is a USA Today bestselling and multiaward winning author. She also enjoys assisting authors in writing, publishing, and marketing their books with her helpful non-fiction guides on Amazon and her YouTube channel Author Journey.

She's a huge fan of The Mindy Project, Hugh Jackman, and binge eating any and all things chocolate. Who isn't, right?

As a mother of four awesome children, C.J. is usually helping out with homework, going to gymnastics, or delivering her kids to their karate classes so they can learn discipline, respect, and "...kick some serious butt, mom." She loves writing entertaining reads for everyone to enjoy and dabbles in singing and songwriting for kicks and giggles.

Follow her on Bookbub: https://www.bookbub.com/authors/c-j-anaya
Stop by and say hello at http://authorcjanaya.com
Facebook:https://www.facebook.com/cjanayaauthor
Twitter: CJAnaya21

Made in the USA
Columbia, SC
11 September 2019